M000104239

^A*Promise*
Child

^A*Promise Child*

Faith, Loss, and Hope in the 1930s
(Book 2 in Promise Series)

Kathryn Spurgeon

Kathy Spurgeon

MEMORY HOUSE
PUBLISHING

Edmond, Oklahoma

Published by Memory House Publishing
Edmond, Oklahoma 73034
www.memoryhousepublishing.net

Copyright @ 2017 by Kathryn A. Spurgeon

Certain names have been changed in this book to protect the privacy of individuals involved.

All rights reserved. No part of this publication may be reproduced, stored in a retrieval system or transmitted in any form or by any means—electronic, mechanical, photocopy, record or any other—except for brief quotations in printed reviews, without the prior permission of the publisher.

Printed in the United States of America

ISBN 978-0-9973347-5-3 (Paperback) Christian historical fiction

Authors and photographers retain copyright to original work.

Book cover design by Krystal Harlow
Interior design and layout by
Photo Credits: Margaret Pope Akin and Pottawatomie County Oklahoma Historical Society

To Frances Trimble,
the youngest and last living relative
of Sibyl and Fremont's generation.
I appreciate her help and support,
but mostly I appreciate
her love and kindness.

Chapter One

January 1936

I gazed at the latest fashions in Mammoth's storefront window, fashions completely beyond my financial reach. Hats tipped at an angle, embroidered collars, fur-trimmed coats, and long evening dresses with brocade jackets in lovely shades of creamy rose pink and seafoam green. The elegant styles intrigued me.

Shaking my head free of daydreams, I looked around at Main Street, Shawnee, Oklahoma. This peaceful town was relatively quiet for a Tuesday afternoon and I felt safe. I dawdled too long at the bookstore rummaging for *Mary Poppins* and forgot about the grocery list tucked into my pocket. I should not have been pining for fancy dresses and rose-covered cloches. Married three years now, I had too much to do.

My husband, Fremont Pope, might not be wealthy but I would fight to make sure our marriage succeeded. Even if that meant I had to do without a new outfit.

"Why Sibyl, how lovely to see you." My old boss tipped his hat. The only acknowledgement I wanted from him was the money he still owed me.

"Sorry, sir. I have to run." I rushed down the street toward the M&P Grocery Store. Popcorn wagons, street vendors and newsboys vied for my attention. Cinnamon aromas wafted out of the City Café and soft music floated from a women's ready-to-wear store.

I slid to a stop. My shoes scrapped on the sidewalk outside the Public Drug Store.

A commotion rattled inside. Several men huddled around a box tombstone radio that blared the news that King George V of England had just died. The announcer said he had been sick for years and now everyone was curious about who would take his place. Would it be his son Prince Edward? Intensely interested in any news from the outside world, I sidled up next to the door and listened to snippets of the conversation.

"Now his son'll be king," someone said.

"Prince Edward ain't nothing to speak of," another replied.

"Disregards his own church."

"Heard he's living with a married woman."

"Affairs. Reckless. Good-for-nothing fellow."

"Womanizer."

"Not a decent fellow, much less a leader."

The words felt too close to home and I shivered. Had these men used that same language last month when referring to my papa, Malcolm C. Trimble, Sr.? The well-to-do bank auditor who abandoned his wife for a floozy? The man who neglected his children during times of economic hardship? Mama and my young sisters were barely getting by on the small stipend he paid.

I pulled my scarf tighter around my neck. Was my papa *not* a decent man?

I stood at the doorway listening as gossip about Prince Edward's affair spun out of control. Would the Prince leave his mistress for the crown? Everyone had an opinion but no one knew for sure. I could only equate Prince Edward's dilemma to Papa's. My parents' recent divorce was a disaster—still raw and painful. The rumor mill had spit out our family like sawdust when their marriage had failed dramatically. Would my marriage succeed?

I fled the drug store as tears sprang to my eyes, flooding my vision.

I stumbled down Main Street, turned south on Beard toward home and tripped over the railroad tracks. On this side, the side where I lived, the houses became smaller and shabbier. When I married Fremont against Papa's wishes, I chose to live a different way than my father had planned. Papa taught prestige and riches would transform the world. All I wanted was to find peace, especially for the ones I loved.

Fremont had grown up in a different social circle. He grew up poverty-stricken, on the wrong side of town. A drifter and hobo before we met, he found work where he could. Now that we were married, I was no longer coddled, spoiled or affluent. Instead, Fremont and I could barely afford the little two-bedroom house we rented. But we had love. What more did we want?

In fact, Fremont loved me so much that today he closed the filling station a bit early to take care of the children, allowing me to escape for the afternoon and go shopping. He often did that, thought of my needs before his own. Would he always? Even in difficult times?

Fremont was right for me in so many ways. I hurried toward the house where my stable, down-to-earth man could calm my racing mind.

After shoving the front door open, I leaned against the wall, panting and out of breath. Freshly brewed coffee warmed the air along with the scent of fresh baths. I breathed in deeply. Strands of wavy brown hair fell over my eyes and I pushed them back.

Fremont sat amidst chaos on the floor, toys strewn around him as he played quietly with our children, three-year-old Margaret and two-year-old Judson. Fremont, nonchalant as always, ran his fingers though his tousled hair. As I looked at my family, I felt like an outsider, not included in their laughter and joy, my heart still stung by the vicious gossip that echoed what I feared people said about my papa.

He slowly looked up at me but didn't seem to notice my disheveled state. His stunning face and striking crystal-blue eyes still made my heart throb.

"Back so soon?" he asked.

"I just . . . the news . . ." I collapsed onto a chair. "King George died yesterday."

"Why's that important?"

"Why is it important? The King of England dies and you don't care?"

"He's been mighty sick for years, so it isn't surprising."

I swallowed hard. I hurt, but more from the stinging words I'd overheard in the drug store than from Fremont's disinterest in the King's death. After all, Fremont had never been as concerned about world events as I had. But that knowledge didn't help me respond any better. He was my husband. I thought he should understand my ache, the reason for my pain and the flood of feelings that overtook me.

Fremont leaned back against the sofa, his unbuttoned shirt revealing a worn undershirt, undressed enough to be improper in my family. Papa never left his room half-dressed.

I stared at his open shirt, his muscles bulging, and then snapped back to attention. "How can you be so calm? Prince Edward may be crowned king any day now. Changes could happen."

"And . . ."? Fremont buttoned up his shirt.

"Don't you see? No one respects the prince. What with his dallying around with married women and all? A leader should be above reproach." How could Fremont know I was talking about Papa? I pressed my hand against my throat, trying to calm myself with the cool touch. Frustration gripped me.

"Now, Sibyl." He rose and shooed the children toward the bedroom before beginning to pick up toys littered around the room.

"Don't go getting in a tizzy. It'll be all right."

"Nothing's all right any more. We don't have enough money for food, much less shoes for Judson. I can't even find old material to make Margaret a dress." The tears threatened to burst free.

"You're talking nonsense, honey." He pulled me up from the chair and put his strong arms around me. "We still have the filling station and what it brings in. Why don't you go lie down and I'll fix some supper."

"Supper, oh no. I forgot!"

He gave me a puzzled look.

"I never made it to the grocery story." I burst into sobs. How could I let the pain from Papa's poor choices and gossip about a foreign prince upset me? I forgot about taking care of the people who meant the most to me?

"There's plenty of potato soup left from last night," said Fremont with a soothing voice. "A lovely lady like you shouldn't get so upset."

Frustrated, I slunk into our bedroom and fell to the floor. Would Papa's tainted reputation follow me all my life? Why did thoughts of Papa still rattle my mind?

Maybe my real purpose in life was still waiting. Papa groomed me to be important. His training about social reform and political leadership still echoed in my mind. What could I do now? Poor and married. A housewife. A mother.

Would I lose my marriage like Mama did?

Fear surrounded my heart and I cocked my head.

I would not let Papa's disreputable reputation—so like the prince's—define my life. I would rise above Papa's reputation as well as what the world considered acceptable for me. I would not give up. I would not become a peasant, a mere housewife, sweeping floors and washing windows. I would not be stuck in the kitchen baking apple muffins all my life. I would not. There had to be some way to prove my value.

I pressed my lips together. My parents' marriage may not have worked out, but mine would, no matter how difficult it might get.

And I would never forget the groceries again. Never.

Chapter Two

We had purchased a filling station a few months back, thanks to Papa's influence at the bank, and Fremont kept busy there, working up a good sweat. With strong, steady hands and skills he'd learned on the job, he could replace any broken part on most makes and models of vehicles. People noticed, and at first, the station brought in enough funds for a hopeful future.

New sleek automobiles were Fremont's favorites. He loved them almost as much as he loved me. Once a gentleman drove a Pierce Arrow in for gasoline, and that night Fremont relayed the details of the sleek body and new devices like the built-in radio and heater. His knowledge impressed me. He could talk for hours about transmissions, chokes, hydraulic brakes and gear shifts mounted on steering columns. Things I knew nothing about.

The blighted economy created a lack of money everywhere, not just in Oklahoma, and with rumors of more bank closings, fewer people purchased motor cars. Instead, people tried to repair vehicles on their own when it became necessary. When a family jalopy broke down, it might be months before the owner could afford to take it to a mechanic. And when things got really bad, a family car might sit abandoned in a dusty field, unusable.

Fewer people drove by our filling station. Soon, only stragglers stopped for gasoline or repairs. Our income grew smaller and smaller each week. Even still, Fremont stayed late at work many nights, cleaning an old farmer's dirty carburetor or patching extra inner tubes in case someone dropped by. On days like that, he would trudge home with his hands in his pockets, a frown creasing his forehead.

One evening, after a long and fruitless day at the station, Fremont came truding home in his grimy clothes. He brought the filling station smell into our dining room, a mixture of gasoline, dust and petroleum. He ran his fingers through his thick, dark hair and handed me the week's earnings without looking me in the eye. "Don't look like we made enough for the mortgage."

I dropped the money in an old cigar box and set it on the top kitchen shelf. "We barely have enough to buy beans. Maybe the bank will understand if we're a little late on the mortgage payment."

"The payment was late last month, honey. The banker may not understand again."

"We should ask." I hated missing a payment. We couldn't afford to lose the station, our only means of support. Hopefully, people would travel more often once spring weather hit. Folks liked to get outdoors and go on road trips after being confined all winter.

"This feels like a mighty big boulder around my neck," he said quietly.

We'd been through a dozen hardships and learned to work together. Fremont had stuck by me when the children were born and when my parents divorced and when a leaky faucet flooded the kitchen floor. I would stick by him now, although I might have to forgo purchasing used books and shorten my grocery list to a bare minimum.

"Go on down the street and see Mr. Adams," I suggested, handing him a cold bologna sandwich. "He should be home by now. He still owes for that fender you fixed on his Ford last fall."

Fremont looked crestfallen. He hated collecting money, but after cramming his worn hat on his head, he plodded back out the door.

In my family growing up, we always had an abundance. We even owned two fairly new automobiles. Now, not only was my family in dire straits, but ever since Papa left Mama, she was poor. Fremont's parents—poor. Friends—poor. Neighbors and a slew of strangers begging for crumbs on the streets—poor as barn mice. There had to be a way out of poverty. So many people lost farms or jobs, their only means of support, that scarcity pervaded every corner of our world.

Fremont didn't return home for nearly two hours.

"What took you so long?" I asked. "Did you get the money?"

He held out two crinkled, one-dollar bills. "It just doesn't seem right, Sibyl, taking money from the poor. They have less than we do and have all those kids hanging around."

I looked at his strong, sturdy hand holding those two measly dollar bills. I touched them with my thin pale fingers. Looking up, our eyes met and his sorrow drew me to him. Here was a dedicated man who put everything he had into taking care of our family. He tried so hard, working from dawn to late evening, laboring to bring in enough funds to support us.

I put the dollars with the rest of the month's savings. Gritting my teeth, I hoped and prayed we had enough flour for tomorrow's breakfast. We ate a lot of biscuits and gravy, but it kept our family fed.

Somehow, we scraped enough money together to pay the month's mortgage. But the way times were going, we might not have enough for next month's payment. How would we survive if we lost our business? How would we feed the children?

Chapter Three

February 1936

Gossip multiplied like mosquitoes on a hot summer day. Many people had read about my parents' divorce in the *Shawnee News* or heard about the embittered battle from neighborly chit chat. For the first time in my life, people turned away when they saw me, Sibyl Trimble, the former society queen. A scandal was a scandal after all.

Eventually walking down Main Street became painful. But I had to do it, so I hitched up my shoulders and moved past the gawking gossipers in front of the busy Woolworth's store. I leaned into the baby carriage where my toddler, Judson, squirmed to get out, while Margaret walked along beside me.

We arrived at Mama's house on North Beard Street by mid-afternoon. A newer housing addition on the north side of the tracks. I tried to visit her once a week. I lifted the carriage up the stairs and through the front door without knocking. Margaret trailed in behind me and Mama helped her remove her outer coat.

Mama looked young for her age, her sandy-colored hair rolled into an artful hairdo on top of her head. She worked part-time at First Baptist Church. Although brighter than many women (at least she thought so) she hated menial work.

"You're smart enough to do the work, even if you've never fancied numbers," I said when she complained.

"Why, thank you." Mama primped her hair back as if she were a movie star. She liked compliments and loved being the center of attention. "That's what the preacher said, too. But the work doesn't pay enough to live on. Singing, which I'd rather do, brings in doodly-squat."

"How's choir? When's your next solo?" We walked into the kitchen where a pile of dirty dishes filled the sink. I expected to be enlisted to play the piano so she could practice.

Mama's mood instantly changed and her eyebrows drew together in a frown. "Won't be a next solo. The choir members got together and decided a divorced woman should not be singing in front of the church, especially not a special."

"Oh, that's just gossip." I poured glasses of water for the children and handed them a freshly baked snickerdoodle cookie.

Mama ran a sink full of hot water and began to wash dishes. "No, I'm telling you, those hussies want me kicked out of choir. I hope some old she-devil teaches them a lesson."

Working in tandem, I dried a plate with a tea towel and put it away. "Now, Mama. I'm sure not every member insisted you stop singing." I couldn't tell Mama that many Shawnee residents thought the divorce had been her fault, when Papa was the one who had left.

"The song leader likes me. I have a better voice than anyone else." Mama pushed her shoulders back. Musical performances kept her afloat through her marriage crisis. Everyone knew Mama's outstanding talent, that she had sung opera on stage. That she'd sung at the fancy Aldridge Hotel for the KGFF radio station.

"Did he stand up for you?"

"I'm sure he tried, but he took me aside and said too much controversy abounded. He wants me to take a back seat until the ladies simmer down." Mama rolled her eyes.

"That seems reasonable."

"Not to me! I stomped out, and I'll never set foot in that choir room again. Not even if I have to quit my job."

"Mama."

"I'll never trust church people again either. And it's all your papa's fault."

As Mama gestured to solidify her point, a glass flew out of her hand and broke. I knelt and cleaned it up for her. When we finished the dishes, Mama had calmed down and shed her apron.

Our conversation deteriorated. Mama hated Papa for leaving her stranded. She raved about disgraceful men and the decline of morals in our society. She ranted about the unfairness of the divorce and the humiliation Papa brought upon her. She seethed about the choir members unkind, judgmental words that devastated her.

My younger sisters, eight and fourteen, were at school and would be home soon. I knew there were times when Mama didn't have enough to feed them. What it would feel like if I were unable to feed my children? At least we had money coming in from the filling station. I could depend on Fremont to get us through these lean times, but Mama had no one. The $50 monthly child support stipulated by the divorce helped some, but it wasn't enough to cover the house payment, utility bills and food tab, much less provide the entertainment Mama was accustomed to.

We sat on the cushioned living room sofa, set our drinks on the coffee table and continued talking.

"Have you kept up with that big corruption case? With Bank Commissioner Barnett?" Mama loved gossip, if nothing else, especially what concerned her society friends or was related to banking articles and Papa.

"The scandal in the paper? Why do you ask?" I took a sip from my glass of tea, hesitant to get into a conversation about this.

"Well, it looks like your papa has been more involved than he let on."

"What do you mean?"

"While the family was distracted with the shenanigans and back-and-forth bickering of the divorce, Papa got further involved with this crime."

I heaved a sigh. Wrestling with Mama's suspicious nature turned my mind to mush. "Papa would never get involved in anything illegal."

"Don't be too sure. You don't know your papa like I do."

Papa had audited banks for his boss, former State Commissioner Barnett, and now Barnett was accused of corruption. Was Papa involved with this scandal? If so, it would make it even harder to hold our heads up in society.

That evening after dinner, I talked to Fremont about Mama's near-poverty situation and rumors about Papa.

Fremont didn't choose sides. He also didn't want to discuss the banking scandal. Instead, he merely listened, nodding his head and encouraging me to be patient.

"Patient! What if Papa did something underhanded?" The idea festered inside me. What if the rumors were true? What if Papa was more involved with the banking corruption than I thought?

"Trust God through these mighty hard times," Fremont said. "That's what I did when riding the train to California. The Lord'll get us through."

His no-nonsense, unemotional attitude infuriated me.

"How can you be so calm?" I blubbered while Fremont watched like a bystander. "Can't you help me through this struggle?"

"You're mighty upset now, honey. What do you want?"

I ignored him and stood, not wanting to discuss it any longer. "I have to get the children to bed." I hurried from the room.

I didn't know what I wanted except maybe a life without the worries that followed me throughout the day. Where was the comfort God had given before?

From the bedroom doorway, I watched them—my two darlings. Margaret helped Judson maneuver his pajamas on, talking to him in a comforting voice. A serious child, she hardly ever laughed. My heart ached. I wished to be a better mother. More attentive. More affectionate.

I walked into their bedroom. "Let's read a book." The children climbed into the small bed and I tucked them in. Their wide eyes peeped over the patchwork quilt Fremont's mother had made for us. I chose their favorite reader, *The Pony Engine,* and read with expression. Afterward we prayed, and I kissed them on the forehead.

Once they were asleep, I returned to the dining room table, wondering why I still struggled to please my papa. I wanted to dwell on the good memories. I wanted to recall his laughter when he brought gifts, his confident bearing and slicked-back good looks, like Clark Gable walking through our living room. He was my father, after all, and I felt sorry for him and all he'd lost: his family, his reputation, and his standing in Shawnee.

Fremont sat still, observing me.

"My whole family's struggling, can't you see?" I heaved with frustration. "None of my siblings are adjusting. How can two people go separate ways after being married for so long? How can they destroy each other and their family?"

Fremont nodded sympathetically. He'd heard this before.

I propped my head on my hands and mumbled. "Everyone's been affected. Mama lets Frances stay in bed all day, which means she misses a lot of school. What other eight-year-old is always sick all the time? And Blanche is angry at the world and may never get over it. Marjorie's mind is lost in a cloud. And please, don't even get me talking about Calvis. If that brother of mine isn't careful, he'll give up his music to work for Papa at the bank. And Papa! What has he gotten himself into?"

"You can't fix everything, honey. That's a mighty big job."

"Then what *can* I do about it? I feel helpless, caught in a family that's disintegrating into the quick sand." I sighed. "It's hard keeping the family together."

Why were my feelings so jumbled? So out of control? Even though I was an emotional person, I should have been able to take charge of my problems. These sentiments overwhelmed and exhausted me.

I loved my family, but I was losing myself in all the demands. Could I trust God or was it up to me to find a way to make life valuable?

Fremont stood up from his seat at the table and stepped behind me. He stroked my unruly hair and then leaned over and kissed the top of my head. Warmth flooded through me. At least I had a calm, reassuring man by my side to keep me level. His faith in God created a foundation to our marriage. A rock.

Suddenly, I had a solution. Maybe it wouldn't solve all my family's problems, but it would give me a purpose, a plan. I would become a perfect mother and housewife. I might not be the leader Papa had groomed me to be, but I could be a perfect example of a well-trained homemaker. I would never lose my temper. I would ensure no dish lay out of place. I would keep the laundry caught up. I would be an adoring wife and attentive mother. No one would be better at this than me.

The goal of a well-oiled, smooth-running household would give me something to work toward. Determined to be proud of my life, I would show Papa and everyone else my worth. Nothing could keep me down.

I would work so hard, even God would be proud.

Tightening my hands into fists, I determined to make a model home, the kind I saw in *Good Housekeeping* magazine, spotless and perfect. Yes sir, nothing would be able break up this family. Nothing.

Chapter Four

Blanche stormed through the screen door of our house, cracking her knuckles. Her lanky teenage body strode around the living room. She kicked the flowered armchair and slammed her books on the side table, making its legs wobble. Mama was taking Frances to the doctor today to determine what could be done for her turned-in feet, so Blanche had come in alone.

Before I could ask about her day, she threw her coat in the corner and blurted out with a mocking tone, "People are despicable. I never want to speak to anyone again."

"What's wrong?" I asked.

"My friend came to visit and claimed she could never come back to see me again. Her mama doesn't approve of divorce." My sister's pain from our father's abandonment had settled into confusion. She was growing resentful, bitter as green persimmons. "It's a disgrace. My own papa just up and divorces us."

"Don't let Papa's behavior color everything in your life," I said gently. "You have to get over it."

"Oh, and you're fine with the divorce? You don't have any hard feelings?"

"You don't know how I feel." I would not admit my struggles to Blanche.

"Well, I for one didn't ask for any of this, and you haven't been the best support, you know." Blanche glared at me, her long arms gesturing wildly. Her accusations shot like arrows.

"You have to choose your attitude," I said, leaning forward. I wanted to shoot an arrow back at her, but it wouldn't help either of us.

"That's just like you, always against me. A puppet would be more helpful."

Surprised at her coldness, I said. "It doesn't matter what people say. God knows the pain in your heart and can comfort you." I didn't realize until then that I also needed to hear those words. Words from Fremont's Mother. His parents, the Popes, were full of wise sayings.

"Papa's ruined my life." She stormed to the other side of the room. "I hate him!" Her eruption carried a sharp edge.

"That's not true. You might not like your father, but you shouldn't hate him. Just give it time."

Blanche lowered her head and narrowed her eyes like she didn't believe a word I said. If she wouldn't let the past go, time might not heal her heart.

My children burst through the door, Margaret chasing Judson, momentarily distracting us. Continuing their game, they fled into the bedroom, leaving us alone again.

My sister and I were opposites in many ways. While I loved the tragic *Les Miserables* film, she preferred *Top Hat*, a musical comedy. I was more like Aunt Betsy in *David Copperfield* while she tended to be as melodramatic as Greta Garbo in *Grand Hotel*. We were definitely disconnected.

I had been Papa's confidante and Blanche his favorite, but now Papa had become the antagonist.

"You'll stay for dinner, won't you?" I asked. "We're having cheese sandwiches."

"Why not? There's nothing better at home." She followed me into the kitchen.

"How are your classes at school?"

17

"We're *required* to purchase bloomers and a one-piece gym suit. They look ridiculous. The instructor said we start jogging next week."

I buttered two slices of bread, laid the cheese between them and put the sandwich into the cast iron skillet. I remembered the mandatory gym classes I had in high school. Awkward. Maybe most young girls felt the same. However, knowing Mama's situation, Blanche's problem might be more about finances than embarrassment.

"Can you afford the bloomers?" I asked.

"Idiotic question. You know we don't have a dime to spare for something so mundane. It's a waste if you ask me. We do good to put food on the table. Just the other day I had to put cardboard in the bottom of my Oxfords."

I looked down at Blanche's shoes. The scruffiness and loose stitching told a sad story. "You still have those? What about the ones Mrs. Collins gave you? They're in better shape." Not long ago a kind neighbor noticed Blanche's shoes and gave her a pair of tri-colored high heels with pointed toes. Mama couldn't even afford to buy worn-out booties from the dozen shoe repair stores in town.

"Girls at school said they looked funny. Mama told me not to worry about what others say, but I'll never wear those heels again. I went back to wearing these shabby shoes."

"Don't worry. We'll find a way to buy you some bloomers for gym and maybe some new shoes," I said, trying to cheer her up.

"I don't care. No one speaks to me anyway."

"What about Irene? She goes to gym too, doesn't she?" Fremont's younger sister, Irene, attended Shawnee High with Blanche. They had classes together but seemed incompatible. Blanche ranked at the top of her class, while Irene ranked near the bottom scholastically. Irene hated to study but chose to play whoopee instead. Blanche's words.

"Irene is about as senseless as a ladybug. All she does is giggle and flirt with the guys. She's a mindless clown if you ask me. I'll be surprised if she graduates."

18

"Maybe she needs encouragement." I took a deep breath. Irene with her nonstop talking and many curves attracted more attention than Blanche's intelligence and lankiness.

"She just bats those big blue Pope eyes and the guys come running."

"Well, you won a Wewoka baby contest, didn't you? Your big brown eyes should mean something." This elicited a smile out of her. The doll she won still lay on her pillow.

My sister had a difficult time fitting into high school. Being a nonconformist with an uppity mind didn't help. A bit antisocial, she didn't hesitate to call out the weaknesses of others. School friends probably tiptoed around her because of her short fuse. Now they would laugh at her for not having the proper attire.

"It doesn't matter." She shrugged.

I knew better.

I felt sorry for her. I'd grown up with luxury and comfort, other children weren't mean to me, and I had a lot of upper-class friends. Blanche had been through so much for a fourteen-year old. One of Papa's favorites, her world shattered like thin glass after the divorce. I still remembered Papa saying in court that he'd never wanted his youngest daughters. Blanche's face had registered shock. Spurned and abandoned by our previously doting father, disillusioned by his betrayal, her pain projected on anyone in her path.

How long before she recovered? Could I help her see life through a different lens?

What about me? Would I ever forgive Papa for the hurt he caused our family?

Part of me still yearned for approval, needed to feel important and valuable. Actually, what I really needed was to address my pain before it turned into a deep well as sour as Blanche's. Now, that was something to think about.

Chapter Five

March 1936

Marjorie came to visit. A year younger than me, my sister and I were always close. We snuck out to dances, flirted with dandies and giggled together in the dark. She married a few months before I did, but her husband Kelley wasn't the sticking-around kind. He vanished a few months ago when Marjorie lost her second baby.

I never liked Kelley. He was a deadbeat who spent his evenings cavorting at speakeasies, ignoring Marjorie and their son Larry. Secretly, Mama and I celebrated his leaving. At least we wouldn't have to listen to Marjorie cry about his affairs anymore. Of course, I didn't say that to Marjorie.

"Sis, can I borrow a bit of cash. I'm down to nearly nothing," she said after I poured her a cup of coffee.

"You know I don't have two coins to rub together. Why don't you ask Papa for help?"

"Papa disapproves of everything I do."

"And . . ."

"Gladys, Papa's girlfriend, called me a slut, saying I sleep around with every Tom, Dick and drunken Harry in the county. Ballyhoo. She doesn't know beans."

Gladys had no right to speak to my sister this way. My opinion of Papa's live-in plummeted, not that it was very high. "Surely, she doesn't mean it. You've been staying with Papa since the divorce."

"I'm leaving, sweetie." She took a sip of the hot liquid.

"Leaving?" I opened my eyes wide in surprise.

"I'm going to find Kelley. I heard he moved to Phoenix and has a good job. Larry and I need someone to support us. Can't find decent work around here."

"I thought you were filing for a divorce? My old boss Mr. Weston agreed to help in exchange for money he owes me. I worked weeks for that—"

"I know, dearie, but I changed my mind and withdrew the petition."

My mind reeled. Bouncy, blond Marjorie was so unpredictable. Desperately seeking a divorce just last week, she'd cried about how her husband abandoned her and their son, and now she was dropping the petition to run back to him. "Does Kelly know you're coming?"

"Nah, but I can persuade him to think it's a great idea." Marjorie wiggled her shoulders. "I'm good at convincing men."

I noticed her new hair style—soft finger waves down to her shoulders—and wondered where she got money for the perm. Naturally, she would look fashionable in a worn-out petticoat. No. I should hide my jealousy.

For the next hour, we discussed the pros and cons of her leaving. I grabbed my paper and wrote down all the reasons she should not leave Oklahoma. Lists made me feel in control by helping organize my confused thoughts.

Her family was here.

She couldn't depend on Kelley.

Her three-year-old son should not be dragged around the country.

She had no moolah to get back if things went wrong.

I would miss her.

But Marjorie pulled a trump card. "With this depression, it's hard to survive, sis. I gotta leave. There's nothing else to do. Papa threw me out, said he couldn't afford to keep me any longer. He's preoccupied with work. Gladys hates me and Mama doesn't want me around. I have absolutely no place to stay."

She was right. Even I didn't have a room to offer. None of my words could convince her to stay in Shawnee. The only thing I could do was pray for a safe trip.

"Try to understand. Kelley and I are still married and there's no use staying in this forlorn town any longer. A change will do me good. Besides, I still love him."

I didn't understand my sister. How could she love a man like that? One who clearly did not care about her? Unlike Marjorie, I had a stable, God-fearing husband. He would not abandon me like Kelley did Marjorie. Fremont and I were going to create a good family, no matter how hard times became. With persistence and hard work all my efforts would pay off. We would eventually have a happy, ideal home. Wouldn't we?

Luckily, Fremont's love didn't demand that I traipse all over creation to find him.

Two days later, I left to meet Marjorie before she hopped a train. I hoped to leave my children with my mother-in-law, but it was her grocery shopping day. I knew she also liked to saunter for hours through Woolworth's Five and Dime because I sometimes went with her. I would just have to take the children with me.

I met Marjorie at the Hamburger King, a narrow cafe on East Main Street. They made the best hamburgers in town, complete with toasted buns, homegrown tomatoes and sweet onions. So delicious. I bought two burgers and fries and shared mine with Margaret and Judson while Marjorie shared hers with Larry.

"Sis, do you remember some of Papa's house rules when we were growing up? No elbows on the table, and couldn't stand up when we ate hamburgers, we had to sit down."

I laughed. "He had the silliest rules."

As we ate, we chatted about family, the latest fashions and new movies, especially Carole Lombard's love for a bum in the movie reel *My Man Godfrey*.

Love. Marjorie knew nothing about love.

My sister wore her best day-dress, its puffed sleeves and belted waist matching the hat over rows of flat curls. "Where did you get the eye shadow?" I asked, knowing she used most of her funds for a train ticket.

"Oh, I make do, dearie. I smoked the bottom of the cold cream box with a candle and mixed in a dab of charcoal. Works well, don't you think?" She batted her eyes.

She looked nice, as usual, but I wondered if her rose-red lipstick would look as perfect when she arrived. Would she keep track of her hat? Her gloves? Larry? It was a long trip with many stops along the way.

After lunch we walked to the prominent Santa Fe Depot and waited inside on a bench. When the "all aboard" announcement came, she pulled on her doeskin gloves, tucked a bag under her arm and grabbed Larry's hand. My children and I followed her outside. I hugged her for a long time and then bent down to give Larry a tight squeeze. His eyes widened as he stared at the huge locomotive, black smoke pouring from the engine. The horn blast startled us and Judson put his hands over his ears. We stood in awe as the engine roared.

I yelled as Marjorie walked toward the train, "You can still change your mind!"

She didn't hear me. I watched as the conductor helped her and Larry up the steps into the car.

A minute later, they leaned out the train window and we smiled and waved. Goodbyes were tougher than I'd expected. I had no idea if I would ever see my sister again.

"You can always come back," I hollered over the noise as I ran to Marjorie. Our gloved fingers touched each other. "You don't need an invitation!"

I stepped back and watched the train depart. Tears ran down my cheeks. Family meant everything to me. Now my little sister and nephew chugged away to discover the wild blue yonder. When would I see them again? What would she find as she traveled to a different city, to a different state? Would she be happy? Would Kelley take care of them?

Questions kept reeling in my mind as the caboose thundered by and the train disappeared out of sight. My shoulders slumped. So many Shawnee people left town never to return. Many left the dusty plains without even sending back a postcard.

I grabbed my children's hands and meandered through downtown on our way back home, passing old men sitting under storefront awnings, Indians wrapped in shawls and shabby, barefoot children playing kickball in the alleys. A busy, dusty town, the center of the country, where farmers brought wheat to the flour mill and bonneted women examined bolts of printed cotton. What would happen to Shawnee if everyone left?

We walked over the Toonerville Trolley track, as we called it. It was being paved over, destroyed. Back when we were dating, Fremont and I paid a dime and rode that trolley almost every weekend, out north to the Oklahoma Baptist College, west to St. Gregory's, and back around south toward Tecumseh. At intersections, a bell rang to warn motorists and pedestrians. Not a smooth ride, it jerked and swayed, but it also provided a small amount of privacy for us to talk.

Marjorie was gone. It felt like she and the trolley tracks were disappearing into the past.

That night, I tossed under the covers, pulling the blanket up to my chin. Sleep evaded me. Nonsensical thoughts haunted me. I dreamed about running in circles through desert patches in search of water.

I worried about Marjorie. I worried about collecting money from people who hadn't a penny to spare. I worried about how to feed and clothe our children and help Mama and my younger sisters. So many worries.

Though we had a little money trickling in, not enough materialized to pay all the bills. Our filling station was drying up like the countryside. What were we to do?

Everyone seemed caught in the bad economy. The nation lingered in a downturn. I read every scrap of newspaper I could find and listened to Roosevelt's fireside chats on our Crosley radio. Hundreds of Shawnee families headed west with their jalopies piled high, carrying what household belongings they could. Neighbors—the Wilsons, the Bedfords, the Thompsons—all pulled up stakes one after another and headed west.

Fremont rolled over in bed, restless too. He sat up. "Did I tell you the Smiths came by today? They're heading out."

My heart sank. "I didn't know they considered leaving. Thought they were doing fine."

"Yeah, they were loaded down. Beds strapped on top of their old flivver and a chair sticking out the trunk. They stopped at the station to say goodbye and fill up before leaving."

They must be taking Route 66, the road that took hundreds, maybe thousands of folks who wanted to escape the dusty plains and stiff heat. It led nowhere. People disappeared down that highway and we never heard from them again. Luscious California seemed like a myth. According to Fremont who had been there, it wasn't a fable but how could I believe that?

Fremont ran his fingers through his hair, a habit when he puzzled over things. "Maybe we should leave with them."

"We can't give up yet," I pulled my long gown around me. "As long as the station is bringing in a little money, we should stick it out here."

No more big jobs arrived that month, at least not enough work to make the mortgage payment. Maybe we were not meant to be business owners, not cut out to take risks. Anxiety weighed heavy and I felt like the oak trees at Benson Park had fallen on my shoulders.

I liked to keep my mind busy. I liked debates and I liked to argue. Fremont didn't like the slightest disagreement so I never knew whether we agreed or not. He flat refused to discuss our financial problems. I decided to find a way by myself to see us through. A perfect mother needed funds.

I took a deep breath. We would not only survive but thrive in this restricting environment. We would create a family to be proud of. I heard that overcoming difficulties makes you strong. Well, now was the time to be strong.

Chapter Six

Sunday afternoon I encouraged Fremont to borrow his dad's Model A and drive us out to Bethel to visit his cousin Inez. A few days ago, she'd given birth to a baby boy and convalesced at home. I wrapped up some homemade cinnamon rolls, the smell dancing around me, and then rounded up Margaret and Judson to put on their jackets.

Fremont had grown up in Waco, Oklahoma, a tiny community ten miles west of Shawnee. At one time, the town had had a post office, a gristmill and a church for which the Popes had donated the acreage.

The Popes were a close-knit family. Fremont's Aunt Woodlie and Uncle Raleigh had stayed with them in Waco before building a cabin near Bethel, about five miles away. Their one and only child, Inez, was four years younger than Fremont. As children, the two walked together to the one-room schoolhouse and stayed close while growing up.

When we pulled into the farmhouse driveway, Fremont saw Uncle Raleigh down by the barn and took off after him. They loved to spend time together, sharing a knack for telling tall tales. Margaret and Judson ran ahead, jumping up and down.

Aunt Woodlie welcomed me into their small country home, thanking me for bringing cinnamon rolls. Her eyes sparkled, excited to have her first grandchild. "Inez is ready for a bit of company."

As I turned down the hall, Aunt Woodlie whispered hoarsely, "The children haven't been exposed to any sicknesses, have they? No colds? No runny noses?" She had lost a second child to diphtheria. She'd refused to let Inez be around anyone ill while growing up, overly protective of her daughter and apparently now her only grandchild.

"They haven't been sick," I answered.

"Good. I'll fix some lemonade," she said. "You just wander on back and visit Inez and hold that sweet baby."

Inez grinned when I walked in the door and I bent to kiss her cheek. Baby Marvin was about the sweetest thing I ever saw. I remembered when my own children had been this small, the joy of holding that tiny bundle. Had it been just a few years ago? I picked up the baby and sat on a small wooden chair by Inez's bed. I drew Marvin near my chest and held him close. His soft blond hair felt like the fuzz of a newborn puppy and his eyes shone as if he knew the answers to all the mysteries of the universe.

"Here, I'll take him back now."

I handed the bundled baby back to his mother. She beamed. Like Fremont, Inez had the family's large, blue Pope eyes and calm spirit. She'd married Clyde Hensley in '33, the same year Fremont and I married. She had a real wedding, though. She didn't run off like we did. She married at Blackburn Chapel three months before graduating from Bethel High School. Their pastor told the church he would marry any couple for free if they would help start a Bible class, so three couples walked the aisle and started meeting that month.

"God sure blessed me, Sibyl. Been looking forward to the day when I could hold my own little one." Inez, her long hair falling around her shoulders, was one of the proudest mamas I had ever seen. After Fremont and I married, Inez and I became fast friends. She visited me many times, brought homemade potato soup and rocked my two little ones. Even then I could sense her underlying melancholy because she didn't have a child of her own. She'd had three miscarriages before finally giving birth to Marvin.

"God pulled us through some tough times, didn't he? I heard how sick you were last week. You should have called Dr. Fortson about that high fever."

After Inez married and left her mother's protected home, she was exposed to the panorama of childhood diseases, including this last round of measles. Poor Inez. As an adult, she caught everything. I hoped she didn't pass her illness on to Marvin.

"Don't be silly. It's only the measles and everyone gets the measles sometime. I'm feeling better now. Anyway, God has been my helper since I was twelve."

Such a specific age, I had to ask. "Twelve?"

"Did I ever tell you about my first encounter with him?"

"No, you didn't," I settled into the chair. Listening was the best gift I could give.

"Our family went to a tent revival outside of town at Bethel Church. You know where that is?"

"I've been there."

"We had enough gasoline to get to the revival a time or two. But during the service, I kept thinking that something was missing. I went to bed that night and worried that something was seriously wrong with me. I kept thinking 'something's going to get me.' I was trembling and so scared, I couldn't sleep."

"Because of the revival?"

"Not exactly, but it made it worse. You know how terror feels? Like a black widow spider crawling up your leg?"

I shuddered.

"That night toward the end of the revival, I prayed real hard. Desperate to get rid of the fear. My whole body was shaking, and then I sensed God's presence nearby."

Inez sat up straight in her bed and clutched baby Marvin tight.

"Sibyl, my fear left. All of a sudden, as I was praying, it just left."

My mouth fell open. "God did that?"

"Yes. I'll never forget. Jesus helped me that night. The next evening at revival, I shook hands with the preacher. I have no idea who he was, but my anxiety was completely gone."

"Did it come back? The fear?"

"Oh, I still have normal fear, like when I lost my baby girl last year, that was heartbreaking, but nothing like before the revival. Nope, that overwhelming fear has never come back."

I smiled with joy and decided to cuddle baby Marvin one more time before we left. Even though my hair-brained sister had skedaddled across the country chasing a no-good, rotten fellow and didn't have time for me or the family, I still had a sweet cousin living in Bethel with her precious baby full of promises.

I left feeling encouraged and calmer than I had in months. I had been so frustrated and depressed lately that I felt almost buoyant after basking in Inez's cheerful mood.

Two weeks later, Uncle Raleigh brought news into town. He dropped by Fremont's parents' house and told them that tiny Marvin had caught the measles from his mama. His fever soared and he was scalding to the touch. After a full day, his crying ceased. He lay limp, his face flushed. That poor, miserable newborn. Neither Inez nor Aunt Woodlie knew what to do for him. They decided to keep him home and bundled up, having no extra money to take Marvin to the doctor. It was only the measles, anyway, they said. Children recover.

I wondered if high fever was damaging to an infant. I remembered holding that sweet bright-eyed baby and my heart ached for Inez. I'm sure she and Aunt Woodlie were worried to pieces, afraid of losing another baby.

A week later, we heard the sickness went away and the fever went down. Most of the family breathed a sigh of relief but I determined to wait and see how the child developed.

I sensed how fragile children can be. I'm not sure I would have been calm if Margaret or Judson had been that ill. But they were healthy. Nothing would happen to them. Right?

The next morning I cooked up some chicken and dumplings and a spice cake to take to Inez's house. After dressing the children and packing a bag, Fremont and I borrowed the Pope's car and rode all the way to Bethel again to take Marvin a baby blue layout I crocheted.

Chapter Seven

Sears and Roebuck's was having a sale. Mama and I perused the hats—they were her weakness. Even though smaller pillbox hats and snoods were in style, she preferred large-brimmed felt hats with bow-tied flowers.

"I found a new job," Mama told me excitedly, rounding a corner.

Mama needed something to do, especially after leaving choir. She and my younger sisters had stopped going to First Baptist altogether. They sank deeper into gloominess. I encouraged them to visit Calvary, the church I joined when Fremont and I married. Caring people attended Calvary and Fremont's parents had been involved for years. I thought our sisters, Blanche and Irene, might become closer if they went to church together.

Mama had refused to go.

"A job is good news. The extra money should be helpful," I said from the next hat rack. "What kind of job?"

"I'm selling Spirella corsets. We have to survive, my dear, after your father's unfortunate desertion."

"Corsets?" I walked around toward her.

"I tote around a large suitcase filled with corsets of different materials and colors with a variety of prices, including several corsets for overweight women."

"How belittling. Look, here's a hat you might like." I modeled a one-dollar green felt cloche with a pheasant's feather.

"I can't see myself in that one," said Mama. "Anyway, I drag this heavy corset bag into someone's home, chat a while to make them comfortable, drink a glass of tea, and then ask the woman to strip down to her undies and lie on the bed."

I rearranged my own hat in a jaunty angle, refusing to picture the scenario in my mind. I couldn't imagine why society women succumbed to that embarrassment.

"It takes all my strength to lace the corset on her, pulling the whalebone so tight the woman huffs like a stuck pig. I pull and pull." Mama leaned back, pulling an imaginary rope.

I couldn't help the giggle. Mama could be so funny sometimes.

"Finally, the woman stands up and checks the mirror to see if she looks thinner. That's when I tell her how beautiful an hour glass figure makes her look."

"I hope it pays well."

"Isn't my job a dandy?" said Mama.

A guffaw burst out of me. Mama, trying to be serious, ignored the hilarity until she finally broke down and laughed with me.

"I have to hold my breath to keep remarks from coming out of my mouth," she admitted. "Honestly, I don't think selling corsets suits me too well. I'll have to find another way to make a dime."

I agreed, but we all needed a good to laugh during these trying times. And we needed stylish hats.

"All laughing aside, after what your papa did, I'll never trust another man again. They're not worth it. And your papa's the worst." A henna-colored brimmed hat fell off her head and I caught it, feeling the texture of the felt and fluffy quail feathers.

A church acquaintance looked at us from the next aisle and turned away. Mama humphed and left the hat displays carrying the henna hat and headed toward the check-out counter. The dated cartwheel hat was a bargain at five cents but a bright colored hat might lift her spirits.

"You'll make it through, Mama. I know you will." People, especially old society friends, looked down on Mama for her position, but it seemed ridiculous to me.

"I make the most of it. Do what I can to get by. Can't respect a man who won't feed his own kids. Course, can't respect a man who conducts business the way your papa does either. Men. I hate 'em."

I struggled not to catch Mama's hostility. Bitter words are better left unsaid. I wished she'd let go of the anger against Papa, let it slide away. Sick of her whining, I wanted her to set aside the hurt and not bring it up every single time we talked. At the same time, I sympathized with her poverty, aching over the horrible situation.

She had stooped low to care for my two young sisters. I mean, selling corsets? I decided to visit Papa and give him a word myself. A strong word. He needed to stand up and do right.

Mama purchased the monstrosity of a hat and we walked to her house.

"Come in," she said. "I need to discuss your brother."

Within minutes we were in the kitchen sipping a shared bottle of cold soda pop and discussing what to do with Calvis, my brother who perpetually found trouble. After the divorce, Calvis lived a few weeks with Papa in the City but returned to finish his senior year at Shawnee High School. At seventeen years old, he was hard to control. Mama blamed Papa. Papa blamed Mama.

"Papa dropped by the other day to visit Frances and Blanche." She hugged her glass with two hands. "But all he wanted to do was talk about Calvis. Humph. What does he know?"

"Calvis will be able to graduate, won't he?"

"Your papa wants the boy to come live with him again. As if that's a good idea," she said. "However, a boy does need a man around. Someone to teach him a few things. Come to think of it, Calvis might be better off if I send him back. He's caused me a lot of heartaches."

From boyhood, Calvis seemed unable to escape difficulty. He rode bicycles in his Sunday suit, fired his pea shooter at smaller kids, demanded to be the leader or he wouldn't play, and got arrested for following too close to a firetruck and interferring. Mama bailed him out of jail.

As the only boy in a home where Papa was often gone, Mama blamed her son for anything that went wrong. Then when Papa returned from his trips, he would lecture the boy.

I loved my brother, but sometimes I felt jealous of him. He received decent attention from our father, although maybe not the right kind of attention. Papa wanted a boy and as the oldest child in the family, I disappointed him by being a girl. Trying to please Papa had shaped my life. Maybe it had shaped all of our lives.

Chapter Eight

Mama and my sisters needed financial help. Their cupboards were nearly bare and I needed to tell Papa about it.

He lived in Oklahoma City and I'd never traveled outside Shawnee alone before. I had to find a way to get there. Fremont had only a few customers at the filing station but he needed to be available.

A couple of days passed and before I could find a ride, I heard a knock on my front door. I opened it, and there stood Papa. Of all people. Suave, debonair Papa, straight out of a Sears and Roebuck catalog. He seemed out of place on my dingy front porch.

This was the first time I'd seen him since the divorce three months ago. He'd visited Frances and Blanche, but hadn't dropped by our house since I'd refused to testify for him. Honestly, I wasn't sure if I was ready to face him. He'd hurt every member of my family, and I'd been left to pick up the pieces. The divorce proceedings had been a farce. Papa and Mama yelling at each other, and demanding each of their five children choose between them. I cringed when I remembered my youngest sister, Frances, crying, "No! No!"

"Papa, what are you doing here?" After all that happened, he was my father and I had missed our chats.

"I'm passing through town on my way to audit a bank down in Maude. Thought I'd stop in." He wore a homburg hat, a dapper suit and spit-shined shoes. A forceful man.

"Come in. Come in." I tore off my splattered apron and scanned the house. While he stepped inside and stood, I rushed around to pick up toys and clothes, wiped off the kitchen table and sent the children outside. I glanced down at my torn house dress, one Mama made from scraps. She'd sewed ruffles on the front to cover the stain. Embarrassed, especially with Papa looking so debonair, I crossed my arms to cover it.

Papa looked around the kitchen disdainfully but agreed to sit for a cup of coffee. I made it like he liked it, dark and strong. I updated him on the children, and then I thought I would talk about religion and politics before jumping into Mama's circumstances.

"I've learned so much at Calvary Church. Just this past Sunday, the pastor said—"

"Traditional religion hinders progression," Papa blurted out. "Most faiths are unconcerned with the truth and disregard the welfare of their brothers and sisters. Self-righteous churches are to blame."

I shifted away from him. "I don't understand, Papa. What's wrong with the church?"

"As a universalist, I believe we should gather together to share ideas. However, one of the gravest errors is that traditional church members give too much importance to saving individuals. Our forefathers could have saved humanity from self-destruction rather than teaching a man how to save his own soul. How self-centered, to focus on the individual rather than on what's good for mankind."

Papa toed a toy out from under the table.

I walked to the window and looked out. Margaret and Judson were swinging on the porch swing.

"It's like your children," he continued. "If left in poverty, as your life now stands, they will fall into a life of disrepute. They will have no opportunity to do good."

I couldn't believe Papa was talking about the poor—my family—when he wouldn't support his own children. "You're wrong. I can teach my children, Papa. I'll teach them right and wrong."

"You can't give them all they need. You're poor as a beggar yourself. Soon you'll be one of those do-gooders asking for the Social Security money they allotted last year. You won't be able to make this marriage to a poor man succeed."

I wanted to argue but Papa continued. "Do you understand this whole state has been scourged with bank failures over the past few years? As a bank examiner, I help liquidate the banks that can't continue. And for that I'm despised. Do you think it's an easy job?"

"I didn't say that, Papa," I said, trying to appease him. "You have a difficult job and these lawsuits against your old boss, Barnett, must have been hard on you."

Papa leaned back in his chair and looked exasperated, as if he had explained it many times before. "Dishonest men have made a fortune from this bank fiasco, and I've done what I can to make it right. December was not a good month, what with testifying against Barnett only days before your mother dragged me off to court for a divorce I never wanted. She hardly considered what was best for my career. She only considered herself—as always."

I had no desire to talk about the divorce. Papa had an affair. He acted recklessly. He left my mother and abandoned our family. What more was there to say? I had set aside the pain and didn't want to resurrect it.

However, I was interested in the banking rumors. "I read in the newspaper that you were enmeshed in the scandal. I didn't realize you were a primary witness."

Papa stood and paced the kitchen, dismissing the dirty cake pan and unclean floor. Why could I never keep my house spotless?

"Your mother is the least of my worries," he said with a flip of his hand. "Barnett's a scoundrel, pure and simple. I think he absconded with more than what I discovered. More than the fourteen thousand."

I raised my eyebrows. That much money could purchase three houses.

Papa and I had not discussed matters like this since my parents' separation. It felt good to delve into political banking issues. "The destroyed bank records could have proven Barnett's innocence. Do you think they were destroyed on purpose?" I asked. "Why would anyone do that? Have pertinent documents burned? It looks suspicious."

"Enough of this talk." Papa grunted and rocked back and forth on his feet. "No need to talk about the case's merits, one way or the other. I did nothing wrong. And no one can get me to change my story. Bribery won't work on me."

Papa's short attention span left me unsure how to continue so I remained quiet, waiting for him to speak again. He grunted a second time and I wondered if he was hiding something. Maybe I didn't want to know.

"I say, Sibyl, you should find a job and help your family during this time of need." He plopped back down in the chair, seemingly satisfied that the bank discussion was over.

Papa had lied in the past. Lied for years about seeing other women while married to Mama. Was he lying now? Lying about his involvement in the scandal?

It would do no good to push him for answers so I said, "I tried to get a job in town, but there aren't any."

"Then get out of this backward town and come to the City with me. I'll set you up with a banking job—secretarial, of course. You can send money back home."

I hoped for more than secretarial work since Papa had groomed me to take charge, to be a leader. But any banking job would be helpful.

"Just until the economy improves," said Papa. "I take care of family, even when I'm knee deep in bank closures. Didn't I help my brother Glenn find a banking job in Vici?"

The prospect of a job excited me. Even though I'd gone to Shawnee Community College and worked for several years as a legal secretary, no one in Shawnee would give me a job. After all, I was married and most jobs went to family men or single women who needed to support themselves. If a job meant giving my children and family much needed funds, I might go.

Papa prepared to leave. He looked at me, his beady eyes drawn into a frown. "I failed to teach you and your sisters correctly. I see you're all floundering in the mire. Remember, a job's waiting." He grabbed his homburg hat and stuffed it on his head. "Think about it."

I stepped in front of him, blocking his way to the door. I had almost waited too long to bring up Mama. "Papa, you probably don't realize Mama's desperate situation. If you knew, you would help. She has very little money for food, much less anything else. The family's barely holding on."

His face hardened like the clay mud in our back yard. "Your mother made her own bed. I've walked away from her problems and I won't turn back."

"But Papa, you can't let the girls suffer because you're angry at Mama. They need your help." This was my chance to show Papa how his stubbornness affected our family.

"That's of no consequence. Those hooligans are her responsibility now, not mine. I never wanted them to begin with."

"They're still your children." This statement alone should pierce through Papa's conscience. At least he couldn't deny the fact.

"Agreed. I fathered them." Papa sighed heavily. "Therefore, I will do what my conscience dictates." He stormed out the door.

Thank God. Papa would do what was right even if he had to grit his teeth to do it. My papa may be a scoundrel at times, and keep secrets, but no decent father could ignore his children's needs. No more than I could ignore the needs of Margaret and Judson.

Chapter Nine

April 1936

"Dance class at school?" I asked Blanche while we sat on the front porch and dangled our feet over the side. "Do you like it?"

"It beats push-ups." She hesitated and lowered her voice. "But could you please give me a few dance lessons? I don't want to look like a fool. Irene makes fun of me as it is. She thinks it's ridiculous to study so hard and make good grades when a D will do. I'm not sure she'll make it through the semester."

"Surely it can't be that bad," I said.

Irene had gone to Washington Grade School on the south part of town while had Blanche attended Jefferson on North Kickapoo. The schools were on opposite sides of the railroad tracks. But now the students went to the same high school and must get along, no matter their economic status.

"When I signed up for art class, Irene laughed at me," said Blanche. "She said, 'Who takes art classes during this depression? It won't help you get a job. And with your bean-pole figure and long face, you'll need a way to support yourself for a long time.'"

To be sure, Blanche was a talented artist, but I also knew her talent would not keep classmates from laughing at her.

"Sure," I told her. "We can practice dancing." Marjorie and I snuck out to dances before we married and I must admit, many a fellow stared at my long legs doing the jitterbug.

"You won't believe this," said Blanche, "but Irene's mother won't let her dance. It's against her religion."

"How do you know?"

"Everyone knows. Mrs. Pope went to the principal and asked for Irene to be excused from gym."

"There's nothing wrong with her mother pulling her out of class. She has that freedom."

"I know, but it wasn't Irene's choice. She sneaks out and dances at Friday night parties all the time. She was furious with her mother."

I felt sorry for Irene. Mother Pope tried to keep a tight rein on her, maybe too tight.

The next day, I brought my Crosley radio to Mama's and set it up. We rolled back the Persian rug, revealing a slick wooden floor.

A new song began to play and I found my feet tapping and my shoulders swaying. Music did that to me. I decided "Don't be that Way" by Benny Goodman would be one of my new favorites. I loved the rhythm, the swirls, the movements. I didn't realize I had missed dancing so much—missed letting go, missed feeling the beat reverberate through my body. Music was part of me—an expression of myself. I gave up dancing for Fremont while we were dating, and we never discussed it again.

Though I wanted to connect with Blanche, I was hesitant about spending a lot of time with her. I hated my sister's sarcastic, cutting remarks. So far, my efforts to guide her heart had not made a difference. I hoped dancing lessons would help.

My youngest sister, Frances, slipped into the room. One of her feet turned in a little, and although she was a pretty child, the turned foot didn't look good and no one wanted to see her limp through life. Mama heard that ballet classes could straighten out Frances's foot, so she talked to the ballet teacher and made a deal with her to do washing in return for tap, toe and ballet lessons. Frances turned out to be a swell dancer, graceful and rhythmic.

"Can I dance, too?" Frances asked.

"Join the party," I said.

Frances' special sandals made it hard for her to move smoothly so she kicked them off and danced barefoot.

Blanche, Frances and I laughed like sisters should. The song, "Thanks for the Memory" by Bob Hope warmed me inside. I enjoyed spending time with the girls, and fortunately, I didn't have to worry about Blanche's negativity. She was on her best behavior. While we danced, she never said a nasty word.

I started to comment on her improved attitude when Mama walked into the room, followed by Margaret and Judson. They stopped to watch as we danced to "The Dipsy Doodle" by Tommy Dorsey.

The song stopped and I took a deep breath, panting. "Mama, I think she's going to be a great dancer. We've been practicing for hours."

"All my girls are good dancers, dear."

"Just Sibyl. She's the best dancer ever." Blanche beamed and I could see she'd enjoyed the time together as much as I did.

Mama agreed with Blanche. "Sibyl, you could have been another Ginger Rogers, dancing your heart out with Fred Astaire. Too bad that day is long past. That's one more thing you lost because of Papa."

"One more dance!" exclaimed Blanche. "Just one more dance and you can quit." About then, "A Tisket, a Tasket" came on the radio and I grinned. Just one more dance.

Mama joined us, her housedress swirling around her like a tent while the children held hands and jumped up and down. The wooden floor bounced from all the activity. Life was lighter with a little play.

Fremont believed like his mother, that dancing was of the devil. I understood why he didn't like barrooms with their drinking and carousing, but what was wrong with a little rhythm in private? I didn't want to tell him about the lessons, but I also didn't want to hold anything back from him. Open communication, as I learned from my parents' problems, seemed important to a good relationship. But perhaps I could wait until the end of Blanche's semester.

While doing long jumps in gym class a few days later, Blanche sprained her ankle. Mama soaked her foot and ankle in hot water and rubbed it with the horse liniment we had used for generations. Then she wrapped a bandage around it.

Blanche had to use Grandpa's walking cane to ambulate the nine blocks to school and grumbled about the end of her dancing career.

My conscious pricked me, and I told Fremont I'd given her dance lessons. He wisely gave me leeway to make my own choices, not responding one way or the other, even when the children danced around the house mimicking the Trimble sisters.

Chapter Ten

Saturday morning I peeked through the bedroom curtains and watched the dented fender of Dad Pope's Model A Ford pull into our driveway. Fremont slid out from the driver's seat of the tin can. He looked particularly handsome this morning, a wave of dark hair falling across his forehead. My heart skipped a beat.

"Hurry honey," he called as he entered our bedroom, his blue eyes sparkling. "You don't have to get all fancied up. We're just going out to the farm."

Wanting to impress Fremont's parents and not look foolish, I spent an hour deciding what to wear. Preoccupied with babies and housework, I had not had time to visit their farm in Waco until now, although I heard much about its attraction. Tall oak trees, cool porches and wildflowers. Finally, I'd be able to go.

I settled on an ankle-length print dress, a brown straw hat and a light jacket. Impressive, but not too swanky.

"Mother and Dad are waiting." Fremont escorted me to the car. He seemed more reserved than usual, not that he usually displayed affection in front of others.

I nodded and said hello. They looked older than their years as they sat in the back seat. The Popes dressed simply and owned few possessions, so different from my own parents, Papa with his dapper suits and Mama in her fur coats. Margaret squeezed between my in-laws, while our rambunctious toddler sat on my lap.

Fremont attempted to start the Model A several times, pushing in the clutch and grinding the gears. Finally, the engine roared to life and we rambled down Beard Street and turned west onto Hardesty Road. Like most rural dirt roads in Pottawatomie County, the narrow lane went straight, going up and down hills like a lazy roller coaster.

The farther west we drove, the more accentuated the red clay ruts in the road became. Loose dirt lay piled high along the fences from the fierce winds, and roadrunners scurried in front of us. Fremont dodged holes and rampant sagebrush. We passed New Hope Cemetery and a few houses scattered among patches of post oaks, the budding trees interspersed through plowed-up pastures. The recent dust storms had done damage, but they had not destroyed everything in their path.

"Good driving, son." Dad broke the silence. "Hope this jalopy makes it back home." The engine sputtered every time Fremont went over twenty miles an hour.

"We'll make it, just have to take 'er mighty easy," said Fremont.

During the bumpy ride, ten miles west and two miles south to Waco in Brenton Township, Fremont waved out the window to a driver headed in the opposite direction, the only other vehicle we saw on the way. Waco was named after an Indian tribe, but that's about all I knew about it. We turned south on Okay Road.

"That's where the old post office used to be." Mother pointed to the right. "It closed before my time. And there's the gristmill."

"And here's the church." Fremont pointed to a faded white clapboard building with a cross on top.

Fremont turned around at the church and pulled right into a dirt driveway of the old Pope place, his grandparents' original home.

"Welcome to the old farmhouse," Mother spoke as we stepped from the car. "Couldn't make a living here. Had to move to town." Her voice sounded warm as if disclosing family history to a bosom friend. She looked different as she stood, no longer dowdy, but prim and proper, carrying herself well.

Beside the worn pathway, overgrown honeysuckle covered a barbed-wire fence and released a sweet, pungent smell. The path led to wooden steps, and a long porch stretched across the front of the house.

"Ollie grew up here where John Pope and his wife Amanda homesteaded," said Mother. "Back when it was Oklahoma Territory. Got the hundred and sixty acres from an Indian who couldn't make a go of it. John registered his land once he'd stayed the five years. Later, he sold this eighty acres to us." Mother—Eva Katherine Castleman—met Ollie Pope here in Waco.

Fremont and his father headed to the rear of the house, the children following. Mother Pope opened the door to the wooden house and our steps echoed as we walked through the empty rooms. A thick layer of dust carpeted the floor. I touched the faded dull apricot walls, and saw that it was once been painted a creamy yellow. I removed my hat and fanned myself while Mother pushed open a tall window to air out the musty smell.

"Fremont's grandparents used a corner of this living area as a bedroom," Mother said. "There's another room upstairs. Quite a large house, if I do say so." We wandered through the bare kitchen toward the back while Mother continued to chatter, her gathered skirt swishing around her feet. Comfortable and easy-going, she made me feel at ease.

The house needed a good cleaning. It had no indoor running water, no place for an icebox and only a pot-bellied stove to cook on. I stepped daintily, tiptoeing over the grubby floor. I should never have worn fine clothes to an abandoned farmhouse.

We stepped onto the back porch where Mother pointed to a large kettle. "This here's the black pot for the washing," said Mother. "We set it over a fire to boil water, and eventually we bought an agitator. That sure cut down on the work." She yelled around the corner. "Ollie, when are you going to carry this pot into town? I sure could use it!"

"Don't reckon I know," Dad yelled back. "My clothes seem fine without all that much trouble."

"Next week?" Mother asked.

"Right, right. We'll get her done."

Mother turned back to me. "We moved here when we first married. His mama taught me how to churn butter, wring a chicken's neck, and lay white clothes on the grass to bleach 'em. Things like that."

We walked toward the rusted tin roof of the chicken house, and I held my dress above my knees and stepped around bull nettle and dandelions that covered the path. My high heels left tiny holes in the hardened ground. I felt like a duck landing in a dried-up pond. The large vegetable garden had transformed into a sticker patch.

"We used to have a fairly good crop, but so did everyone else, and prices got so bad I couldn't sell a nickel's worth," said Mother. "Farmers grew more food than people could afford. So we let the garden go to weeds and don't gather except what we can give away or store for the winter."

Dad pointed to the fields behind the house. Wheat fields dotted with wild thistles and Indian paint brush. We could see a quarter a mile to the top of the next rise. "Lots of work to do." He hitched his thumbs into his overall pockets. We gazed over the horizon, quiet for a few minutes. The farm was nestled in a hollow. Whippoorwills whistled from the patch of woods, and the wind sang through the crooked post oaks. Children's laughter sounded in the background. An almost magical peace enveloped the farm.

Although not a farm girl, the homestead intrigued me. The possibility of living away from close neighbors, gossip, and judgment about my family's ordeal sounded inviting. By the time the tour ended, I also realized the heavy work required to live on a farm, back-breaking for men and women alike. I felt pride knowing Mother Pope had taught me so many physically challenging tasks. I could manage here. For the first time, I understood why Dad wanted to move back, understood the joy such a life might bring.

Mother brought out a picnic lunch, and we gathered on a patchwork quilt spread under the maple tree. I folded my dress carefully under myself, positioning the material so as to not touch the red dirt. A cool breeze fanned away the worst of the heat, a reminder of the breeze in my bedroom window this morning. Breezes bring change, Mama often said.

We pulled out cold biscuits and crispy fried chicken from baskets. Mother poured lemonade from a jug. As I bit into a chicken leg, Dad started praying. I swallowed my bite, hushed the children and looked down, examining the hand-embroidered tea towels covering the food.

"Lord, thank you for this farm and the time we have together. Bless this food and help it nourish our bodies. In Jesus' name. Amen."

Everyone repeated, "Amen."

Dad lifted his head and laughed, "Ain't it good to be here!"

"I remember the mighty hard work it takes." Fremont's head cocked toward his dad. "Most days from dawn to dusk." Even as a young boy, Fremont had tilled the farm along with his dad and granddad. He had been brought up with a strong work ethic. One of the things I admired about him.

"Hard work ain't nothing. Ain't no rest for the weary." Dad grinned. "However, I do recall your interests lay more in fixing old Mr. Stephen's broken-down tractor than in hoeing weeds."

"Guess I'm not the farmer you are, Dad."

"Don't worry. We'll come back, all right. Yes, sir, we'll come back. Got to plow this land under again so it'll be ready for the spring rain."

Something about Mother's countenance lit up like fireflies when they talked about returning to the farm. The same as when Dad looked over the fields and spoke of working the soil or pulling buckets of cool water up from the well. Even Fremont reminisced about the good old times when he'd lived there as a boy.

I had never slept in a leaky loft or used an outhouse or ridden a horse across the countryside. I would never have memories of being ten years old and leading a team of mules to work the soil. Fremont's childhood was different than mine. My papa had money, dressed us fancy, and allowed us to be introduced to high society, even when he was too busy to spend time with us.

As we picked up and gazed over the farm one last time, I studied Fremont's strong, pleasing profile. He was the handsomest man I had ever seen. He slipped his arm around me, and I felt his warm breath near and thought—*this is him, his way of life*. He stared far away, past the empty clapboard structure, the overgrown garden and the dusty fields. A solid, dependable man. Was he thinking of moving back to the country?

As much as I loved him, adapting to this way of living would be hard. I wanted to live life to its fullest, not become some drab housewife with a passel of kids, especially if it meant living on a hardscrabble farm and canning blackberries for the rest of my life.

"Not what I want," I muttered to myself, recognizing the vast ravine between our two worlds. Could we find a way to come together? Could success be found in the middle?

"Son, we need to buy seed for this year's crop," Dad said. "Weather permittin' and the economy improves, we'll be moving back come summer."

Did 'we' include Fremont and I? Hopefully, Fremont wouldn't ask me to move to a destitute farm. But what if moving to the farm was our only choice of surviving through this down-turn?

Chapter Eleven

May 1936

Calvis got a singing part in the Shawnee school play, surprising all of us. The potential star of the show strutted around until a week before the play, when he came home with his ego busted.

"They're not going to let me perform," he said, throwing his hands in the air.

I was standing by the window at Mama's house, watching Margaret do somersaults on the front lawn when Calvis returned from school that day. "Not let you perform? Why? You already have the part."

"One uppity school teacher talked to the principal about it," said Calvis. "She said I should not be allowed to perform due to my parents' disgraceful situation."

"Because of the divorce?" I asked.

"It sets a poor example for the others." Calvis' youthful face scrunched up.

Mama walked into the house and Calvis updated her on the latest problem.

"I know all about it," said Mama. "The principal and I discussed it in the school office today. He told me about the complaint."

"Am I in trouble?" Calvis looked sheepish. He had often been called into the principal's office to explain his shenanigans. Naturally he expected to be admonished.

"I told the principal what happened between your papa and me. It wasn't your fault. You had nothing to do with our divorce." Mama took a deep breath as she took off her colorful hat. She set it on the coffee table. "It isn't even my fault. Mr. Trimble is to blame for this one."

Expecting Mama to go into a rant about Papa, I turned back to the window to watch the children playing. Judson tried to imitate Margaret but fell on his rump and both broke out in giggles. They made me smile. Too bad my brother and sisters couldn't be as carefree as my children. Constant somberness can leave a bitter taste.

"Well . . ." Calvis said, impatient to find out the results. Would he be able to sing or not?

"The principal said, 'I'll see that he can sing in the play.' So keep practicing. I think you're in."

Calvis let out a holler. I'm not sure how, but he was allowed to sing in the school program.

Calvis was a pretentious young man who loved nice clothes. Mama bought him a new shirt for the event, and he borrowed one of Papa's jackets, which had a narrow waist and broad shoulders. He completed the look with cuffed trousers that tapered into wide angles.

I left the children at the Popes' for the evening. The crowded auditorium was no place for two young children, especially an unruly little boy. Besides they loved staying with their grandparents, listening to Grandpa tell wild stores and helping Grandma bake brownies.

We walked up the concrete steps to the Shawnee High School auditorium and entered the auditorium. I saw Mama and the girls in their Sunday-go-to-meeting clothes. They wore tailored dresses, gloves and shoes to match. Fremont and I sat behind them, and I leaned to see around Mama's broad-brimmed flowered hat. In front of us, a sea of millinery covered the room.

We enjoyed the play, especially Calvis' solo, "The Object of my Affection." The crowd responded as we did, clapping loudly. I fought back tears because he sang so splendidly. His baritone voice could beat Bing Crosby's any day. He always said he wanted to sing for a living, and he had the talent to do it. Although all my siblings could sing, Calvis was the one who could impress a crowd. I swelled with pride.

Papa sat in the back and after the play, he cornered us in the hall.

"It's time Calvis moves back to the city with me," he told Mama. "Young men need guidance. He needs to be taught an effective means of earning a living. A boy needs correct influence to be important in this world."

My heart dropped. I knew Papa wanted Calvis to live with him because he hated Calvis' interest in music and wanted to discourage it.

Gladys, Papa's bouncy girlfriend, stood a few steps behind him, tapping her foot.

"He does need a man in his life, I'll say," Mama said, clutching her pocketbook in front of her. She avoided looking directly at Papa or Gladys.

"If he comes to live with me, I'll make sure he obtains a college education and a good job," Papa said. "I promise. He can attend any school he wants. Back east, best education money can buy. Course, if he doesn't come, well . . . I can't assure anything."

Mama nodded her head and mouthed *okay*, then turned and stomped away.

I ran to catch up with her and shot her a questioning look.

"What can I do?" Mama shrugged. "After all, he's the father. I don't have enough money to pay for college and your papa owes him that much."

Calvis was shuffled off to Papa's house once again, back to Oklahoma City, toward the end of his senior year. I remembered the many times Calvis would sing along with the radio and Papa would tell him to shut up. What would happen to his music now?

The next weekend, Papa picked up Blanche and Frances from Mama's and took them out to Bell Street Cafe. Mama had an Eastern Stars social to cook for and wouldn't be back until supper time, so I was enlisted to be there when they returned. The children and I had been waiting for an hour. It gave me time to clean Mama's kitchen and dust the end table where her knickknacks rested.

When they walked in, Frances said in her little girl voice, "Blanche wouldn't tell Papa 'thank you' for taking us to the restaurant or the soda shop afterward. I got the biggest chocolate malt they make and thanked Papa for it." Her dress flared as she twirled.

"I shouldn't have to thank him. He owes us," said Blanche. "He *should* be taking care of us."

"You should mind your manners," I told Blanche.

"He spouted so much about liberalism and needing funds to march toward the Kingdom of God, I could hardly stomach it." Blanche's tall lanky arms flapped in the air, narrowly missing the porcelain vase sitting on the end table.

I didn't want to get into a discussion about Papa's beliefs so I changed the subject. "Did you see Calvis?"

"He didn't go. Gladys didn't come either. She had shopping to do." Frances took her shoes off and dove toward the couch.

"Did Papa say how Calvis was doing?"

"Calvis lives at the YMCA." Blanche used her mocking voice. "I assume his waywardness didn't suit Gladys. They probably had another one of their full-blown squabbles and Gladys wanted him gone for good this time. It's only been two weeks!"

I gasped. "He's living at the Y? Calvis isn't living with Papa?" The YMCA was an organization that cared for transients, homeless people and men with nowhere else to live. Not for high school brothers who had families to care for them.

"Papa said it was awkward around his house, what with Gladys and Calvis arguing and all," continued Blanche. "Papa explained it to us. He found Calvis a place to live in a nice room that's close enough for him to walk to school. Papa's paying for it, obviously."

My heart ached for Calvis. No home, shuffled back and forth between Mama and Papa, and now banked up in a community room. I splurged my pennies and called the YMCA and asked for Calvis Trimble. I waited at least ten minutes for them to find him.

"I'm not sure where I'll be living next month, sis," said Calvis. "But hey, neither Mama nor Papa want me. I can make it on my own. I got to be hard boiled, Sibyl, tough like Papa."

The phone call didn't help me feel better. Calvis sounded dejected. But I couldn't blame him. His disjointed home life would cause anyone to feel dejected.

A few weeks later, Calvis graduated from Central High School in Oklahoma City. Calvis' friend Joe told us about the graduation. After the ceremony, he had gone out afterward with Calvis and his buddies to celebrate. I would have liked to attend, but we didn't know until too late. Even then, we didn't have money for gasoline even if we had borrowed the Popes' car.

No one in the family went to the graduation. Mama didn't have a vehicle to travel there. Papa didn't watch Calvis graduate because he was too busy with private affairs. More like too busy getting remarried.

Papa and Gladys Shell Means married on May 16, 1936, six months after the divorce was final. He was forty-seven and she was forty. They had a private ceremony at a Universal Church in Oklahoma City. None of his children were invited.

Blanche saw the article in *The Oklahoman*. When Mama saw it, she hissed through her teeth.

Chapter Twelve

"Recovery Looms just around the Corner" the newspaper headline read and I wanted to believe it. Springtime promised hope. Daffodils popped up early. Redbud trees began to bloom. Quick showers came. If a full rain fell, we might have a decent harvest this year.

I worked hard to manage our house money, stooping over the dining room table, my head bent low over bits of paper. The scraps were covered with numbers and names and lists of amounts due from the filling station work. The bookkeeping I'd learned at the business college years ago was being put to good use. Part of my desire to be a good mother involved managing our home's finances. Hopefully I could find a good job soon.

I wrote and rewrote lists of income and expenses but no answer came out positive. I fought for every penny we had and remained determined not to touch my emergency stash of money unless absolutely necessary.

Flyaway curls fell around my face and I brushed them back, hoping to find a solution to our monetary problems. Fremont and I hardly ever argued but when we did, it was over the lack of money. No money meant no food and no clothes for growing children.

Dismayed at my failure to reconcile our spending and income, I set aside my lists and took the children for a walk. We sauntered down the

Main Street sidewalk. I pushed our ornate stroller, my oldest tot trying to keep up with me. A vendor touted hot tamales in corn husks wrapped in newspapers, and I was tempted to splurge a dime. Weary horses clopped along the street pulling carriages. Old bearded men sat on stools under the eaves of downtown drugstores and looked up at the sky and shook their heads. No moisture today. I understood their dejection. I, too, felt like the dull days would never end.

Late afternoon, my children should have been taking a nap. Instead they trailed me wearily to the Safeway Grocery Store on Main and Broadway. Judson threw a fit just as I was searching in my pocketbook for change. The clerk waited patiently while I pulled him off the floor. I paid for the hamburger meat for the night's meal and rushed home.

Fremont, always hungry after a long day at work, scarfed down every spread as if it were his last. Therefore I tried to have dinner ready at the end of the day when he walked in the front door. Despite all my rushing, Fremont came home late. The potatoes looked like mush and the hamburger gravy was cold. My frustration simmered and boiled over. I turned my back, hiding my anger as he sat down at the table. The children, having already eaten, played in the other room.

I wanted to discuss a serious problem that Fremont insisted on ignoring.

I took a deep breath and turned toward him. "We don't have enough money for this month's mortgage payment."

"I know, honey, I know." He shrugged his shoulders.

"We should not have bought this filling station in the first place." I said, accentuating each word. "Papa knew better. He gave us bad advice."

"We didn't have to listen to him." Fremont's voice remained low and steady even when I got upset. "*We* made the choice, remember."

"Well, we made the wrong choice." My voice rose even though I tried to control it. "Or else we can't do anything right. What are we going to do? No money for next week's food and the mortgage payment is coming due."

Guilt for my outburst overcame me. "I'm sorry. I didn't mean it to sound like that." Unkindness popped out of my head like a torch sometimes, burning everything. That wasn't the kind of person I wanted to be. My mother-in-law declared emotions were not sinful, but I experienced emotional ups and down that made Judson's temper tantrums look like entertainment. There must be a better way to handle anxiety.

Fremont had the patience of Job, I thought, but my fears crowded out the compliment.

I was upset with Papa for getting us into this situation and angry with Fremont for our failure. Right in the midst of this misery, I stopped. This was my fault.

If I hadn't gotten pregnant . . . . If I hadn't gotten married . . . . If I hadn't had a second child . . . . If I had kept my job . . . . Why, I'd encouraged Fremont to buy the filling station, for mercy's sake. The blame fell on me. If I had kept better account of our money . . . . If I hadn't spent so much on food . . . . If I'd helped Fremont collect what was due . . . . If any one of those things or all of those things . . . then maybe life would have been different.

I dropped my head in defeat. We were going to lose everything.

Who was I to blame others? It was my fault we were poor.

"I'm so sorry." I shook my head and tried to stop my racing thoughts. Why did I act like a shrew when life got tough? Why couldn't I be composed and trust God the way Fremont did? Would I ever have a calm and secure family?

I cradled my head between my hands. Fremont put his arms around me and pulled me close. I felt his warm breath as he whispered, "We're going to make it, honey. It's mighty hard now, but we're going to make it."

I tucked the tired children into bed and kissed them goodnight. Then I sat down at the foot of my bed. "Lord," I prayed silently, "help me understand the anger. Help me let it go."

I liked to use my mind and had little outlet. Tonight, I wanted to discuss with Fremont what the Bible taught about finances, and consider God's plan in all this. I wanted to rethink our financial situation based on what I had studied.

Fremont saw only black and white. Either we trusted or we didn't. He was a concrete thinker, a what-you-see-is-what-you-get kind of guy. Definitely opposites, he was a plodder and I wanted to go further and faster. Like the rabbit and turtle story, I was the rabbit. But needless to say, in the book, the turtle always won.

"Maybe the economy will recover as the newspaper promised," I told Fremont when he sat down beside me. "Maybe business will pick up at the station."

"I'm doing all I can, honey." His voice deepened and his blue eyes turned sad. "I'll look for a second job tomorrow. Old Mr. Simpson may need some plowing this year. His sons have up and gone west."

Then I had an idea. I couldn't keep the excitement out of my voice. "Let's talk to Papa. He said he'd help if we needed it. He offered me an office job, but I don't want to leave you and the children. Not unless I absolutely have to. Maybe he can give us a loan."

"Not sure it'll help," he said.

"It'll help. And he's the only one we know with enough money to get us through."

"You're a might smarter than I am and if you think that's a good idea, I'll go along, but I'm not sure it's for the best."

Papa had made it possible for us to purchase the filling station. And Papa said he respected Fremont for his fortitude in the midst of family difficulties. Papa the social-minded, although I had seen no action on his part, claimed he wanted to help the downtrodden. Maybe he would help us now. He might not help my mother, but I hoped he would be willing to pull his oldest daughter out of the hole into which she'd fallen.

Good deeds were buried deep inside Papa somewhere. With a little prayer and a lot of begging, he might acquiesce and help us through. After all, he'd been my hero since I was a little girl.

One Sunday when I was young, as we were eating the midday meal, we heard sirens wailing. Fire wagons tore by and screeched to a halt in the next block. Papa and all of us kids ran down the street and found an old lady's house on fire. She was screaming for somebody to save her trunk because it had all her treasures in it. My dad consulted with another man and the two of them bounded into the burning building, flames lapping around them. We were biting our nails and about to cry for fear we would lose Papa. A few minutes later, the men came out carrying the lady's trunk. Mama, pregnant at the time, didn't even know what was going on. We ran home and told her that Papa was the biggest hero in town.

My hero wouldn't let me down now.

Or was I being too optimistic?

Chapter Thirteen

June 1936

Fremont hated to ask for help. "A man feels degraded when he scrambles around trying to find mortgage money or scrape food together," Fremont said as we walked to the Popes house with our children, Judson riding on his shoulders.

Mother Pope gathered Margaret to her large bosom as we entered the house, exclaiming how big she had gotten, greeting us with enthusiasm like she forgot we had been there only a week ago.

We explained our situation, borrowed Dad's jalopy and kissed the children goodbye.

As we drove the Model A to Papa's home in Oklahoma City, I rehearsed how we would ask him for money, repeating the words several times to Fremont.

We drove up the long driveway and saw hundreds of irises, Papa's favorite flower. They bloomed in the front yard—yellow-toned Chickee Irises and red Siberians, just like the ones at Mama's house. Papa loved his flowers. He'd spent more time caring for them than he had his own children. I dismissed my negative thoughts.

Their new two-story rock house sat on an acre. It seemed showy to me, considering the dire situation of everyone else in the family, not to mention the thousands of jobless, homeless people forced to live in shanties along the North Canadian River.

Gladys greeted us at the front door, and I immediately saw the difference between their lifestyle and ours. Their house was shiny, newly painted and smelled of fresh lilacs. Quite a contrast to our house with its worn furniture, scratches on the walls and smell of sour milk and sweaty children.

"You might be interested in what I just purchased." Gladys' voice was an octave too high as she pranced in front of me through the living room. Her permanent waves bounced and her ready-to-wear outfit swayed.

I smoothed down my curls wishing I could afford a good haircut.

"I'm enjoying setting up house," said Gladys. "This is a special made, three-piece Angora Mohair living room suite."

I followed her around the house and she described her new Gibbard dining room set and jade green Steuben candlesticks. I watched her red lipstick move on her pale face.

She told me about her dishes—Staffordshire dinnerware. She clamored on about how difficult it was to choose the right paint color for the interior rooms. I stood quietly and nodded, looking at the expensive items, afraid I might vomit. The cost of any one of these items would feed my family for a month.

Eager to get away from her chatter, I joined Papa and Fremont as they walked into his office.

"Times are slow," Fremont said as we sat in front of a large oak desk, slick and shiny, glowing with importance.

Papa considered himself a big shot, wearing double-breasted suits and giving advice to small bankers. "I agree, but the state's financial problem could be eliminated with a few changes." He clasped his hands behind his head and leaned back. "I frown on overdrafts and question loans extending longer than is considered wise. Foolishly, people usually listen to my advice and promptly dismiss it, which gets them in a worse bind." Papa's laugh didn't sound funny to me.

"Sibyl and I are between a rock and a hard place, sir." Fremont looked at me and I nodded.

"It's too bad for poor old Herbert Hoover that he happened to be where he was," said Papa. "Times are so tough a monkey could have been elected against him. Not calling Roosevelt a monkey, you know, and I still judge the New Deal to be a gateway to communism." Blathering on about his disapproval of President Roosevelt and his deficit spending plan to revive the economy, Papa didn't give attention to our dire situation.

"Sir?" Fremont said.

But Papa went right on talking. "Not that I have anything against communism, you understand. It has possibilities if administered correctly. Not sure Roosevelt's the man to lead this country, but his plans might just work. Equality for all as I believe it. We hold the fate of our existence right here in our hands."

He paused long enough to take a breath. Fremont jumped on the moment. "We're trying to make our payment on the filling station. We're in a mighty bad predicament."

"I've spent most of my life as an analyst and studied all aspects of economics, especially the banking industry. People of goodwill have an obligation to succeeding generations to undo what we have stupidly permitted.

"Take the former bank commissioner Barnett for example. He finagled the system to his own benefit and look where it got him. Court marshaled. Corrupted of all things, even after Governor Murray trusted him. Stole money from investors."

"It doesn't look good," said Fremont.

"I say. You're correct. We must overturn greed to lighten the burdens of the less fortunate. As I've said many times, social justice can be attained if good people simply follow the Golden Rule and help one another. Yes sir, if people would just act on that, we could have a better society."

"We don't have enough money for the mortgage payment this month." Fremont glanced at me.

I shrugged. Papa wasn't paying attention at all. Had we come all this way for nothing? Didn't he understand what we were asking?

"Banks all over the country are struggling," said Papa with a tightness in his voice. "Besides that, many people hear of bank closings and run to take out their money. Bankers are hard-pressed to pay off these demanding depositors."

Irritated, I gritted my teeth to keep a scream from coming out of my mouth. What was wrong with Papa? We didn't care about bank closings. We needed a loan.

"Sir, we were wondering if you could help." Fremont leaned forward. "At least talk to the bank about extending our note? I know the economy's not doing well, sir, but I'm sure it'll improve. We just need more time."

Papa finally seemed to hear us. "Frankly, I'm disappointed in you and it wouldn't be right for me to ask the bank a favor, placing my own family above the many who are suffering. Also, I'm trying to keep my position secure, so that's a priority. I'll be glad to help Sibyl get a job at the bank, or even better, let me help with the children. You don't want them to grow up as disadvantaged as you are, do you?"

I seethed. How could he even bring the children into this conversation? The man had the manners of a mountain man.

"No, Mr. Trimble, sir," said Fremont. "You misunderstand. We're not here about a job for Sibyl or the children. We're just looking for a loan to help until times get better." Fremont balled his hands into fists, uncomfortable with begging.

"I see no reason to support a failing filling station. I've done my duty. If you can't make a go of it, that isn't my concern." Papa sounded as if he were dismissing a business meeting. "Wish I could help, son, but—"

"Please, Papa." I said quickly, thinking Papa would listen to me and understand the importance. "We're in a crisis. We need this station."

"Sorry. Can't do it." Papa pushed his chair back and stood. "Should have known you couldn't make it work. No training. No business experience. But I might say, I'm proud of the way you're handling these burdens. You are lucky." He looked at Fremont. "Sibyl possesses more common sense than most people."

Averting my eyes, Fremont staggered out the doorway with his head hung low.

My own Papa didn't care. All my life I'd sought Papa's approval, ever since I'd followed him around the country like a loyal puppy to political meetings. And now he refused to help us? I bit my tongue to keep from saying words I'd later regret.

How had Papa changed so much since I was a child? He had been a fun, debonair, happy father. I didn't want to give up hope that Papa, deep down, didn't want to act this way. Yes, he was behaving like a bull dog and I was disappointed. But he was my papa. I loved him.

I lagged behind Fremont and looked back at Papa when he came out of his office. I couldn't dwell on our problems. I needed to summon all my diplomacy tactics to discuss Mama's dreadful predicament. Money. Money for food and clothing. Money Papa owed Mama for taking care of his two youngest children. He was two months behind on his child support payments again, and he'd told me he would take care of them.

Papa would disapprove of my inquiry, certainly. Claim I was meddling or choosing sides. I didn't care. It had to be done.

The hallway seemed darker than it had earlier. I took a deep breath and blurted out, "Papa, Mama's having a hard time making ends meet."

He looked at me, his familiar sinister countenance raising my concern to high-wire level. Could I handle any more of Papa's negative comments today?

My heart pounded as I continued my rehearsed speech, certain I could convince him of their need. Every problem had a solution and if I could communicate Mama's situation, I was almost certain he would help. "Mama and the girls need money for basics, like food and clothes. They can't even afford school supplies, and I'm sure you agree those are important. Can you help? Please, it's very important."

"My matters with your mother are none of your concern." Papa gave me an icy look, his eyebrows drawn down into a scowl, his beady eyes as sharp as ever. "And the last time I tried to visit, the girls didn't want to see me. That godless woman has turned them against their own father. Why should I give her money for that?"

It hit me like cold water in the face. Papa didn't want to share his wealth with Fremont and me or with Mama or my sisters. Did his Christian charity theories not include his family? Did he not have a personal, moral obligation to feed his children? His lofty ideals lacked substance. I should have known after the divorce that he wanted nothing to do with helping his family. But a thread of hope still lingered.

I stumbled into the living room, numb and confused. Before we left to drive back to Shawnee, I kissed Papa's cheek goodbye.

"There's a bank job here if you decide to move out." Papa mumbled in my ear. "Poverty's no place for a girl like you."

I lowered my head before turning around and sliding into the smooth Model A.

We were in worse condition than before we started the trip. "We have to fill your dad's car up with gasoline," I reminded Fremont.

He grimaced. That was money we couldn't afford to part with.

"I'll go to the bank, honey," said Fremont. "Maybe the banker will help."

I said nothing as I mulled over my father's waxing philosophy and the following refusal to help us. We were impoverished, but so were many folks.

Papa's last words echoed in my mind. "Poverty's no place for a girl like you."

How could I pull me and my family out of poverty?

Chapter Fourteen

The next day Fremont and I walked into the two-story State National Bank on Main Street, our footsteps echoing against the massive room's tall, high ceilings and shiny counters with a mezzanine overlooking the foyer. A huge chandelier hung in the middle of the colossal area and teller stalls stood on each side. We stopped and asked to speak to our banker.

"Please wait. I'll tell Mr. Branson you're here." The teller was a middle-aged woman who seemed to have been at her post since the President Taft days.

We hoped the bank might waive the foreclosure of our filling station.

Recently, I heard on KGFF that banks needed cash. Some banks took over businesses and tried to run them themselves, but since bankers knew little about operating businesses, they usually lost even more money. Although many people had received free homesteads a few years ago, they'd had to mortgage the farms to buy equipment. Short-term loans with high interest rates caused many farmers to fail. With so many farms and businesses foreclosing, I hoped our banker would allow us to keep the station a little longer. That's all we needed. A little time to make it succeed.

After spending an hour waiting and pacing the stone lobby, the teller finally brought the message that the banker would see us. We walked into Mr. Branson's office, but the wiry man with horn-rimmed glasses kept his nose stuck in a document. We sat and waited for him to speak first.

"How can I help you?" he asked without looking up.

"Sir, can you give us more time to make the payment on the filling station?" Fremont begged, his face drained of color. We hoped Mr. Branson would see the situation as we did.

"I'll work extra hours and keep the station open seven days a week." Fremont fidgeted and jingled the change in his pocket. Surely, a smart banker preferred to leave a business in the owner's hands instead of taking it from us. "Hear say, things should be picking up soon. We'll be okay if we can just hold out a mighty bit longer."

Mr. Branson looked up, harried. "Sorry, but we don't get any slack from the state. Those auditors are watching over our shoulders, and we don't want to get put out of business because of folks like you. A deal is a deal, and business is business." He pushed his glasses back up onto his long nose and resumed reading the papers in front of him. "You either make your payment or we foreclose."

We were abruptly dismissed. How dare he? "Mr. Branson, don't you know that the filling station is a vital part of the community?" I raised my fist and my voice grew loud. "Not only that, but our family depends on it for survival. Are you going to turn us away?"

The banker ignored us.

Fremont grabbed my arm and dragged me of Mr. Branson's office and through the bank's heavy front door. He looked straight ahead as he walked home beside me, his face pale and stony.

My anger collapsed into a pile of defiance. All the way home, I repeated, "We *will* make it! We will. We will. We will."

The State National Bank foreclosed on our filling station at the end of June. I understood a bit about banks liquidating around the state due to the severe economic depression. Papa had a huge hand in whether one of his banks would stay open or not, and in this decline, the banks were set to lose as much as other folks. But I still felt betrayed. If I didn't know better, I'd suspect the big dog bankers of taking advantage of the downtrodden, skimming off the top, so to speak.

Fremont gathered his tools and other belongings.

Mr. Branson walked around the station. He took off his spectacles, folded them, and tucked them in his front shirt pocket. "Sorry to have to do this to such a gentleman, son, but times are hard. Never saw such a year when banks couldn't help a man down on his luck. But I have my own family to think about."

Fremont's head nearly dragged the ground. "My luck with banks has never been good."

Years ago the bank refused him the ten dollars he needed for college.

I felt sorry for my husband and his dashed hopes. As I watched Fremont, a flood of relief swept over me. With the station gone, I wouldn't lie awake at night worrying about whether we would succeed or how to collect money from people who barely survived. Fremont wouldn't have to worry about making sure Mr. Johnson's Buick would make it to California hauling a trailer full of furnishings along with his wife, four rag-tag kids and a grandmother. Now, undoubtedly, Fremont would work on their car for free.

That night we lay in bed long after the children fell asleep, Fremont tense as a mortar board on his side of the bed. There was a chasm between us, widened from the tension of losing the station, and I found it difficult to share my fears.

"You're disappointed. I know this is hard on you." I put my hand in his big, working-man hand and pulled him to me.

"I'm sorry I failed you." His voice held a despair I'd never heard from him before.

"Don't say that."

"But I've failed," he moaned. "I can't afford to lavish you with gifts like you deserve or take you traveling in style. I'm lucky if we'll be able to buy oatmeal for the young un's."

I rolled over, laid my head against his chest and listened to his heartbeat. Steady. Like him. "Fear makes the wolf bigger than he is."

"What?"

"One of Mother Pope's sayings. Don't listen to fear, life is not as bad as it looks. And I'm sorry about the loan. I'm truly sorry."

"Those words mean more to me than 'I love you,'" he said, stroking my hair. "I'll find work somewhere. I won't let you starve. I've been doing a lot of praying lately. Hasn't helped much, but things have to look up sooner or later."

We continued our normal routine and went to church Sunday night. Blanche sang a duet with me and then cornered me at the back of the sanctuary. "I heard you went to see Papa." Her voice was low and accusatory, her hands on her hips.

I wasn't sure where this statement was heading. "Right. Fremont and I drove to the City to talk to him about helping with the filling station. Why do you ask?"

"So, you admit it? You went to see Papa, who ran off with a floozy, left Mama high and dry, and refuses to support us in the middle of the worst bust ever. You call that a papa?" Blanche crossed her arms. "I wish I was as dead as Thelma Todd. My own sister doesn't give a hoot about me."

The movie star had been found in December of 1935, dead in her motor car inside the garage. But Blanche wasn't suicidal. Bitterness was more her style. Manipulative, prone to dramatizing and apt to get inflamed quickly, but not self-destructive.

"Blanche, dear, I asked him for help with our filling station. What's wrong with that?"

"What's wrong? If you don't know, then I won't tell you."

She made me feel like I'd betrayed the family. Her accusations grated like a rusty door hinge needing oil. Had I failed as a daughter and sister? Should I have avoided Papa? He may have been acting like a heartless grizzly bear, but he was still our father. "No. I don't believe we did anything wrong."

"That's what you say. After all that's happened, you need to choose Mama's side or Papa's. You can't choose both." She turned and hoofed out of the church.

Blanche was about as frustrating as my two-year old. Didn't she know I loved all of them? Her included.

Chapter Fifteen

Quilting women met weekly on Tuesday mornings at Mother Pope's house. The Women's Missionary Union project was to finish a quilt for the pastor. Each lady in the church submitted a quilt square with her family's name embroidered on it. Several weeks ago, I'd given them my square of autographed scraps. The ladies painstakingly assembled the quilt block and sewed the squares together to make the colorful quilt top.

Now the quilters were ready to sew the blanket together. The backing on bottom, the warm batting sandwiched in the middle, topped with the spread of quilt blocks. Then it was all pinned together waiting to be quilted.

I arrived early and instructed Margaret and Judson to not get in the working ladies' way.

Mother Pope wore her good wrap-around dress. Her white hair braided and wrapped around her head. Fremont said she'd been white-headed since her thirties. I hoped I looked as good when I got old.

Mother's best friend came in and placed a covered dish on the counter. Mother called her Mrs. Stapp and she called Mother, Mrs. Pope, never using their first names. This must have been a formality learned long ago. They'd met when they both lived in Waco. Mrs. Stapp was a lot like Mother, from a genteel family, serene and composed, traits I admired. A small lady, Mrs. Stapp was active in town. Her husband owned Martin's, a small grocery store on Beard Street I often frequented.

Several other ladies showed up before we began stitching. They brought sewing baskets and dishes for the potluck lunch to follow. My friend Effie brought her children, who were near Margaret's and Judson's ages. Another woman, Mrs. Harrington, brought two of her grandchildren. I hoped the children would play well together. Sometimes Judson pulled other children's hair or refused to share his toys.

Mother pulled down the square quilting frame Dad Pope had made for her. It was a few inches bigger than the small bed in their bedroom and it hung from the ceiling. When not in use or at nighttime, she pulled the frame up out of the way with a pulley. When she wanted to work on the quilt, like today, she would let down the square and friends would gather in the bedroom around the quilt to work.

I pulled a needle, some thread and a thimble from my sewing kit and sat on a stool next to the frame. Around me, conversation fluttered. Talk was the most important part of the quilting party, more so than the quilting itself. Social interaction was one reason quilting existed.

I listened to the women talk about recent church programs, where to purchase fresh fruit at the best prices, and the disturbing increase in homeless men and women in town. I couldn't help it—my thoughts went straight to my family. We desperately needed funds to survive the next year. If Fremont didn't find a job soon, we could end up homeless like the people they talked about. I hoped this group of wise ladies could help me decide what to do.

"We're having trouble making ends meet," I mentioned cautiously.

"You and the whole universe," one of the women replied.

"Yeah, Mr. Branch and I are rubbing elbows with the hobo crowd. That's something to tell my grandkids—if we ever get some."

"I know what you mean, we can barely pay rent."

"Food is scarce nowadays. The store ran out of day-old bread by nine o'clock yesterday morning."

"Can't find a rotten apple in any grocery story in town."

"I'm thinking about looking for a job," I said. "Maybe in the City."

The chattering stopped. It got very quiet. No one spoke or even looked at me and I felt like falling through the thin floor out of sight. Did no one else think of working? Or moving to the City to find jobs? Or were we all expected to stay at home manufacturing gravy and encouraging our husbands to find work?

The only sounds came from the women poking their needles in and out of the material.

Finally, Mother spoke.

"We all could use cash, dear. I bought some lemons to make lemonade today. You won't believe where I found them."

Everyone chirped, glad to change the subject. "Where?" they asked.

"Please tell us," said Mrs. Stapp. "It's so hard to find lemons this time of year."

And that was the end of the conversation about working. I would never broach that topic again during a quilting group.

The women continued to talk, talk, talk. But this kind of talk reminded me that life goes on even with the hardships around us. An hour later, we stood, stretched and took a break. Mother Pope hurried to the kitchen to set out glasses for tea and lemonade and cut the pineapple upside-down cake.

As the ladies filled their plates and mingled, Effie pulled me into a corner to chat. The windows were wide open but no breeze came in. We sat on the love seat, pushing printed cushions behind us. "What's this about a job in the city?" she asked. "You aren't thinking of leaving Fremont and the kids, are you?"

"Need to earn some extra money for the family. Papa said he would help me find a job."

"Mrs. Harrington's daughter-in-law found a job," said Effie. "That's why she's taking care of the grandchildren. She gets a check every once in a while but it's hard on an old person."

I shook my head. I felt stifled, like my existence was futile, meaningless. It was so hard to take care of my family's needs. Work seemed a viable choice, but I struggled with the decision. I could make a difference. Make sure my family wasn't hungry or left stranded in the cold like so many people I saw around town. I wanted to scribble the pros and cons on a note, but I would have to wait until I got home.

"There are no jobs in Shawnee, especially for married women," I said. "But the thought of leaving my family makes my stomach ache."

"I could never do it," Effie said. "I couldn't leave my family, no matter how hard it gets."

"But if I get a job, we would have more money to survive. Mama and my sisters need help, too. Heaven knows, we all need the extra funds."

"I don't know. That may not be the best thing to do."

"I want to stay with them but common sense tells me I should leave and send money back home. Mother could watch the little ones. Probably teach them more than I could."

"Be sure and ask God if that's best. Ask if that's what you need to do."

I nodded my head, feeling guilty. Effie was right. I hadn't prayed about it yet.

My goal of a successful family seemed impossible to reach, like trying to play a tune without knowing how the song ended.

As I walked home with Margaret and Judson, I considered all that Effie had said. The children were not to blame for our problems. I loved them so much and I couldn't dwell on how it would feel to leave them. I should stick to my self-inflicted vow for the time being. My goal of motherhood and homemaking. I would focus on having the cleanest house in town and such well-behaved children that no one could complain. Bed sheets needed changed, closets cleaned out and summer dresses made for Margaret.

I would build a well-run home, become an attentive mother and make my marriage work—even if I had to chew nails.

The next morning when Judson climbed halfway out of a window and I scrambled the last eggs, I was again filled with doubt. Success seemed to be slipping through my fingers like a slick needle and thread. For goodness' sake, I had become one of the destitute myself. How could I take care of others? How could I obtain a well-cared for family?

Fremont and I had limited choices since losing the filling station. Moving in with our parents wasn't feasible. A crowded house with in-laws was too stressful. No one had room for four more people and couldn't afford to keep us, not even Mama.

We had few other choices. We could try farming on the Pope's land or we could pick up and move to California like so many others. No. We weren't that desperate yet.

A job in Shawnee already proved futile.

Fremont could apply for a government program job like with the WPA but he and Dad hated government handouts.

Or I could follow Papa's proposal and move to the City to work while Fremont stayed here with the children.

Hopefully, Fremont would find a job soon and we wouldn't need to make a choice.

Chapter Sixteen

July 1936

I walked into our bedroom, pulled out a drawer and reached way into the back for my small black pocketbook where I stashed pennies. I counted out three dollars and seventy-two cents. Not much, considering I took out nickels here and there to buy day-old bread. Definitely not enough to live on. It had already been a month since the filling station closed. We'd been surviving off the little income from Fremont's hit-or-miss jobs. Paupers had more money than we did.

Lately, I'd been dropping hints to Fremont about jobs I saw in the newspaper or heard from acquaintances until I sounded like a vinyl record scratching on the phonograph machine.

"I'm feeling mighty awful, honey," said Fremont after another one of my suggestions. "Time rages against me. Jobs are so scarce."

"At least you're trying. That means a lot."

"I have my dad's strong back and good arms. I can always find a way to put food on the table." He turned to me and put his arm around my shoulder. I could tell depression hadn't totally overcome him like it had many jobless men I'd seen. He hadn't given up.

"Maybe Mr. Wilson can use some help in his truck garden in exchange for fresh vegetables. That okra is growing mighty good in this hot weather. I know. I know. It's a dirty job out in this hot sun but I'll do anything. And be mighty glad of it."

"Picking rights," I said about a common tradition in our area. If someone helped harvest vegetables, they were entitled to take home a few.

To tide us over, Fremont's parents brought over a chicken and a few eggs. The eggs came from Mother Pope's box under her bed where she kept them cool until she took them to the store. She traded eggs for other staples.

The Popes also had a milk cow and supplied us with milk. They sold quart jars of milk to a few neighbors. Mother would seal the jar with a paper stopper and set it on the front porch in the evening. When neighbors would come get the milk, they would leave the old milk jar with a dime in it.

"Your parents help a lot," I said. "If it wasn't for their garden, we'd be haunting the woods like the Marshalls and so many others."

"Dad said we'd butcher a hog this fall. He'll sell most of it or give it away. But we'll keep enough meat to get us through the winter."

"Every bit helps, even those chitlins." I couldn't stomach his favorite snack, fried pig skins.

Fremont's face lifted. "Best food on God's green acre, except your biscuits, of course."

His words and silly smile could always brighten my day. He was a positive in my life. An outstanding man, if I ever met one. A good man who trusted in God to get us through. I felt lucky to call him my husband. In fact, I didn't feel worthy of him, but I sure felt grateful.

Fremont still needed me. My family needed me. That made me feel important.

I took the children to Mother Pope's to help prepare supper while we waited for the men to arrive from the field. Fremont had been working on odd jobs with his dad around the countryside, baling hay, mending fences, herding cattle.

Mother fried chicken, the smell permeating the room, while I peeled boiled eggs to make deviled eggs, crushing the shells for garden fertilizer.

Dad walked through the back door, hung up his hat and removed his work boots. Fremont followed behind, also shedding his dirty hat and boots. Dust settled around them.

"Do you think the relief programs will help us?" I asked Dad. "Maybe Governor Marland will bring in some funding."

"I'm worn slap out, child. Wait 'til I get washed up." Dad scrubbed his hands in a bucket and dried them before he turned back to me. "That last governor, Wild Bill Murray, disagreed with anything the president thought up. Not sure our current governor'll do any better."

"Folks are sure struggling to make ends meet." Mother hurried to set the table. "Makes a family hang on to each other a little closer."

"This here depression's enough to turn a good farmer to communism, I say," Dad paused to drink a full glass of water poured from the water bucket. "After all, us farmers supply food for the rest of the country, don't we? And we've shipped out enough cotton to clothe the state of Texas."

Margaret and Judson, playing in the living room, noticed the men and came running in. Fremont bent down to give them hugs, Judson climbing all over him.

"Can't find a job steady enough to support a flock of sparrows," Fremont said turning his head up to me. "We even tried baling hay behind one of those new-fangled, steam-powered machines going from farm to farm."

Dad shook his head and sat down at the table. "Can't make a living doing that. Now let's quit chatting like magpies and eat some vittles."

Later that evening, Fremont and I joined Mother and Dad to listen to the scratchy national radio broadcast. We pulled up chairs close to the tombstone radio with our heads leaning together in a semi-circle to hear the commentators. Even the children sat on the floor expectantly.

Like most Oklahomans, we were glad President Roosevelt had been elected. He chatted on the radio through his "Fireside Chats," making us feel like a part of the first family, and we speculated as to how his changes would affect Oklahomans.

Though Dad claimed he'd never waste a minute with a talking machine, the trying times had changed him. News was news. He could hear the news reports tonight and read the details in tomorrow's paper. While fiddling with the knobs, he turned the radio up as loud as possible.

"Turn that thing down!" Mother yelled over the static.

"Don't have a duck fit, Mother. I'm trying to hear it." He kept twisting the buttons, losing the sound and bringing it back. I think he liked making Mother shake her head.

Finally, the radio burst out with news about the current Oklahoma governor. The announcer outright stated that since Governor Marland was a personal friend of Roosevelt, the public works money should come more quickly to Oklahoma. Always with a pencil in hand, I scribbled down snippets of the news as we listened.

The newsman blasted out about another huge relief program coming, a five-billion-dollar works bill passed by Congress to expand the New Deal. Soon the unemployed could find jobs anywhere working on new public projects, and a man could support himself and his family.

Dad sat up straight. He'd heard this before but he had never been so long without work. Like many men, he would never take unemployment relief. Never. He claimed the Bible stated a man should work for his living, therefore he refused charity. He believed working people shouldn't support a lazy man. Relief discouraged self-reliance and hard work, rock-solid basics of American life.

The possibility of working for a share of government money caught his attention. "Might be something to this," he said. "Might be more new jobs coming to Pott County after all." Work was acceptable. Relief was not.

Since the district director of the WPA program lived in town, Pottawatomie County was in a good position to obtain more projects than other areas around the state. The government could provide money for projects that otherwise would cost our town thousands of dollars. One of the WPA's latest projects was Shawnee's large, brick auditorium. With a full stage and a seating capacity of three thousand, it loomed quite immense for our town.

"Maybe I ought to look into this," Dad said. "Pays a dollar fifty a day. Not bad, if I do say so myself. The job might not last, so I might ought to jump in while the getting's good."

For the next two days, Dad discussed the programs with people who worked with the government. Most fellows liked their jobs. All were grateful for the work. The New Deal was working. I agreed with Dad— supplying jobs helped us all.

"Can you help me with this?" Dad asked the next time we visited them. He pulled out some papers and laid them on the kitchen table.

Mother set down her knitting and looked up. "He's been going down to the WPA office for days on end now."

"Have you found anything?" asked Fremont as he pulled his chair beside Dad at the kitchen table.

"I hear about work here and there, but no WPA jobs are available. I did get privy to another program called the PWA."

"What is that?'

"The Public Works Administration. They supply funds for bridges, dams and schools. I need help to fill out this application." Dad waved a form in the air. With only a third-grade education when they married, Mother had used the Bible to teach him to read. But still, I knew Dad would appreciate Fremont's assistance.

Fremont looked over Dad's shoulder and read the questions out loud. Then he helped Dad write the answers.

"I'll take it down first thing in the morning," said Dad.

Dad's habits probably had not changed since we lived with them as newlyweds. I could see him pouring warm well water into the wooden bucket hanging by the back door. He would smear lather over his face and pull out his straight edge razor to shave. Then dressed in his Sunday suit, Dad would take the application down to the PWA office.

Two weeks went by. We despaired of Dad getting a job. Not that we were much better off. Fremont was still unemployed, scraping by from odd jobs he could find. He became discouraged. An overwhelming amount of people scraped by like us. They also needed jobs.

Then one day, while chatting with Mother on the front porch, Dad scrambled up the front steps waving an envelope. "I got it. I got the notice. I got a job."

Fremont, who'd been working in the garden, rushed over.

"I don't mind working for the PWA," said Dad. "No shame in getting paid for a job well done, even if it's working for the government. This job's a gift from God."

"The good Lord be praised," Mother Pope exclaimed.

Chapter Seventeen

I mulled over the last conversation I'd had with Marjorie. At times I wished I could flee to Phoenix with her. Run away. Start over. Life couldn't get much worse, could it? Dad had a job but Fremont still struggled.

Maybe when Marjorie returned we could go dancing. I had a rhythm inside that still wanted to jump out every time I heard a jazz song. I could never explain that to Fremont.

I should have completely given up on my dreams by now, like Calvis and so many others in Shawnee. I sighed. Responsibility tired me out. If I'd married the man I was first engaged to, grocery store owner James Fleming, I'd be sitting high in the City. Mama was still upset about our breakup, even though it was years ago. But then I wouldn't have Fremont and my two sweet children.

Jobs were as scarce as hen's teeth. If I found work in Shawnee, the pay would be minimal. Fremont and I discussed the possibility of me moving to Oklahoma City to a job Papa could find. He said I should do whatever I thought best. The look on his face showed differently.

I set aside the afternnoon for cleaning, which I hated to do. But to have a perfect household it must be done. I trudged through the house with a mop in my hand, stumbled over the rocking chair and caught myself. I growled at Margaret, who sat quietly in her cotton frock looking up at me. Judson seemed oblivious to the tension. He simply continued stacking blocks and knocking them down.

"Stop!" I shouted when Judson jumped up from his blocks and ran out the back door. "You get back here now. Margaret, go get him."

Margaret ran after Judson. I felt rotten for yelling.

That evening, Fremont walked into the room with his head down. "Did you find a job?" I asked.

"Job? Oh yes. I was supposed to be looking for a job, wasn't I?" He smiled when he said it but I understood all too well. Times were tough and he wanted to lighten the load.

"Maybe you should try harder."

He immediately recognized my accusations. He kicked a chair. It hit the cabinet and tumbled over.

"Daddy, that's my chair!" Margaret ran across the floor crying.

Fremont mumbled and then looked down at our daughter, her dark curls unruly and her frock wrinkled.

Margaret, still a mite of a child, slid into a corner and crouched on the floor. She folded her arms around her, put her head between her legs and pouted. A picture of sadness.

Fremont looked at me but I looked away, unable to control my own sad heart. Tears threatened to spill down my cheeks.

He went over to Margaret and got down on his knees. "I'm sorry, girl." He touched the top of her head with his big strong hands. She had dark curls like his own when his hair grew long. "Daddy didn't mean to. I'll try my best to never scare you again."

Margaret forgave easily and hugged him tight, but I didn't forgive as easily. I took everything personally. Each time Fremont came home without money for food or bills, I drew a little farther away from him. My shoulders tensed and my mouth tightened when we discussed finances. I couldn't relax. My misery was obvious from my behavior, and I didn't like myself this way.

If only I could persevere until things got better. But would the situation ever improve? "God, please help us," I prayed that night. "Help us survive."

Could I do that? Be patient. Learn to trust the good Lord through the hard times, like Mother said. Not give up. But how could I, with no money, no job, little food and dry, dusty wind storms assaulting our lives?

I felt like David when he wrote in the book of Psalm. He who cried to the Lord so many times, "Give me understanding according to Your word." And in his time, God always answered David. Surely, he would answer my cry too. My cry for relief in this drought and economic disaster. My cry for my family.

What else could I do? I determined to trust God to get us through.

Since marrying Fremont, my days were consumed with scrimping, saving and worrying about the next meal. For heaven's sake, I had once been a member of the country club, worked for an attorney in town and lived the life of a banker's daughter. How could I have stooped this low?

I imagined the worst. Losing our house. No food, not even beans for my family. Begging like one of the urchins on the streets. I'd seen plenty of down-on-their-luck people the past few years, especially when I helped on the food line. I wondered if we would end up right there in line beside them.

Nope. We would survive even if I had to dig potatoes from the neighbors' garden. We would make it through this difficult time. I prayed for help, but I knew flour for a loaf of bread couldn't just magically appear.

I went to the store only when we had spare money, which wasn't often. Even then, I bought the bare minimum. Flour, salt, beans and oatmeal. We ran up an account at the grocery store, owing even for our dab of bacon.

Fremont walked around in deep thought for the next few days. Then he talked about his back hurting while picking cotton on those hot dog days of summers past. I loved to listen to him.

He told me about the harvest seasons when he was a boy driving a truck while his dad threw seventy-pound alfalfa hay bales onto the truck bed. Even in those days, he felt rotten about merely driving the truck. Now he felt useless again with Dad working at the PWA. Dad brought in money for the family while Fremont hardly contributed anything at all.

Dad was assigned to work on the dam on Deer Creek Road, nine miles west of Shawnee. He shoveled dirt, moved rock and mixed concrete. The Shawnee dam, owned and operated by the City of Shawnee, was intended to cover 1,336 acres and had sixteen miles of shoreline. Newspapers gave details like that. Our town needed the clean water it would supply.

Dad suggested that Fremont look into the program. "It's hard work but it makes a man feel like a man again," he said with more enthusiasm than he had shown in several years. The job allowed Dad to accept help without damaging his pride.

"I reckon I might look into it," Fremont said.

"Now's a good time," Dad said. "They need men out on the lake project. The good Lord willing and the creek don't rise, by this time next week I'll have money to pay the taxes on the old homestead."

As Fremont watched his father bringing home a paycheck, his opinion about working for the government changed. Finally, several days later, he turned in his application.

The PWA kept good men off the food lines. Many Shawnee projects used local material, mostly sandstone like on the swimming pool and pool house in Woodland Park, and a short wall around the Oklahoma Baptist University. There should be plenty of materials around for a dozen more projects.

A week later, Fremont came home with his face beaming.

"So, tell me," I asked, "How did it go?"

"Dad steered me right. I got a job and even a PWA job's worth celebrating. Come Monday morning, I'll be working with Dad."

I jumped up and down glowing with happiness so much the children thought Santa Claus had come. He grabbed me and swung me around the room, laughing.

"See, the Lord won't let us down."

"That's true," Fremont said. "He hasn't failed us."

Once Fremont had a steady paycheck, we could help others more. I believed God provided the job and gratefulness brought out some of my finer characteristics, which had been squelched in all that poverty. Both of us wanted to do something for unfortunate people around us.

The next Saturday morning, Fremont noticed Mr. Buckmaster repairing his back-porch roof and he climbed up to help. Later, he mended Mama's broken window and cleaned the neighbor's carburetor for free. Meanwhile, I babysat a lady's three kids whose husband broke his leg and took a loaf of bread to a family whose youngest had died of consumption.

Fremont and I joined forces and began to look outside our own struggles. Hundreds of needy people lived under bridges, in alleyways or in wooden sheds in our home town. Before, we had ignored them, inattentive, distracted, enclosed in our cocoon of survival. But not anymore. I begin to give more than cold biscuits to vagabonds who came knocking on our back door.

The job transformed me, my relationship with Fremont and our entire family. It was downright good to find something positive in life.

Hope was something we could share with others. Hope that might or might not last.

I daydreamed about what it meant for Fremont to have a job. A larger home with a garage for him and a bigger kitchen for me. Hot running water in the bathroom. A wringer washing machine so I didn't have to carry laundry down to the Popes' each week. A job would allow me to be a Susy Q homemaker and make gingham curtains and throw pillows, brightening up a dull house. I could plant irises in the front yard and sit in a rocking chair watching them grow.

With steady income, I could buy McCall's new leather shoes for Judson and purchase rayon fabric to dress Margaret like a princess.

I would take Mama shopping and buy her a new hat each month. I would be proud. My children would be well fed and clothed. We would walk hand-in-hand down Main Street, me and my dignified prince of a husband. People would turn and look at such a good-looking couple and well-cared for family.

I wanted it all. To be happy. To be carefree. To have a loving home. No squabbles. No worries. Just pride and contentment knowing God watched over us. This was my dream.

Chapter Eighteen

August 1936

The year started out with Roosevelt sworn in for a second term as president. He promised a stable year. It never happened. The wheat fields in Pottawatomie County dried up. Lawns turned into bleak stretches of monotonous earth. Red soil flaked into dirt powder.

Life didn't improve as I'd hoped after Fremont started working for the PWA. Even after working a month, our accumulated grocery bill had not been lowered. We still bought food day to day.

Our Crosley radio sang out news in a static monotone. The KGFF radio keeping me informed about the economy, the state, and the nation. I shared these tidbits with Mama.

When Fremont trekked home in the evening from working on the reservoir, he was downright worn out. Red dirt clung to his arms and face like war paint. Oklahoma heat burned his skin and drained him of energy.

Then of all the bad luck, PWA funds were cut back. The project slowed to a crawl. The newest workers lost their jobs first.

Fremont and Dad were let go.

Fremont walked into the house slumped over. He wouldn't even talk about it.

The job had lasted almost two months. Just two months. I should have been glad when it ended, because those had been exhausting hours for Fremont. But it also meant Fremont was once again among the unemployed. Poverty stared through a fragile window. One little gust could easily break us.

Other government jobs in Pottawatomie County already had enough men working and didn't need help.

The job search began again.

One evening, I stirred together flour, lard and milk to make biscuits for supper. We would have them with gravy. I didn't know when money could come our way again. I took a deep breath, pounded the biscuit dough, remembering that God said he would never leave us. Never. Leave. Us. I prayed it was true.

We ran low on flour, so I made only one flat biscuit apiece. The gravy was thin, made with a dab of leftover bacon grease from my tin. It smelled delicious, but I knew it wouldn't fill empty bellies. Four hot round biscuits didn't look like much. I rummaged around and found a can of green beans.

I took off my apron and called the children to the table. Sitting down, Judson, his huge eyes almost level with his plate, surveyed the food in front of him. He looked up at me and asked, "Is this all?"

"I've done the best I can. We should be grateful for what we have." I tried to hold back my emotions. I didn't want to cry in front of the children.

Fremont offered to say a blessing, and we bowed our heads as he gave thanks. When I lifted my head, Margaret was staring at me, hunger written on her face.

I caught my breath, pushed back my chair and stood. I cut my biscuit in half and dished it to the children. "I'm not hungry. Go ahead and eat." I rushed to the bedroom.

My poor little family. I couldn't feed the children enough food to keep a dog alive. I would starve to death rather than see them go hungry. I felt like the bottom had fallen out of my life. A lump tightened in my throat as I thought of my hungry family. My shoulders shook with sobs. I couldn't stop.

I heard the bedroom door slowly open. "Honey, you need to come eat with us."

"I don't want a bite. You go ahead," I turned away so he couldn't see my tears.

Fremont took my face in his hand and turned me toward him. He wiped my wet cheeks with his shirt sleeve. "We're in this together. I'm not eating if you don't."

"Then please, just give the food to the children."

"I tried to make them eat, but they're as stubborn as their mother. They refuse to eat unless you come eat with them."

I caught my breath and looked at him helplessly. I couldn't even starve myself. The thought made me want to cry more.

"This isn't your fault, and the food's getting mighty cold. Come on back to the table. We'll make do."

I followed him back into the kitchen and sat at the table.

Sniffling, I picked up my fork and served myself a few green beans, avoiding my children's eyes.

I hated our predicament. Hated that I couldn't keep myself together. Hated that I would never be a Mary Poppins perfect nanny, magically giving the children a perfect life. I fell apart at any provocation, a complete failure. I hoped my efforts at homemaking were worthy, but the possibility didn't look good. I didn't want to be poor. Didn't want my children to be hungry and certainly didn't want my family to fall apart.

The next day, Fremont stumbled through the front door and plopped down in the usual chair, his hat falling to the floor.

I nagged Fremont about money. I could tell he wanted to react, but as a stoic man, he remained calm.

"How can this be happening to us?" I fussed. "Why can't you find a job? Don't you care? Surely Mr. Winters needs some help down at the corner."

"I've gone to every filling station in town," said Fremont, frustrated. "What am I supposed to do? It's mighty hard out there. The Rock Island repair shop moved to El Reno. That leaves a hundred jobless men standing on every street corner in Shawnee."

The Rock Island train, one of three trains running through Shawnee, employed hundreds of people, what with maintenance and repairs shops. Closing the Shawnee shop would create an enormous job loss.

"The gristmills might have openings."

"Already checked there, Sibyl. Nobody wants me."

"Do you think someone's just going to come along and offer you work?" Oh. I should shut my unruly mouth. I handed him a sandwich for his lunch—tomato and mustard between two slices of leftover biscuits.

"I'm a mighty hard worker."

Fremont shoved open a window that earlier in the day, I couldn't budge. A slight breeze came in. I looked outside to see the children sitting under a shade tree playing in the dirt, Judson putting hand fulls of dirt in his hair. "I know you are," I said. "I'm just trying to help."

"I'll take any job—mowing yards, hoeing weeds, painting fences. I made a dollar last week fixing flat tires. I get paid pennies compared to what I used to get."

He grimaced as he took a bite of the tomato sandwich. "I feel like the whole world keeps me from providing for my family. I'm trying to stay calm. I really am."

I tried to sympathize with him, but fear clung to my mind. Things had never been this bad before. Dread seized me and I panicked. Asthma gripped my lungs. Breathing came hard. We would be stuck in Shawnee on the poor side of town, dreams unfulfilled, and our family blowing away with the sand.

"Honey, calm down. Breathe slow."

I breathed in through my nose and closed my eyes to relax. Better.

Fremont leaned back his head and stared at the ceiling. "This job hunting is getting mighty pointless. It's no use. Can't find a decent job this side of the Mississippi."

"Almost a quarter of the work force faces unemployment. I read it in the newspaper. So you're not the only one looking."

"Knowing that don't put food on the table. It's my job to take care of the family. I'm responsible, and I'm a mighty big failure at it."

"You aren't a failure. These days have been harsh." Fremont seemed as overwhelmed as I was. We were both frazzled. He not only felt rejected by the economic system, but he felt he'd let his family down. His bewilderment deepened.

"There just aren't any jobs," he said. "Can't you understand?"

I turned my back to him and started peeling potatoes in the kitchen sink for the evening meal. The paring knife needed to be sharpened.

"Why is God doing this to me when I've tried so hard? Why?" Fremont asked. "Doesn't he care?"

I was alarmed by his doubt. His faith had sustained me through many trying times. He'd held my hand, listened to my worries and reassured me. I didn't have an answer, but I knew I must hold onto the faith God had given us. Hold on tight.

Fremont seemed to feel our dreadful situation more deeply than I'd thought. When he lost the PWA job, his attitude had changed. My calm, self-assured husband become a self-conscious man, doubting his worth. Perhaps he had been acting like a bear, grumbling because he couldn't fix the problem.

He was downright crotchety. Even more so than me.

Gruff words didn't sit well with me, and I was afraid I'd say sharp words back that I'd later regret. I tried to hold my tongue, but his despondency deepened every day he came home without a job. With Fremont more dejected than I had ever seen him, I looked up and said, "Lord, what do we do now? Give up? Call it quits?"

Fremont stormed out of the house without finishing his sandwich. "Going to Sutherland's Lumber before they close."

The door slammed behind him. I held my breath, afraid I would break down and cry.

But instead of crying, I pulled my shoulders back. True, I could do nothing about the rest of the world—at least not now—but I would try to be the best wife and mother possible with what we had. We were a family and we would go through this together.

My priority was caring for my family.

Focus, I told myself. Focus.

Chapter Ninteen

Mother and Dad Pope wanted to keep Margaret and Judson at their house Saturday evening so I let them stay. The children enjoyed their grandparents. They spent the night so often that they ran about like it was their second home. In fact, Judson behaved better with them than at our house. My mama had busied herself with work and outside activities since Papa left, and she hardly had time to watch the children.

Fremont seemed preoccupied that night, not interested in talking. The romantic meal I had planned fell flat and tension stood between us like a hundred foot brick wall.

Sunday morning, Fremont left early to go fishing with his friend Doug. He said he needed to get away, to catch a catfish in the river and think a while.

I put on my best sun dress and stuffed a straw hat on my head. I tried to get to church before the crowd, knowing the Popes typically arrived thirty minutes before the service started.

I walked into the auditorium and past the small classrooms to the side cordoned off with curtains. Calvary had two areas on each side of the vestibule and a baptistery in the front. The ceiling fan right above the pastor's head whined when he turned it on every Sunday.

I opened the door to Margaret and Judson's classroom to find them already there. Mother stood holding a Bible and a black handbag hung on her arm.

"Mommy, mommy." Judson ran to me with open arms.

I squatted and put my arms around him. "You smell good this morning, clean as a button. Grandma must have given you a bubble bath."

"Where's Daddy?" Judson squirmed away from my hug. Margaret came and took my hand, standing beside me like a sentinel.

"Yes, where is Fremont?" asked Mother.

"He didn't come to church today. He had other things to do."

Mother's face clouded over. Even if Mother disapproved of her son's behavior, she would never say so. I knew her well enough to know that.

The last few weeks, Fremont had missed church for one reason or another. Was he doubting his faith? I couldn't imagine him stepping away from the church. Before losing the filling station, he never missed a chance to attend the service. But not anymore.

"I'm glad you're here, girl." Mother's eyes crinkled fondly when she looked at me. The dainty wrinkles caressed her eyes. "Every cloud has a silver lining."

"I wish Fremont took God a little more seriously." When I finally began to trust Jesus to see us through, Fremont became distant and uninterested in talking about spiritual matters.

"Now, don't you worry none," said Mother smoothing down her wrap-around dress. "God has never stopped watching over that young man."

"If only we can find a way to make it through."

I took the children to class and told them I'd be back after the service and then walked into the sanctuary. I prayed earnestly for God to intervene and lighten our load. Poured out my heart. Then I felt selfish for such a prayer and prayed for the many homeless vagabonds I saw around town. *"Lord, could you help all of us?"*

After church, I rushed the children home to check on the meal I'd put in the oven early that morning. When I opened the front door, the house smelled like a hometown cafe. I roasted a plump rabbit with a potatoes and onions. I tried to cook a hearty meal after church on Sundays, just like my mama. We would use the leftovers to feed us for the next few days.

I put on a smock, choosing the peach one that matched my dress. With potholders, I opened the oven door and slid out the small roasting pan. As I took the lid off, the steamy smell of meat made my mouth water. Ah. The juices would make delicious gravy.

Fremont burst through the front door, chattering about the many catfish Doug caught. Thankfully Doug shared his catch because apparently Fremont's fish all got away. He kissed me quickly on the cheek and went to clean up, unaware of my cold, stiff look. I watched as he came back in and sat on the floor beside Judson, who was arranging a pile of sticks into a teepee.

"How would you like to go fishing with me sometime?" Fremont asked the boy as he tousled his hair.

Judson grunted and I couldn't hear his answer. Fishing. Fremont was talking about fishing when he should feel guilty for not being in church this morning. It irritated me.

I needed to talk to him about his lack of interest in our spiritual lives. He was supposed to be the leader of the family, wasn't he? He had grown up learning about faith, had solidly grounded parents and been exposed to good teaching. His was the opposite of my upbringing. Why was he being obstinate?

"Fremont, your mother asked about you this morning. Wondered why you weren't in church."

"She already talked to me about that, honey. I'll take care of it."

"Seems like you've missed a lot lately."

Fremont stood and a stern look crossed his face. "I go sometimes, that's all I need. Not sure why we bother going at all. Feels like God has forgotten about us." Fremont avoided looking at me. "He's not listening to anyone's prayers. Least of all mine."

My mouth fell open. My husband was wavering in his faith? When we needed him to stand by us, he was drifting away from Jesus?

"That isn't what you were taught," I said. "Didn't your mother say God is still in control and we should trust him to take care of us?"

Fremont didn't reply but helped the children sit down at the table for dinner. I pulled biscuits out of the oven.

"Do you know how bad it is out there?" said Fremont after he said the blessing. "Thousands out of work. Literally starving. I don't want that to happen to us. I plan on working as hard as I can to feed you all. I trust I can do that. God's left us high and dry."

"You don't mean those words. The Lord is as real as you or me."

"Oh, I still believe in him, honey." Fremont cut up the meat I dished on Judson's plate. "He's just so far away. All that praying I've been doing hasn't helped a lick."

Who was I to judge him? My own faith felt as weak as Mother's iced tea. If Fremont couldn't be strong in his belief, how could I stand alone?

After the meal, I cleaned the table and examined my doubts as I washed dishes. I decided to let Fremont's lack of faith slide. He was having a rough time. Once he found a job, he would begin to trust God again.

Chapter Twenty

The number of dirt storms increased and the temperature broke the 1934 record high by soaring above 120 degrees. The sweltering heat. The whirlwinds. The dust gales. I was happy to read that Roosevelt had approved the Great Plains Shelterbelt, a CCC program to plant trees as windbreaks to keep the soil from blowing away. Many trees were brought to Oklahoma for the project. At least the government was attempting to help.

I read in the paper that one giant dust storm had rolled two miles high. It stretched out for a hundred miles and moved faster than fifty miles an hour, completely destroying vast areas of farmland.

I saw the next storm coming. Clouds appeared on the horizon and the thunderous noise rolled along the ground. Turbulent dust clouds would spin in from the north and dump silt over the land like dirty flour being sifted from the heavens.

"Fremont!" I yelled out the back door. "Hurry and get those clothes off the line. A storm's coming!"

Fremont dragged chairs from the backyard into the house so they wouldn't blow away. Then he ran to the clothesline behind the house. Dust from the flying earth clung to once-clean sheets as they blew in the wind. He unpinned the sheets, draped them over his arms and ran toward the back steps.

I opened the door and helped him inside. My thin house dress blew up around me.

"Here, hang this blanket over the door," I said. We had suffered through so many storms, we had a routine.

Working together, we plugged every crack in the house, wedging clothing tight against the onslaught. We hung towels over the windows and blankets in front of both doors. We shut the house so tightly against the dust that it became extremely hot and stuffy inside.

Fremont, the children, and I tied handkerchiefs over our noses and mouths. I wet the handkerchiefs nearly every hour. I swept the indoor air with soggy gunny sacks and tied damp sheets over our beds. Silt managed to get in anyway.

The children huddled together. I re-wiped their sticky faces with wet clothes to cool them, but it only produced mud. Margaret whimpered and coughed while Judson hugged the towel to his face, with only his frightened eyes showing above the dingy cloth. My poor children had trouble breathing. I read about black pneumonia, the inability of children to breathe in these storms. Some children died because of it! The thought of losing a child scared me senseless.

How did homeless mothers fare through these storms?

The temperature stayed high all day. Sand mixed with sweat made a body miserable. I felt sticky and my mouth tasted of dirt. I could even smell the dirt—dry, flaky, desert-like air.

I took shallow breathes, laboring under the lack of oxygen until my chest hurt. Fear felt like knife stabs in my stomach. As my anxiety escalated, I caught my breath, unable to think clearly. Short bursts of air puffed through my mouth, my childhood asthma resurfacing. It happened when I felt stressed, the threat stealing my air. My heart beat fast and I intentionally slowed my breathing, counting slowly to myself to calm down. I would not die with my children sitting on my lap.

All we could do was wait it out. Sit and pray.

I felt like a tiny drop of sand blowing in the middle of life's storms, tormented. Not only physically—filthy, grimy, and miserable—but emotionally. Time raged against me. All my life's efforts, my struggle to succeed, seemed useless. Lands, I couldn't even protect my children.

The dryness of the countryside mirrored my inner life. Dry. Dusty, barren and dried up. Farmers' wells ran dry. Animals died. Corn stalks turned brown. I became desperate for sustenance. Sips of water from the pitcher tasted gritty.

I squeezed my eyes closed while the storm raged around me.

More dejected than at any time in my life, I prayed silently. Lord, what do we do now? Give up? Call it quits? Move away? Please help us, Lord, please.

I wasn't sure how much longer I could go on.

Where was God through all this? Had he abandoned us?

A verse I read yesterday came to mind. Psalm 50:15. "Call upon me in the day of trouble. I will deliver you and you shall glorify me."

I must trust God to deliver us. How? How would he deliver us through this?

My thoughts wandered. Shawnee was ruined. Filthy, scorched and withered like a California plum dying on the vine. Wrinkled. Burnt up. I was impatient for some relief.

"California was never like this," Fremont interrupted my thoughts. "I can catch a train and make a mighty lot of money. Why, I could even purchase a car."

I looked at him. His face streaked with mud, his hair gray from sand. He looked as miserable as I felt. Maybe he had the solution. We might have to leave Oklahoma to stay alive. Pack up and move our meager belongings west.

Fremont liked to talk about the Rosens, the family he'd worked for in the San Joaquin Valley, and how good they were to him. He remembered Mrs. Rosen's cooking and his long talks with the Mister. Fremont talked about green pastures, abundant gardens of fresh vegetables and luscious fruits. Cool, refreshing rain and thriving meadows. I practically salivated over the idea of a cool glass of ice water.

We had watched many families pack up and move out west over the past few years.

I'd always resisted. I didn't want to travel with little money and go out to a land of fantasy and make-believe. I thought our family should stay here, come what may. But I couldn't erase Fremont's dream of a better place for us. Was it possible to uproot our family and take the kids on the road?

A long time had passed since the last time Fremont talked about going back to the valley. Today the notion seemed tempting. A possibility, always in Fremont's mind, remained a vision I had not shared. But if times continued this way and Fremont didn't get a job soon, I would grit my teeth, pack our bags and move on down the road.

I felt Margaret's hand squeeze mine and looked down at her pale, sad eyes. I would do anything necessary to keep these little ones alive. Even move west.

Fremont's head drooped between his hands as the storm raged around us. I glanced at him and wondered what he was thinking.

The thick black dust settled a few days later and the children and I scurried around dusting windowsills and sweeping piles of silt out the doorway.

Chapter Twenty-One
September 1936

A few days later, the postman brought a letter while Fremont was out searching for work. We seldom received mail, so I examined the white envelope. *Fremont Pope* was clearly written on the front along with our address.

I turned the envelope over and read the return address. *Rosen, San Joaquin Valley, California.* I gulped. Why had Fremont received a letter from the Rosens?

Fremont came home early after hoeing and hauling water for Dad's dry garden. He washed up and sat down at the kitchen table, his normal spot.

"What was California like?"

Fremont answered cautiously. "Well, times are a mighty lot worse these days I hear, but I still hold out for good opportunities for hard workers. Why do you ask?"

"You got a letter today." I pulled the envelope off the shelf where we kept papers and the new seed catalog. I held the letter in my hand.

Fremont look chagrined. "I've watched dozens of families move west and wondered whether to uproot you and the children. Why, I loved it there. When I thought about the Rosens and how good they were, I knew you might not like it, but I wrote a letter to see if they had a job. I figured we could catch a train, make a bundle and even build a house."

"Why didn't you tell me?"

"I didn't want to tell you until I heard back. I thought you'd agree to leave once you read about the green valleys."

Hope rose inside me, hope coupled with fear. My fear arose from the many horrible stories I'd heard of Okies who didn't fare any better in California than they had here. Many never arrived. Most never came back. I read that one million people travelled on the motor drives trying to get somewhere, anywhere. People died and were buried on the way. It sounded terrible.

But life wasn't getting any better in Oklahoma. I would consider going west if we could save enough money for gasoline to travel that far, if we had a place to live when we got there and if Fremont had a job waiting.

Fremont stepped back. "I'm sorry I didn't tell you. It's an option, one of the choices always in the back of my mind. I know you're mighty afraid to go. And you're right, it could be worse in the valley than here, but I had to see."

"Maybe it's good news."

Fremont took the letter, tore it open and read it out loud.

Dear Fremont,

We were happy to get your letter and surprised you're married and have two children. Mrs. Rosen and I are in good health. We waited for you to come back but had to hire help when you didn't. Things are dreadful here. This is not a good time to move to California. Destitute people living in ditches and church yards, many sick and dying. Hope times get better and we can see you again. In the meantime, keep on being the good person you are.

Sincerely,

Mr. Rosen

Fremont dropped back into the dining room chair nearest him. How long had he dreamed of going back to the San Joaquin Valley? He had loved it there, the climate, the ocean, the people. The promising future. His dream, his last hope, had been yanked out of his grasp.

"Fremont?" I whispered as I sat down across from him.

He covered his face with his hands.

"We'll make it." I reached out and touched his hand.

"I know," he said. "I know. I just thought, after losing the filling station . . . I thought God might have a way out . . . but I guess not."

"Sometimes it's hard to tell what God is doing." I was more shaken by his despondency than the unannounced letter.

Fremont didn't glance up. His tears fell onto the table. "Where is God in all this? Where, Sibyl? I give up on him. He doesn't want to help us."

"You know that isn't true. Don't doubt him now," I dug for encouraging words. Fremont had always been there for me.

God could get us through. Fremont was the strong, steady man who kept the family together. How could I be a good homemaker and mother without his support? How could the children and I survive without his strength? We were in this together.

"Like you always tell me, we may not understand the Lord's ways, but he sees the future better than we do. Just trust him."

"I don't know, honey. I don't know. It's getting mighty hard. It feels like he doesn't care." Fremont was a good man and he would not slide far into doubt. The Lord would strengthen him.

We sat together for a long time without speaking.

Margaret and Judson came in from the yard and stood in the doorway, and I roused myself to prepare the evening meal.

"Don't know what to cook," I said. We were tired of the same routine. Sliced leftover oatmeal, fried and served with simple syrup for supper. It was getting downright repugnant.

"Wake up!" I shook Fremont's shoulder gently that night, forcing him to stir. "You're having a nightmare."

He gulped, his chest rising and falling rapidly.

I touched Fremont's shoulder again. Softly, so as not to startle him.

"You're not on the train anymore," I said. "You're not a vagabond. You're married to a beautiful socialite. Fremont. It's Sibyl. Wake up."

The soft feather bed bounced as he thrashed about.

Since our untimely marriage, Fremont sometimes woke sweating and shaking uncontrollably. Nightmares ate at him. Memories rambled through his mind from the year he rode the rails as a penniless hobo. I could only imagine what he'd seen. What horrors he'd experienced. He hardly talked about it.

Half-asleep, Fremont popped up straight, looking out into the dark night.

"Another nightmare?" I asked.

His voice was tense. "Hands reaching out. Children screaming. Pleading. Starving." His voice broke. "Tattered clothes."

"Take a deep breath."

"Oh, honey. Their begging gets louder and louder. Crying. 'Help us! Give us food!' Children faint at my feet." Fremont shook his head as if to get rid of the images. His chest rose in heaves.

"It was just a dream."

"No! No it wasn't. I should have saved her. I think about it every day. It wasn't a dream, Sibyl, it wasn't a dream." Fremont scrunched his eyes shut, his face drenched in sweat.

"Who? Who should you have saved?"

"The little girl on the train."

"Fremont." I touched his face. "Are you okay?"

"Pain." Fremont opened pale blue eyes, then grabbed at his throat and slid his hand down to cover his heaving chest.

"It's past. It's over," I certainly didn't want my husband to have a heart attack before he turned twenty-five. "You can't do anything about it now."

"I want to help them." Fremont turned to me, panting. "Help the children traveling across country, but I can't even hold down a job making pennies." He looked at me, his blue eyes darkened into deep lakes of sorrow. "I can't even take care of you and the children. I can't do anything. I'm nobody. Nobody."

I held him as he trembled and my heart ached along with his. The compassion and sadness we both felt for others bonded us together. Trials do that, join hearts in a common emotion.

It took an hour for Fremont to calm down. I cuddled close and placed my cool hand on his forehead. It was my turn to remain calm and supportive. He had remained calm for me through all my problems. A slipknot tied us together.

I read that riding the rails made a fellow self-reliant, compassionate and frugal. Fremont had learned to love freedom and his country. Those were good qualities, but I also knew for Fremont, riding the rails had brought fear of destitution uppermost into his mind.

Fremont's time of homelessness was behind us, wasn't it? If nothing else held our family together, I would pull us through. Trained by Papa, the bank auditor, to handle finances and lead others, I couldn't default now. We would absolutely not become homeless like the alley beggars along Union Street, pitifully clothed in rags with sunken cheeks and sagging shoulders.

I took a deep, determined breath. Fremont and I would succeed. We *would* be somebody. We had to.

However, my first, most important task was to take care of my husband. Let him know I believed in him. I loved him.

He fell asleep and I tucked the blanket tight around him.

Chapter Twenty-Two

Mama lost her part-time job at the church offices.

"I know you need money." I said as I opened Mama's cupboard to get a glass for water and took inventory. A little flour and oil, a small bag of dried brown beans and a couple of potatoes. Despite a few other canned goods, there wasn't enough food to last the week.

Gossip about the Trimbles had calmed down in Shawnee, the divorce forgotten amidst the larger weather and economic disasters. Mama took in washing and ironing, hanging other people's underwear on her backyard clothes line.

"The city's giving away free bread in Woodland Park," said Mama. "Will you go with me tomorrow morning?"

"As long as we're home before breakfast."

We left in the cool, icy dawn while few lights shone through the neighbors' dim windows. Mama, still a beautiful lady, donned her best clothes and wore the mink fur Papa gave her so if anyone stopped her, they wouldn't suspect how low she had stooped.

We walked around the corner to the park north of the stately Carnegie Library. Volunteers sat behind picnic tables under the elm trees. When I raised my eyes, I saw a long row of people in the relief line. I paused. I knew we had a homeless problem, but where had this many people come from? Hundreds of poor, raggedy beggars, thin women and gaunt children? Had I missed them around town? We queued at the back of the line and I stared at the frosty ground in front of me, feeling out of place.

After waiting over half an hour, we reached the people passing out free loaves of white bread. My stomach growled. At least my children would have bread today.

Mama stood in front of me.

"Sorry, ma'am," someone behind the table told Mama. "Can't give you any bread. This here's for poor folk who need it."

"What do you mean?" Mama's voice grew loud. "I wouldn't be standing here in the cold, embarrassing myself, if I didn't need bread."

"Look at that fur coat you're wearing. Now don't tell me you're in need. You sure don't look like it, wearing that fancy dress and coat."

Mama's eyes steamed wild. Someone behind us yelled for her to quit holding up the line, though those were not the man's exact words.

"What choice do I have?" Mama drew herself up straight. "Do you want my little girls to starve to death?"

"Now missus, don't get in such a huff," said the bread lady. "Just go on, and we'll forget all this happened."

"Go on? Without bread?" Mama yelled this time. "How can you give all these good-for-nothing folks food and refuse an upstanding citizen like me a loaf of bread? What's this world coming to?" Drawing attention to herself only made matters worse.

I ducked my head, my clothes too simple and homemade to be noticed.

Mama walked away empty-handed.

I could accept my loaf of bread or leave with Mama. Thinking of my children, I took the bread. How long had I wanted to help poor people only to become one of them? The thought stung. Stung like wasps.

"How humiliating," said Mama as we walked off. "And it's all Papa's fault. The next time he visits, he's going to get an ear full. We still have bills to pay whether he's here or not."

We arrived to Mama's house and split the loaf of bread. "Don't worry so much. God will supply our needs. He promises."

Mama turned to me in a combative stance, her arms crossed. "As if you know," she said, "since you don't live here anymore. I might tell you, Sibyl, we're as poor as Job's turkey."

"Papa doesn't know how bad it is or he would help. I would hope so anyway." Although I doubted the likelihood of Papa helping Mama, I wanted to lift her spirits.

"Last time I saw him, that man said, 'If you want to eat, go sell your diamond ring.' Then he turned and skedaddled away without saying goodbye to the girls and without leaving the month's check. That's how much help I get from him! We have a thirty-dollar account at the Butler's Grocery Store on Broadway. Our situation is atrocious."

I raised an eyebrow. "That's a lot of money to owe."

"The grocer let me run up the bill because he knew us before the divorce and feels sorry for us. Already exchanged about everything I own."

Mama looked at her hand, at the stunning diamond ring Papa had given her a few years earlier after one of their fights. She never took it off. "This ring ought to pay off the account so we can get a few groceries—though it's worth much more than thirty bucks. Don't know where the grocer's going to sell it."

"Are you sure you want to trade it?"

Mama blew out a long sigh. "Can't worry about it now. But that ten-cent-a-pound ground beef is going to cost me a mint."

Papa rushed into our house the next morning. Fremont had gone with Dad to Tecumseh to bale hay north of town. Many farmers had plowed under their fields for federal cash payments but a few still produced crops.

"Just got a minute," Papa said.

He stayed long enough to remind me of his imposing presence, his new fedora hat and all. He seemed excited, but then he always talked like the house was on fire. This time he rattled on nonstop about the banking business, a chance in front of him as a possible state bank examiner. "There are opportunities out there. While the average man sees only the land blowing away, those of us with vision see a promising future."

Papa and I did not see the world exactly alike.

He held up a ladies' watch. "Brought you something."

He put the watch on my right wrist, took a tool from his coat pocket and adjusted the band to fit. He smiled like he had given me a Cadillac. I was thrilled. I'd never owned one.

Later, Blanche told me the wristwatch had belonged to Gladys. Gladys had been given seven watches by different men before they married and Papa wanted to get rid of them. He also gave Marjorie and Blanche watches. My sisters might complain about where the timepieces came from and about Papa being chintzy, but I could only thank God for the two dollars I got from the pawnshop.

Chapter Twenty-Three

Another storm blew through the night and clear skies came the next morning, bright as a Technicolor movie. That evening, Fremont arrived home rather late. He pushed opened the screen door, stepped inside and slumped into his kitchen chair. His clothing was torn and he had a cut above his eye, blood running down his face. His beat-up hat fell off and he ran his fingers through his hair.

"I can't do it," he mumbled. "I can't go out there anymore. I scrambled with a dozen men today in front of the Masonic Building. Just for a one day job. I got beat out. It's not worth it." He wiped his forehead and put his elbows on the edge of the table.

I knelt down in front of his chair and using a wet cloth, dabbed the cut on his face. A bruise had already appeared. "I've been thinking about this a lot," I said. "We should be thankful for what we have."

Fremont didn't look up when he spoke. "Folks say it's like this all over the country. Don't know what we're going to do. We might have to move in with Mother and Dad, sleep on the living room floor."

"I've been insensitive." I looked at his drawn, wounded face. Fremont didn't need my nagging voice. "When this is over, we'll be closer together, you'll see. Hardships make us stronger. That's what your mother says."

"How are we going to make ends meet? I'm doing all I can." Since we'd heard from the Rosens in California, his mood had deteriorated even farther.

"God will give you a job. Just keep asking him." We did that a lot. He encouraged me when I was down and I encouraged him when he was down.

"Don't you know I have?" Fremont rose, his muscles bulging. "I pray every day for the good Lord to give me a job so I can take care of you and the children. He doesn't hear a thing."

I stepped back and looked away. Fremont's faith still faltered? I thought his doubt had resolved itself. I shook my head.

"I'm not worthy of you," Fremont said, his wide, pale eyes looking up at me. "Never have been. Never will be." He heaved a long sigh, almost like he wanted to give up but dare not.

Had I led him to believe he wasn't good enough? Had I been that callous? Had my nagging led him to believe I blamed him?

He had spent hours coddling me, telling me not to worry. I couldn't tell him money wasn't that important, because it was. Money provided beans.

"I know God'll come through." Mother Pope's positive words flowed out even as hesitation fluttered inside me.

He stroked my hair. Tears appeared in his sad, weary eyes. "I just worry so much."

"I know. But be positive."

He nodded.

"I hear they're selling potatoes a nickel a bucket. That'll go a long way," I said.

Fremont chuckled as he pulled me to sit on his lap. "Just so long as they're not rotten potatoes, I guess. Mind you, fried potatoes will be mighty good with those biscuits and sausage gravy we've been having lately."

"I'm serious. And I'll save everything I can. My motto will be, 'never throw anything away.'"

"Save everything? Don't get too ambitious now, honey." I could see him holding back a smile. "Can't save potato peelings forever."

Fremont looked at me as if he hadn't seen me in a long time. His smile broke out. "I'll cook," he offered. "I want to do something useful instead of sitting around moping." He snapped his finger. "I know. I'll make hobo supper. The tramps along the railroad track taught me how to survive."

I raised my eyebrows. I was about to hear another of my husband's stories. He loved to talk about how he lived on the rail.

"Every bum begged for a tater, onion, bone, anything," he said. "We'd put all the gatherings together in a pot and make hobo stew. Honey, we may be poor, but we're not hopeless. Just think. My dreams of a beautiful wife and sweet children have come true, haven't they? We'll just have to hold on mighty tight through the winter."

I tracked our money to each mil, ten mils to a penny. Store-bought bread cost a nickel a loaf and we didn't have many extra nickels. Rather than take more money from my personal stash, I learned to bake homemade yeast bread like Mother Pope made. I baked several loaves, letting them rise for several hours.

I heard Fremont walk up the steps and through the door of our small house.

"Something smells mighty good. Is that bread? And meat cooking?" Fremont loved coming home to the smell of fresh homemade bread.

Sure enough, on the small wooden table, I had laid out an unexpected meal. Next to a juicy cut of beef sat a platter of steaming ears of corn. Homemade yeast bread. Pickled beets accompanied it, and a pitcher of iced lemonade sat nearby. Wildflowers graced the middle of the table, making it a pretty spread the way his mother always did it.

"What's this?" Fremont's mouth dropped open.

"I thought it was time to get up and get going again," I said. "Your mother's keeping the children for the evening." I had taken a long bath and washed and curled my hair. The calf-length dress I wore, my best one, had been starched and ironed stiff.

"But where did you get the money? We can't afford this, can we?" Fremont looked at the table and the scrumptious meal. "And you. You look like sweet apple pie."

"I pawned the Crosley radio down at Cohen's," I admitted. I didn't say how much I missed it. It had brought the outside world into my life. News. The latest songs. Roosevelt's plans. It was my prized possession.

Before he could speak, I continued. "It's only temporary. We'll get the radio back next time you bring home some money."

Fremont strode over to me, put his arms around me and drew me to him. He gave me a tight squeeze. "You're mighty special, honey." He paused, touching my cheek softly with his finger. "And this meal smells mighty special, too."

The warmth of Fremont's embrace provided all the payment I needed for my mealtime efforts. His understanding through our ups and downs sustained me. Unlike my parents, who had never been supportive of one another, we could help each other through this hard time.

I wouldn't give up on my family. Even if I had to make bread every day for the rest of my life.

Margaret sat on the linoleum floor and played with our mutt. A gentle dog, he didn't budge when she put a plastic ring around his head.

"Mommy!" She looked up at me alarmed. "I can't get the ring off."

"Keep trying," I said.

My hands were full of dish soap, but I watched as she tried and tried before giving up. The dear child had a tendency to pout and this was one of those times. She put her head face down on her knees.

Fremont had stepped out to the back porch and when he returned, I motioned to the puppy. Fremont looked at me and raised his eyebrows. I could see the sparkle in his eyes.

He went over, picked up the mutt and said, "Oh no. I can't get the ring off his neck. What will we do?"

No answer.

"Guess I'll have to cut off his head."

"The dog's head?" Margaret's whimper sounded worse than the puppy's, but she still refused to raise her head.

"Maybe I will do that. I don't see any other way."

"Please, Daddy. Please. Don't cut off his head." Margaret kept her face buried and wept.

"Look up here."

Margaret nodded no.

Fremont held the puppy down and pushed him under Margaret's nose. The ring was off. She grabbed the dog and hugged it so tightly, I had to pull her away. We laughed together, as a family should.

I hoped harmony proved better than discord and would help our family move past the bitterness and nagging. Fremont worked around the house fixing broken windows and doors, chuckling at my attempts to hammer a nail. I began to appreciate his help more. In many ways, the quality of our home life improved. I breathed deeply, believing that as long as we supported one another, we could weather this atrocious storm in our lives. Maybe the worst was over. I crossed my fingers and said a quick prayer.

Chapter Twenty-Four

Grass had withered months ago and autumn came early. We sat on the front porch watching the children play. The elderly Watsons across the street waved from their porch. Other families stirred up and down the area. Children played ball in the middle of the packed dirt street. Smaller kids surrounded a tire swing. The neighborhood was alive except for a few houses which stood empty, but even their yards were not off limits to running children.

Fremont wanted to move the family to his parent's Waco farm. "We can stay a few years until the economy improves," he said. "Besides, we would have no rent payments. There'd be fewer bills, and we could grow our own vegetables and raise chickens."

"I don't know," I said. "This dry weather may last forever."

"You're looking at it wrong, honey. At some point, farming has to turn around. If we hunker down for the winter, we'll be there in early spring to get the fields ready."

"Mercy, that house doesn't even have running water." Living on the Waco farm would be difficult. I'd been raised with indoor plumbing and neighbors nearby.

"Mother and Dad are moving out there next month. We can stay with them until we can build our own house. Dad said it takes two hundred dollars to raise a crop, buy a calf or two and live out the year. We can manage if we don't have to pay rent."

"It's a big chance." Didn't Fremont know I had no desire to farm?

"Don't base your decision on last summer. The weather's been heartbreaking and devastating, I agree."

"A terrible year to be sure." I held up fingers as I listed the difficulties. "The rain never came and the corn leaves dried up before the ears formed. The wheat bowed down against the hot wind. Old folks and babies died. No amount of money could help. Everything looked bleak." I looked at Fremont's hopeful face. "And you think it'll change next year?"

"We finally got some rain and it seems the right time to move." He shrugged. "Like you said, honey, be positive. Look for a brighter future. Tomorrow promises better days."

Fremont's cheerfulness might be a reason to give the farm a try, I conceded to myself. "You sound like Mother Pope. But remember how the rain splattered over the dry ground without soaking into the soil?" I raised my eyebrows and stood. Then I turned and walked down the steps to gather the children back into the house.

"But it came," Fremont yelled at me from the porch.

"It ran toward the creek beds and disappeared into cracks in the ground," I yelled back.

I put the children to bed, wrangling with Judson to get his pajamas on. He couldn't seem to be still longer than a minute. It would take all my stamina and imagination to teach this child some manners.

Fremont and I continued our discussion. We bickered for several hours until he convinced me that moving to Dad's farm was our best choice. He had no job. We had no means of support. We should at least try.

I finally admitted, farming was the best choice we could come up with.

The following Saturday afternoon, Fremont and I walked over to the Pope's house. The family took the dining room chairs outside to the lawn where a cool wind kept us content. The chickens in the backyard cackled while Margaret and Judson wrestled on the ground with their grandpa's hound dog and her puppies.

"When are we going to start planning next year's crop?" asked Fremont, balancing a piece of Mother's homemade cherry cobbler on his knees. "We'll have to think about ordering seeds soon."

Dad looked out toward the dirt road and up to the sky. Mother Pope remained still, only her hands moving, engrossed in knitting.

"Dad, I'd like to move Sibyl and the young un's out to the farm. I know it'll be crowded but it won't be for long. Mighty tough making ends meet here in town. Nothing much left since I don't have a job and can't find one."

Dad stared without blinking.

Fremont continued. "Sibyl might not cater to it at first, but I think she'll like it after she adjusts. In fact, we've already talked about it." Fremont's eyes flashed over at me and I nodded. "She's willing to give it a try. Mighty good of her since it's not the easiest way to make a living."

Dad said nothing. I started to get an unsettled feeling in my stomach.

"Dad, what do you say? Is something wrong?"

Dad finally turned to Fremont. "Son, I've been meaning to tell you. I just didn't have the heart."

"What? What do you have to tell me?"

"It's about the farm. We can't move back this year."

"Why? What's wrong?" Fremont grew quiet and his eyes widened.

"It's this drought. A couple of weeks ago I drove out to check on the farm. The well was dry as a bone."

Mother spoke for the first time. "I know you're disappointed, Fremont. We are too, but we can't move back with no water. I know you're having a hard time, but it's best to wait 'til the weather improves. May take a while for the water to come back up."

I sat stunned. Couldn't live on the farm? That meant . . . .

"There's still a chance," said Fremont. "I could go dig the well deeper."

"No son, it's dry. And this ain't the year to be wasting time digging. It's dry over the whole state."

The silence was uncomfortable.

Then I asked, "But what about you, Dad? What about your dream of moving back to the farm?"

"Sure is a hard thing. Don't reckon I understand it all, but we're doing right fine," said Dad. "Me and Mother have learned to lean back on the Lord in times like this. He'll see us through 'til we can move back." Dad seemed relieved to have told Fremont about the well.

I couldn't believe what I heard. The farm was unlivable without a good well. This was the worst drought anyone remembered. Dust blew the soil away. Rivers, ponds and wells were dangerously low. Even if rain came next spring, we wouldn't be there to plant the crops. Another year wasted. Another year lost.

Dad's dreams were put on hold. How could he and Mother sit back and trust in God through this? No ranting and raving. Not even worry or depression. Would Papa react with grace if he couldn't have what he wanted? No, he'd never be this calm. And Mama? Unfortunately, I had experienced Mama's response to loss. She handled loss like a runaway locomotive.

On a deeper level, I was torn. I felt relieved not to be moving to the Pope's farm but I worried about our future. It felt like another choice had dropped out of range. Were tougher times ahead? Would we ever get rain? I couldn't imagine life getting more difficult.

"It's getting mighty hard without some kind of work to do," Fremont said to no one in particular.

"It's in the valleys we grow," Mother replied.

Dad got down on the ground with Margaret and Judson. He sang, "Oh, Susanna." Then he ruffled their hair and wrestled with them and the puppies. The sun went down among a pinkish hue across the wide sky. We gathered our chairs and went inside the house.

Dad sat on the living room floor with the children, where Judson climbed all over him. "I've got a trick for you."

"What? What?" the children yelled.

"Watch." Sitting up straight, Dad pulled one of his legs up and put it behind his neck. The children laughed and tried to imitate him.

A few minutes later, Dad couldn't free himself. He twisted and wiggled around on the rug with his leg in the air for several minutes until Mother finally helped him get loose.

"Land's sake," Mother said, laughing. "I shouldn't have to tell a forty-six-year-old man not to bite off more than he can chew."

Dad and the children laughed with her.

Fremont merely watched, his face stoic. Almost like farm life had been stolen from him. Like he'd lost a chance at making a life for us.

My stomach churned and a familiar ache tightened in my chest.

What was wrong with wanting a happy, secure family?

A PROMISE CHILD

Chapter Twenty-Five

Water ran out. Ponds dried up and their bottoms cracked. People broke out in boils. When the Crosley radio wasn't pawned, it kept me in touch with the outside world. I listened to popular songs like "Brother, Can You Spare a Dime?" Although I didn't dance anymore, the song expressed my family's reality. I scrimped and scrounged every penny, nickel and dime and prayed for rain.

Papa's view of an idealistic world haunted me. How could our country have gone so wrong? In my mind, I could hear him say, "The leaders of long ago should have given more thought to teaching people how to live."

Why, when troubles came, did I think of Papa? Was he right? Did we, as a people, cause this depression? But that made little sense. We may have contributed to the downturn, but we couldn't possibly have stopped the rain. But was God punishing us? Testing us?

I washed my hands and dried them on a flour-sack towel and turned my thoughts to housekeeping. Judson stacked toy soldiers on top of one another while Margaret played with her second-hand kewpie doll, wrapping it in rags.

Fremont had left early to look for a job.

"Run next door for me, Margaret," I said. "And tell Mr. Buckmaster I'll pay him back when I can." I needed a bit more flour for the oatmeal cookies I was making, a treat I hadn't made in months.

I handed Margaret, my responsible child, a list of items—thread, baking soda, flour—and sent her out the door. Next door to us, the Buckmasters had transformed their living room into a store, similar to Mom and Pop stores across the country that supplied essential emergency items. The Buckmaster's living room contained scattered boxes like licorice candy, half-penny nails and shoe strings. Mrs. Buckmaster would give Margaret the items and send her home, adding the amount to our bill. We tried to pay as quickly as possible, even though they were kind-hearted and didn't charge the enormous interest other folks did.

Margaret rushed back into the kitchen carrying the items in her arms, screaming, "He's worrying me to death." She was four and to her, everything seemed a crisis.

"Don't carry on so," I said. "Now tell me what's wrong?" Margaret tended to be protective of her little brother even if she liked to prove she could tackle him to the floor in two seconds.

"He's gone." Near tears, she wadded up the edge of her dress. "I can't find him anywhere."

Judson had been nearby just a moment before. I tried to keep him close because the child tended to find mischief any time I turned my back. I thought he might be playing in the yard, so I stepped out the front door. Margaret trailed behind me and the screen door slammed shut behind us. I looked to the left and to the right, up and down the street. Judson was gone. Flat missing.

"Margaret, run back to the Buckmasters and ask if they've seen him!" I ran around to the back of the house. "I'll check inside."

Margaret took off with her brown skirt flapping and pigtails flying behind.

By the time I circled through the house looking under the beds and in the closets, Margaret was back, her chest heaving between gasps. "He's not there," she said in spurts. "He's not there."

"Check with the Wilsons."

Margaret flew away again, leaping up the steps to another neighbor's front door while I looked around the bushes along the back fence. No luck. I ran through the house again to check every room. No Judson. Margaret returned with bad news. I nearly cried.

Living on the south side of town, I was fearful of the unfortunate people and vagrants who lingered about. Strangers wandered the streets begging for a slice of bread. Most were decent souls, but could one of them have snatched my son?

Another empty house caught my eye. The neighbors had moved away leaving their front door ajar. They must have slipped out of town in the middle of the night like so many others. I looked in the windows but did not see Judson.

Anxiety jumped inside me and I screamed as loud as I could, "Judson! Judson! Where are you?"

I stopped in the middle of the yard. "I don't know where he could have gone," I muttered to myself. Would a three-year-old just wander off? Judson, that impulsive scalawag, could find a million ways to make me worry.

Earlier Judson had asked to go see his grandpa but I never responded. I scolded myself and my absentmindedness. The Popes lived seven long blocks away. Would he travel that far alone?

"Stay here!" I yelled back at Margaret before I darted down the road toward Fremont's parents' house, my heart pounding. I looked up at the sky. The east horizon appeared hazy, a darkening cloud of rust color. A roar rumbled in the distance. Not another dust storm. *"Please, God,"* I prayed. *"Please, keep him safe."*

Panic caused my mind to reel as I cut across a yard. The heat arrived in layers, and sweat trickled down my face and collected along the nape of my neck. I paid no attention.

A group of men congregated at the corner, staring. Fear stabbed my heart. The pest house was on a hill right around the corner westward. Its inhabitants were rumored to be ghosts of smallpox victims and tuberculosis patients. I heard homeless people lived there.

I picked up my skirts and ran. Five blocks from home, I rounded another corner and spied Judson's little body ahead of me. He was sauntering in the middle of the dirt road, swinging a stick as nonchalantly as could be. Blazes, I would have to hog-tie that boy.

"Judson, you little rascal. Get back here!" I caught up with him and grabbed him. "You know better than to run away." Relief flooded me and I hugged him close. White flour from my hands and apron covered him.

He looked at me with his powder-covered face, not sure what he had done wrong. "I going see Grandpa."

I didn't have the heart to scold him. Scoldings didn't faze him anyway. He didn't seem to feel pain like most children. Spanking was senseless. Judson wasn't a bad child, just curious and strong-minded, always doing what he wanted to do.

I pulled him and Margaret into the house and slammed the front door. I leaned heavily against it, thankful everyone was safe inside. Thankful we were out of harm's way. My heart still raced, but I heaved a sigh of relief.

Margaret and Judson's safety was far more important than how much money we had. We had a roof over our heads and food for next week, didn't we? I nearly forgot about the goodness of God. And, heavenly days, we even had cookies for supper! How could I complain when there were people starving all around us?

Chapter Twenty-Six
October 1936

I spent most of my time alone with the children, cooped up indoors. We all needed to go outside. The children were excited when I told them put on shoes because we were going for an afternoon walk.

Margaret and I sauntered north down Beard Street while Judson skipped on ahead of us. He crossed the railway tracks even though I had instructed him to wait for me. We continued on and up to Main's Street brick road. The relaxing day lifted my spirits. We strolled the covered sidewalks in downtown Shawnee, window shopping. I looked longingly at an advertisement in Ideale's Beauty Shop. A Princess wave cost $1.95, but I couldn't spare that much. Another advertisement said, '*Live Steam Permanents' leaves hair soft and lustrous, no electricity*. I ran my finger through my dry unruly curls. Someday I would afford a treatment.

And although I wanted to meander through all four floors of the Mammoth Department store, which would cost nothing, I refrained. It wasn't as much fun with two young ones straggling behind me. Perhaps I could return for the White Sale in January.

We arrived back home in late afternoon without having spent a red cent. I rushed to prepare a meal before Fremont returned from his job search.

Within a half an hour, Fremont opened the front door and plopped down on a kitchen chair as usual. He didn't speak, but he didn't seem as worried as normal. With money scarce, tension had been building between us for several weeks. I busied myself making pan gravy from bacon drippings, which we would pour over mashed potatoes. It would be more nourishing than the corn fritters we had last night.

Margaret played on the floor with paper dolls cut out from newspapers and old *Good Housekeeping* magazines. I laughed silently as she mimicked grown-up conversations among the dolls. She walked over and showed them to Judson, but he grabbed them from her and ran.

"No!" Margaret screamed and sped after Judson. By the time she reached him, the paper dolls were waded into balls. "Mommy," Margaret whined as she looked at me, but I was busy setting dishes on the table for supper.

"Go wash up now, Margaret." I instructed. "You have black ink all over your hands and face. We'll try to find you more cutouts."

An obedient girl, Margaret seldom resisted my directions, but this time she balked.

Fremont walked over and playfully tickled her. He picked the child up with his broad, sturdy hands and carried her to the wash basin. He leaned her over the sink to wash her hands, her long dark curls falling down over her face.

When they turned back to sit down, Judson and I were already sitting at the table. They joined us and Fremont bowed his head, as did the rest of the family, to say a prayer before we began to eat. His prayers hadn't stopped, although the words were like a ritual, always the same. "Father, thank you for all good things, especially for your provision in our time of need. In Jesus' name. Amen."

"Did you find out anything about a job?" I asked as I did every evening although I grew dismayed each time I heard the answer. My emergency fund was diminishing daily, the hidden stash whittled down to some coins. "I heard the Shawnee Mill may be hiring again. Pays two dollars a day."

"As a matter of fact, I did find out something." Fremont grinned from ear to ear. "Joe, who works down at the Buick place, heard about an opening."

"Why didn't you tell me first thing?" I looked up while dishing Judson some mashed potatoes. The mush spilled and splattered onto my blouse in white specks. "The opening wasn't at the Round House, was it?" I teased.

"Making overalls?" said Fremont, a smirk on his face. "No. It's at Norton's down on Union. I wanted to surprise you."

"You really found a job?"

"That's what I'm saying. I got a job working at Norton Motor Sales as a night time watchman."

I jumped out of my chair and ran to give him a hug. "Tell me more about it!"

"Well, good ole' Sam Norton said he needed someone he could depend upon, and Joe vouched for me. I told Mr. Norton about my lost filling station and how hard I tried to keep it open. Mr. Norton sells Chevrolets and Cadillacs and well, a variety of other kinds of cars. Hoping after I'm there a while, I can move on up to a mechanic's job. They don't need one right now."

"But night time?" I stopped before I said more. Fremont found a job. A real job. Maybe we could make progress. Surely, we'd reached the bottom this time and our troubles were over. A job was a job.

"Don't care much for nights either, but it'll put food on the table," said Fremont, his smile bigger than Montana. "I start at seven in the evening and work through the night. The graveyard shift, they call it."

The next day I began to dream of new frocks, dishes to replace broken ones, and one of those new-fangled electric refrigerators my mama's neighbors bought. Counting my chickens before they hatched, so to speak.

Change was coming. Good change. Fremont found a job. Papa would have no complaints if we showed financial improvement. I wanted to telephone him with the good news, to hear that he was happy for us, but his definition of happiness might not be the same as mine.

I could feel progress in the breeze, and I listed all the things we needed.

Then I put down my pencil and looked out the window. "God," I murmured, "thank you." So this was gratefulness, this urge to jump up and down and sing a song, even dance around in circles praising him. I told God I was glad, shoutin' glad, that he'd seen fit to provide Fremont a job.

We could celebrate. I craved the mouth-watering barbeque served down at Van's Pig Stand. It had been too long since Fremont and I had ventured out alone.

Chapter Twenty-Seven

I didn't like Fremont's new job at Norton's Motor Sales. It left me alone at night. Nevertheless, it brought in a paycheck. Within a few weeks, Fremont started driving the nighttime wrecker which didn't alleviate my fears at all. No longer just a security guard, he drove at night to assist with automobile accidents. He never complained, but he struggled with his position for two reasons.

First, as he shared with me, he saw many disastrous car wrecks, especially with teenagers. He wasn't sure how long he could handle the heartbreaking scenes when young people died or had been terribly injured. His heart couldn't take much more of it.

Second, he told me he hated to be away from home at night. Wasn't that a sweet thing for him to say?

However, a job was a job, and he didn't complain again.

Fremont and I had been renting the house on Forrest Street for over four years. The second Sunday in October, the owners of the house came by after church and told us they lost their own home. They needed a place to live and wanted their rental house back so they could move in. I hated to leave this cozy home, but we needed to find another place quickly or we would be out on the street.

We asked our friends and neighbors if they knew of an available house to rent. One that didn't cost much. Dr. Fortson, the doctor who delivered Margaret and Judson, told us about a rental house in the northeast part of the city.

"It's filthy, has broken windows and needs painting," Dr. Fortson said. "Looks like the previous renter had a passel of children and the wife couldn't keep house. It does have possibilities though. The landlord will give you three months' rent free if you fix it up. He'll pay for the materials."

"Tell them we'll take it," Fremont said without looking at the house.

We left the children at the Pope's and walked across town to examine our new home. The house on Draper Street sat on the north side of the railroads tracks. The neighborhood looked decent with sidewalks and clean yards.

We walked in the front door and through the living room. I shook my head back and forth at the terrible condition. "This house is a trash heap. How could any woman let her house get in this shape? I'd never allow it."

"Does that mean you're not up to cleaning for the next few months?" Fremont asked, checking the windows. Several were broken.

"Don't be silly. Look at the possibilities. Hard work never hurt anyone."

"Honey, you're the cat's pajamas."

"What?"

"Something I heard at work. Means you're the best."

We kissed, standing right there in the middle of that wreckage.

Never judgmental, Fremont didn't complain about losing the Forrest Street house or the disastrous condition of the one we would move into.

We stayed at the Pope's while we fixed up the place. Much of the cleaning and painting fell to me since Fremont worked nights and slept during the day. I borrowed Dad's rake to sweep out the big trash. Every closet and shelf in the house contributed to the growing pile. The kitchen linoleum was so worn it would need ripped out.

As I worked, I turned on my Crosley radio that I'd retrieved from the pawn shop. I listened to the news.

Apparently, some New York oil man had donated money for a wading pool at Woodland Park.

The Academy Award went to *The Great Ziegfield*. I had never heard of it.

President Roosevelt thought spending more money would help the economy. That didn't make sense at all.

Fremont worked on our new house during his day off, digging up the old linoleum and throwing away trash. After raking the rooms and pulling up the flooring, the debris pile filled up the back porch.

When we finished cleaning out the trash and worn flooring, I attacked the walls. They needed scrubbing before painting. "How could a mother let her children do this?" Pencil and crayon marks decorated the walls as far up as a child could reach. Wait. Hadn't Judson pulled some pranks just as bad? How many walls had I scrubbed? As much as I tried, I didn't have a perfect child either.

The little two-bedroom house had a bigger kitchen than our old house. Our table and benches would fit perfectly.

Fremont painted the ceilings, which proved too difficult for me to reach. He replaced the broken windows and screens and refinished all the woodwork in the house, doing a terrific job. Finally, we sanded, varnished and waxed the wooden floors in the living room.

I admired the way Fremont worked. My strong, vigorous man could make a living digging ditches if necessary. I glanced at his muscles bulging out below his short-sleeved shirt. Uh-huh. My trusty husband could handle any task.

"I never realized a man could be so useful." I punched Fremont on the arm. "Papa always hired handymen to do the physical labor, but you can do anything. We'll never starve with you around."

Fremont blushed.

We soon finished what became our new dream house. My favorite room was the bright, cheerful kitchen. I had sewn gingham curtains which set off the shiny laminated counter tops. Square-patterned linoleum covered the floor, complementing the print wallpaper. I felt proud when we moved in. Proud of our home. My decorating abilities shone, making me the best homemaker in town. I was proud. This was all I dreamed about.

Our Crosley radio boomed the song "Home, Home on the Range." The song rang through our refurbished house and lifted our little family's spirits.

I stared out the front window through my new curtains. After all the work we'd done to make the inside great, I wanted to add to the feeling of home by growing flowers. Flowers like I remembered.

"Irises," I told Fremont. "That's what I'll plant by the front steps. That'll be a good place for them."

Color was what we needed. More color to brighten our lives.

The next morning after a hopeful mist, I walked north to Mama's house. Papa, an accomplished gardener, had planted hundreds of irises. Since he left Mama, his neglected flowerbeds were overgrown and needed thinning. Mama didn't want the flowers so I dug up dozens of rhizomes. They would bloom beautifully in front of our new home.

I felt relief that the disastrous time in our lives had ended. God had seen fit to bless us. I could purchase the housewares we needed, buy material for nicer clothes and feed my children healthy food. I could focus on being a good parent, disciplining a rambunctious Judson, and helping Margaret with her *Fun with Dick and Jane* book. Not that she hadn't already memorized it.

Now, maybe now, I was ready for another child.

Chapter Twenty-Eight
November 1936

The news blasted from our radio. King Edward, England's new ruler, abdicated the throne. He'd been king since January when his father, King George V, died. The problem was that Edward wanted to marry Wallis Simpson, an American who'd divorced her first husband and was seeking a divorce from her second. Prime Minister Baldwin strongly opposed the marriage. He said Edward was a leader who couldn't act like a leader. Politics verses romance. My life's dilemma.

King Edward famously said, "I have found it impossible to carry the heavy burden of responsibility and to discharge my duties as king as I would wish to do without the help and support of the woman I love." Edward left Britain for Austria the next day. He joined Simpson several months later when her divorce became final. Edward's brother, Prince Albert, succeeded to the throne as George VI.

The news was abuzz about the U.S. presidential election. No surprise that Roosevelt won again by a landslide, but I noticed that Socialist Norman Thomas was on the ballet again. Papa's preferred party didn't do well. It garnered no electoral votes.

The most appalling news came when Calvis, a few days before his eighteenth birthday, announced he was engaged to Evie, someone the family did not know.

Papa would be sorely disappointed in his only son because to him, money, not dreams or romance, kept people afloat. Papa himself was a whiz at the banking business. He could add down a column of numbers, four or five across, in his head quickly. I saw him do it many times. He believed a Trimble man should secure a successful career *before* marrying.

The chit chat began as soon as I entered Mama's house. The family gathered to play a new, little-known parlor game called Monopoly. I, naturally, was the banker. Fremont stayed home with the children for the evening.

"I can't believe it." Mama said when Blanche blabbed about Calvis. "It's all your papa's fault. If that man had been a good father, this never would have happened." Calvis had just finished high school and delayed college for a semester.

"I know all about it," said Blanche. "Calvis was singing with a jazz band at the Blossom Heath Dance Place. That's at the Spring Lake Amusement Park if you don't know. Before Marjorie left for Arizona, she went with two friends to listen to Calvis sing. She tried to match him up with one of the ladies. It didn't work out, but he fell for the second gal, Evie—or Fances Evelyn."

"It seems sudden," I said. "I didn't even know he was dating anyone."

"Evie probably told Calvis she was pregnant just to entice him to marry her," said Blanche.

"That pregnancy strategy wasn't necessary," said Mama, moving her piece on the board. "Calvis wants a home of his own and someone to love him. Can't say I blame him."

"Indeed, she stole his heart." Blanche pretended to swoon as she said it.

"Are you going to the wedding?" I asked as I rolled the dice. I felt self-conscious. Mother Pope would never approve of dice in her home.

"After that fiasco in divorce court?"

"But he's your only son."

"We heard *that* woman's son will be getting married at the same time." Mama rolled her eyes.

That woman was obviously Gladys.

"A double wedding. Isn't that nice?" Mama smirked. "Evie's mother insisted she marry at a Unitarian Church instead of the hotel downtown." Mama said it like she relished someone insisting anything against Papa.

I mulled over what that might mean.

"I wouldn't miss Calvis' whirlwind wedding for all the world," Mama said.

My head jerked toward her. "I thought you didn't approve."

"Of course we're going. The girls and I are driving up with the Cooks. They're going because Joe Cook will be Calvis's best man. Do you want to go with us? They're having a big party afterward."

"I don't think so." Mama's car was full. The Pope's car had broken down again, and we had no other transportation.

The Monopoly game lasted much longer than I expected. Blanche and I, the last two opponents, finally called a draw.

Calvis's wedding took place Saturday evening at eight o'clock, November 21, 1936, at the Unitarian Church where Papa and Gladys attended.

The *Shawnee Morning News* announced it the next week. "Calvis Trimble Wed at Oklahoma City."

College was no longer an option for Calvis, even though he claimed to have discussed it thoroughly with Papa.

Mama waited until she got back home from the wedding to throw another one of her temper tantrums. "No college!" she screamed at me. "Why did I listen to your papa? With all those nice-sounding promises, as usual, he didn't follow through."

"Don't scream at me, Mama. It isn't my fault."

"Papa had a conniption fit when he discovered Calvis was working as a jazz singer," Mama said. "That's when he found Calvis a job."

Papa found Calvis a position at the First National Bank located at the railroad station. The bank set up a window at the Rock Island and Santa Fe Rail windows in Oklahoma City because people needed cash to ride the train. Calvis discovered he had finesse with money matters, a talent he didn't realize he'd inherited from Papa until then. I'm sure he enjoyed dressing for the part also. I could imagine him in wide, pleated trousers riding his waist and held up by suspenders.

"Your papa thinks only of himself. That's the thanks I get for giving him the best years of my life."

I stood and turned around. Mama's house grew more dreary every day.

The other news Calvis had told Mama at the wedding reception dismayed me even more. Words Mama repeated over and over as if unable to accept it.

"I'm giving up music," Calvis told Mama when he kissed her on the cheek over a piece of marble wedding cake. "Papa's right. No money in music."

No money in music.

Calvis had given up more than college. His dreams had sailed out of range.

Just like mine.

At least Calvis had a job. All I had left were dreams of becoming a good parent and housewife. No, I had a better place to live and a sweet family. I could never forget about them. I just hoped we would face no more crises.

Chapter Twenty-Nine

December 1936

Christmas day Fremont and I took the children to Mama's house. Scraps of colored cardboard pictures were glued into the middle of walnut half shells—pictures of horses, snow scenes, Santa Claus—then hung on the Christmas tree. Candy canes dangled from the branches, one for each person. Popcorn and cranberries threaded on string and colorful paper chains were looped around the tree.

Mama pulled sweet, spicy gingerbread out of the oven, the smell filling every corner of the house. Hot apple cider simmered in the kettle on the back burner. Mama, an excellent cook, could make a feast out of nothing. Dressed for the occasion, as we all were, Mama wore a stiffly starched organdy apron over her dark dress.

Aunt Adah and her family came for the day. I was happy to see Thurman. Adah's blind son had begun to attend a special school for chiropractors. Adults filled the table and the children sat at a makeshift bench and trays.

After dinner, Margaret and Judson opened their presents, a pair of second-hand shoes for each. They immediately tried them on and pranced around. Then the adults opened gifts—items previously owned or handmade. Blanche gave Frances a small bracelet she'd received from Papa when she was young, and I gave Mama a hand-crocheted doily.

Everyone squealed with delight. We even enjoyed the presents sent by Papa.

The family gravitated toward the piano to sing Christmas songs. I scooted onto the bench and Margaret slid in beside me.

Amidst the chatter, Fremont grabbed a song sheet from the music stacked on top of the piano. "Here play this song first, Sibyl." "Good King Wenceslas" was one of his favorites.

Frances playfully pushed him aside. "No, play this one!" She opened a hymn book and set it in front of me. "Please, sis."

"Okay, little lady, but I get second choice." Fremont pinched Frances' cheek.

I couldn't resist my little sister and played her song first. I must say, our family had outstanding voices and harmonized as well as a Count Basie band.

By the time I played Fremont's song everyone had chosen a favorite.

We raised the rafters and laughed like we had in the old days. With everyone gathered around the piano, we spent more time joking around than singing. It seemed like the first time laughter had rung out in the house in months.

The time flew by too fast. I helped Mama clean up and then began to pack to go home.

Judson, called "the little imp" by his aunts, disappeared into the back bedroom. He came out a few minutes later with a sheepish grin and Mama's cold cream all over his face.

"I've told you forty-eleven times, son, don't get into other people's things." Fremont couldn't stop a belly laugh as he wiped the white goop off Judson's face. Judson could never sit still for long and ran off within a minute with Margaret chasing him.

Blanche came in from the back room huffing. "That blasted boy had smeared cold cream all over the dresser and mirror."

I left the sack of Christmas leftovers on the counter and ran back to assess the damage. Sure enough, the problem child had left his mark. Guilt over Judson's wayward behavior smashed into me, and I wondered if I could ever be a good mother.

"You should do something with that rascal," Blanche said with a harsh voice when I returned after cleaning up the dresser. "A child like that needs strong discipline."

I looked at her and took a deep breath. "You don't know how often we do just that." Blanche's nastiness cut me and I bit back the frustration.

"Well, it's not working," Blanche stated in a low voice.

"He's not your child, so don't worry about it." I didn't like remarks about my children or, in a round-about way, the way we disciplined.

Mama merely examined her coffee as if nothing were amiss.

"You shouldn't have so many kids if you can't take care of them." Blanche stepped in front of me.

My temper flared and I flinched at Blanche's cold remarks. "How dare you say something like that? Didn't Mama teach you if you can't say anything nice, don't say anything at all?" How could someone so young judge me? I worked hard to take care of my husband and children even if I had not reached perfection yet.

"I always tell the truth, even if people don't like it. You can't afford to feed or dress your children properly."

"Then I won't invite you to my next child's birthing." This was not the way I had wanted to announce my pregnancy.

"See, just as I said. You're having too many kids."

I hoped Mama would congratulate me, but she rolled her eyes. At least Fremont was happy about it when I had told him. He'd be happy with a dozen children.

I had never been able to please a single family member, no matter how hard I tried. Too many misbehaved children were just the beginning.

"And you think you're smarter than everybody else. Well, you're not. Just like Papa, who thinks he's so smart."

Ah. Here was the fuel behind her anger. She believed I'd taken Papa's side because I communicated with him on occasion. "I don't know what you're talking about." I held back from remarks that would make the argument worse.

"Now Sibyl," said Mama, "you shouldn't get so upset. Blanche is only trying to help. Really? Can you afford another baby right now?"

Aguments at Mama's never started until Fremont and I prepared to leave. It was as if no one wanted to destroy the whole visit, so they waited to make their points. By this time, Fremont had bundled up the children and stood by the front door ready to go. He had experienced this contrivance before.

"Well, someone should tell you the truth," said Blanche. "You need to know."

"I'm going home." I turned and stormed out the door.

We walked home in silence, Fremont holding the children's hands. Pain seared my heart. How could Mama and Blanche hurt me so badly? I felt betrayed. Where had I gone wrong? Was I a bad mother? I wanted so much to do right.

"I'm sorry. I'm so sorry." I said to Fremont but my continual apologizes were unnecessary.

When we got home, Fremont pulled me to him and wrapped me in his arms. He didn't have to say he understood.

Fremont left for his night job about dusk. My thoughts raced. I spent hours that night lying in bed rehashing the conversation, wondering if my words were tactless. Wondering why the family mistook what I said. Wondering if God was disappointed in me. And then in a sinking thought, I wondered if Fremont really wanted this new baby.

Fremont had hardly said a complete sentence the whole evening. I blanketed myself in guilt and anguished over what others thought about me. Especially around my family, I worried about what to say and how to say it. I wanted my family's opinions about me to remain stellar. What did they think of my parenting?

The next morning when Fremont came home from work, I sat on the side of the bed. Tired, drained and despondent.

"You're worried about what your family thinks, aren't you, honey?"

I nodded, unable to say the words in my head for fear of unleashing them in a flood of confused prattle.

He sat down beside me and stroked the tousled hair falling about my face. "You don't have control over anyone else. Don't let them define you. What they think is what they think."

I looked up at him.

"And personally," he said. "I think you're mighty fine and I'm thrilled about another baby."

He really did love me.

Chapter Thirty

January 1937

Mama discovered Papa got a raise. He now received three
hundred dollars per month as assistant bank examiner for the
State of Oklahoma. Every month, she got twenty-five dollars each for
Frances and Blanche—when he paid up. She filed a petition to modify
the divorce decree, asking for forty dollars a month for each child. She
needed money for clothing, school supplies, health care, not to mention
food and shelter.

I was explaining this to Fremont when I opened the *Shawnee News*.

"Fremont, listen to this." I began to read the article. "The Court
denies the Barnett Plea. W.J. Barnett, former state bank commissioner,
will go to trial in February on a charge of corruption in office."

"Isn't that the case your father's involved with?" Fremont asked.

"It is. I wonder if he'll have to go back to court and testify again."
Papa had testified over a year ago. As a bank examiner, he'd also audited
the Bethany Bank, another bank in the scandal. He found almost two
thousand dollars missing there.

Was Barnett guilty? Over the past few years, the banking industry
had taken some bad blows. Failed loans. Abandoned farms. Horrible
weather and economic depression. Add corruption on top of that. One
small banker shot an auditor who recommended closing the bank.
Harrison, another bank examiner and one of Papa's co-workers, had

been fired. Allegedly, he'd refused to testify against Barnett. Was Papa worried about losing his job?

I only knew what I read in the paper or overheard through my eavesdropping skills because the rare times I saw Papa, he wouldn't discuss it. Most words I overheard were unfavorable toward Papa, accusing him of being involved in Barnett's bank scandals, being an accessory to the crime, and so on. My heart plummeted. Papa had always been respected. Now that was changing. Would people disrespect Fremont and I because of Papa's behavior?

It was no secret that Papa and Barnett hated each other. I wasn't sure why. I could only guess. After all, Barnett had been Papa's boss. Maybe they didn't see eye to eye on business matters. Or ethics.

The winter proved to be the coldest any of us had ever known. Even the Department of Agriculture had declared it the worst winter in one hundred and seventeen years. A lot of livestock died and hundreds of small animals froze in the fields.

No one in the family had seen Papa in a month. Papa had taken Frances with him to Oklahoma City last December and on the way back to Shawnee, his car broke down. Stuck in Dale, he flagged down a bus and put nine-year-old Frances on it to go home by herself. Mama was furious that he'd put Frances at risk. He had not visited the girls since. Maybe he didn't like the chewing out he had gotten.

I buried the hurt caused by my family and went to visit my mama. That Saturday was a warmer day than earlier in January but still cool.

We heard a car honk outside. Frances peered out the window, recognized Papa's car and ran to the front yard. Blanche followed. Knowing Papa would not enter Mama's home, I grabbed jackets for the girls before I went outside.

"How's my princess?" Papa asked Frances as he stepped out of his shiny, spanking-new black 1936 four-door sedan. He liked to get a new car every few years.

Blanche had on a blue crepe dress and a ribbon around her neck to fancy it up. Frances wore a hand-me-down dress, also blue. Papa had recently purchased a new Kodak camera, and the first thing he did was take a picture of the two girls. We seldom had pictures made. Years ago, Mama had a photo of the girls made holding violets.

After making sure the girls put on their wraps, I retreated and watched my family from the porch steps where it was warmer and I could hear them.

"Here's a package for you." Papa handed Frances a brown-covered box. He looked up and smiled at me without speaking.

Frances tore into the package and pulled out an aqua-green cardigan sweater. "My favorite color. How did you know?"

"Lucky guess. Now Blanche, come get your package."

Blanche hesitated as she stepped back away from the car. "If you really cared for us, you'd come see us more often." She stomped a foot. "But then, if you really cared, you never would have left."

And at a minimum, I thought, you would provide them with proper food and clothing.

Papa ignored Blanche's remarks. He had ignored her outspoken remarks ever since she was old enough to talk.

Blanche moved toward Papa's car, her arms folded across her chest. Her tall, slender appearance accentuated her knobby elbows.

"I brought chocolates." Papa held out a box of Cadbury chocolates. She grabbed it while my mouth watered as I thought of the sweets.

"If you think all I want from you is chocolates, then I don't want them." Blanche threw the chocolates back to Papa, turned and rushed toward the house. Frances followed.

From the steps, Blanche turned around and yelled, "And you don't need to come back. Ever!"

Papa shook his head and motioned for me to come over. I walked toward him and leaned against the spic-n-span curved front fender. He gave me no time to speak. "See what I told you about letting society raise their children to disregard others? It seems the church has failed its people." He leaned against the car door.

Mankind had done a very poor job of taking care of society. Wait a minute, I said, "The church failed? Don't you believe the church has helped individuals?" I began to shiver in the cool air and pulled my sweater around me.

"Instead of the church, the new way is the Kingdom of God on earth." Papa put his foot up on the running board of the sleek sedan. "Civilization must, as far as possible, be untarnished by evil ways. We must take all precautions to prevent people with evil in their minds and selfishness in their hearts to corrupt this new forth-coming society."

I had heard Papa's socialistic viewpoint all my life. It wasn't until I married Fremont and saw true, loving Christianity portrayed in his family that I began to open my heart and change. "What about the little people like Mama, Blanche and Frances? What will happen to them in this 'new' society of yours? What if corrupt people like Barnett decide to rule?"

Papa took his time answering. "Barnett will get his just reward. I'll see to that. You're the one to be concerned about the future. You have a slew of children to support." Papa opened the car door.

As always, before he drove away, he offered me a job at a bank in the city. As an auditor, he heard about job openings before they were offered to the public. A job didn't appeal to me, but what if it was the best thing for my family?

I remembered a childhood experience with Papa. Gypsies had been camping at the park for several days. Out of fear, Mama made us girls stay in the house or on the porch. Rumors claimed the gypsies kidnapped little girls and made gypsies of them. I heard the talk.

After the gypsies left town, Papa took me across the park one night to see a friend of his, a judge. Coming back, he set me up in a tree and said he was going to let the gypsies get me. Then he walked away. Abandoned, helpless and afraid, I started bawling. Papa laughed and came back for me. He had a very mean sense of humor. How could I believe someone who left me for gypsies? It took a while to regain my trust.

After Papa drove off, I rushed back into Mama's house where the open-faced gas heater put off as much heat as a bonfire. I backed up to it to warm myself.

Mama was talking to Blanche. "I understand your reluctance to have anything to do with Papa. I completely understand. The man who fathered my children is a down-right, no-good sham. We don't need him."

She paused. "However, girls, we do need his money. And that box of chocolates would have been nice."

I laughed with them, but inside I felt miserable. Was Papa really a sham? I didn't want to believe that. Even though he treated his family like second-class citizens, maybe he was right about larger issues like the economy. Or banking. Or jobs.

As a child, Papa had always seemed bigger than life to me. A dad I cared about. Along the way, my vision of him had fallen, and I struggled with how to view him now.

Chapter Thirty-One

February 1937

Blanche entered our house with Frances trailing her. "That's the last time I take her to the movies, especially to the Ritz," she said. "She wouldn't sit still and then fell asleep halfway through. Waste of ten cents."

"I liked it," said Frances. She left the door wide open and frosty air swooshed through the room.

"I'm glad you liked it, sweetie." I stuffed my crocheting work into a bag and rose and closed the front door. "Shirley Temple is always fun to watch."

"I've already seen *Bright Eyes* three times. Can't handle any more. I prefer to watch Sonia Henie." Blanche plopped down into my favorite chair, shoving my bag aside.

"The famous Olympic ice skater?"

"She wears the most beautiful costumes and can skate like a dream. I'm a good judge because I've been following her for years. I've clipped out every article I could find about her. She'd make a good actress. I could do that, Sibyl. I could be a movie star."

I pulled Blanche out of my chair. She smelled like Beech Nut gum.

"Now, Frances, run on into the bedroom and play with the children. They'd love to see you." Margaret and Judson thought their Aunt Frances loads of fun.

Frances slouched on the sofa. "Maybe later. I'm hungry. Something smells real good—like steak." Her eyebrows lifted.

"Dinner'll be ready soon."

"Frances wants to stay all night with you."

"Yeah. You have better food than we have at home," said Frances. "I'm awful sick of bean soup."

"Don't complain. At least we have bread." Blanche despised cooking, but when Mama shopped or visited friends, she had to help out.

"Blanche hates taking care of me." Frances stuck her tongue out at Blanche. "Yesterday, I was waiting for Mama at the window and thought she might not return. I waited forever. Papa left and Mama might leave us, too. Blanche just laughed at me and said, 'I don't know, Mama might not want to come back.'"

My heart melted for my baby sister. What questions went thrugh a child's mind when they wondered if their mother might not return?

"You don't have to worry, Frances." I put my arm around my youngest sister, drawing her close while giving Blanche a firm look. "Mama won't leave you."

"You're a tattle-tale, Frances." Blanche grimaced, her eyes darkened and her brow wrinkled. She inched her way toward the front door. "It's time for me to go home."

Then Blanche stopped and pulled her shoulders back. "I forgot. I have another thing to tell you. Papa wrote me a long, typed letter, half of which I don't understand. He wants to turn me against Mama. He thinks I'll trust him again. Ha."

I thought a moment. "He wasn't always like that, Blanche. Don't you have any good memories of him? He used to buy you gifts, take you to meetings. Why, he built you a playhouse with his own hands."

The little house Papa built was a perfectly finished tiny house, painted white with a shingled roof, a full-size front door and windows. The room had a single bed and held space for Mama's trunk full of old family pictures. Blanche loved that little playhouse.

As I said it, I knew Papa hadn't built the playhouse for Blanche. He'd built it for Calvis, who used the small building for club meetings. Calvis formed a neighborhood boys club called "The Chicago Gangsters," and although the shortest and skinniest of the bunch, he would say, "If I can't be the leader, I won't play." He generally got his way, but Papa only boasted about how he influenced others.

Papa never engaged with Blanche the way he did with me. Was it more difficult to grow up without a father or with one who had manipulated you? I was the oldest child and I believed he truly cared. But I was twelve years older than Blanche. A man could change a lot in twelve years.

Frances wandered into the kitchen. "It's liver!" she yelled. Her hopes for a delicious steak were dashed. "I hate liver."

"Well, twit, you wanted to stay." Blanche rushed out the door alone.

Papa and Gladys came by a few weeks later and picked up Frances and Blanche for the afternoon. I was sitting in Mama's warm kitchen waiting for them to return and watching Margaret and Judson color on the back of used envelopes. Mama was in the bedroom trying on a black felt hat with a face net she'd purchased from a used clothing store.

Frances and Blanche burst into the room.

"Slow down, girls. Now tell me, how was your afternoon?" My sisters had obviously been to a beauty parlor. Blanche's shoulder-length hair fell down in waves for a nice attractive change, but I did a double take when I looked at Frances. Her hair stood out from her head in kinky clumps.

Mama walked into the room and let out a scream. "Frances! What happened to your hair? It's a ball of frizz."

"It's okay, Mama," Frances said. "Gladys thought we needed permanent waves, so she took us to a parlor in town."

"She did what?"

"I hate those machines," Frances continued. "Don't ever ask me to sit under one of those again. I sat there attached for hours and hours."

"I can't believe that woman." Mama lightly touched France's curls.

"Mama, you should have seen me," said Frances. "That machine was so heavy they had to hold my head up. I thought I was going to faint."

"I'll never forgive her." Mama ran her fingers through Frances' tangled hair. "Your hair will never be the same. I'll take you down to Faye's tomorrow to have it cut off."

Frances' eyes got huge. She ran to the bedroom to look in the mirror at her hair. I heard her scream.

I didn't dare give my opinion on the new hairstyle. Mama was already too volatile.

Blanche's mouth set in a firm line, which indicated she hadn't enjoyed the afternoon as much as Frances.

"Did something happen?" I asked her. "Your hair looks great, but you look as angry as a mad bull."

"I told Papa off, that's what I did. Told him he's a cruel and terrible person. Told him I didn't want him as a father anymore."

"Don't you think that's extreme?"

Blanche's life might go a little easier if she could control her temper and her attitude, or learn to be polite and not respond so rashly. I looked at the ceiling and prayed. No. It wasn't my job to fix anyone. I had enough to work on.

"Someone needed to tell him off. Arguably, he may never want to see me again."

Chapter Thirty-Two
April 1937

Times had been hard for Lester, Mama's gardener. I didn't know how colored folks survived, because jobs seemed scarcer for them than for us poor white folk. However, I couldn't imagine how you could get poorer than chicken wings for supper.

One Saturday evening, I sat on the concrete front porch steps while Fremont mowed the lawn with a borrowed push mower. He had mowed half the front yard.

"I found a job for Lester." Fremont took a break and sat down beside me on the steps. "You know he's still helping your mama with her yard."

"A job would be a blessing," I said. "Where is it?"

I handed him a glass of water. His face was flushed and the hard muscles under his shirt shone with sweat.

"They need a janitor down at Norton's," said Fremont. "In the evenings, the same shift I work. Think I ought to ask Lester about it?"

"Of course you should." I smiled at him. Here was a good, caring man. "Unless you want to pay him for our yard work. That way you can spend more time with your beautiful wife."

Fremont let out a chortle as he got up to finish mowing. "So you think he's better at this than I am?"

"Well."

Lester Morris, Mama's long-time yard man, walked every week from the southwest part of town up to Mama's house. Mama recently told Lester her circumstances looked grim. Money was tight. She couldn't afford to pay.

"Can't lose a good customer," Lester said, "even if you can't pay much."

So Mama kept him and continued to pay twenty-five cents when he worked, plus a good meal. Usually she sent him home with a little extra food for his family, like leftover biscuits, a few potatoes sprouting in the dugout or a glass jar of sweet buttermilk.

Since meeting Lester, I tried to understand black people in Oklahoma and devoured the issues discussed in newspapers. Over seventy-thousand black people lived in the state and many were not treated fairly. They struggled. But more than that, prejudice was a challenging battle to fight. The last lynching had happened only a few years ago and occurred only sixty miles down the road in Chickasha. That was too close.

A few days later, I sat on a bench outside under a big picture window in Mama's back yard. Red feathery tamarack flanked the two smaller windows, and I breathed in the fresh spring smell of flowers and soil. A springtime drizzle had improved my mood and morning sickness. I watched the children play in a dirt pile near the back fence. They chattered together, pouring water from a cup to make red mud pies, dirt covering their arms and legs.

As Lester trimmed the bushes, he and I reminisced about the first time we met. He and James, my one-time fiancé, had collided on the side of the house. James, in his double-breasted suit and wide lapel, puffed up like a rebuffed rooster. Lester and I laughed at the memory.

"How are Mattie and the kids doing?" I asked. Old beaus were not my favorite topic.

"Doin' right well, miss. Can't complain." Lester always answered that way, but then he added, "Be doing better now since I got a job. Grateful your man helped me out."

"You'll make a good employee." I smiled. "By the way, how old is your son? He's in high school, isn't he?"

"Yes, ma'am. He's doing right well, ma'am. Right well."

"You must be proud of him." I had grown accustomed to our stilted conversations.

"Yes, ma'am. Sure am. First one in my family to make it through the twelfth grade." Lester stood a little straighter. "Goin' to graduate next year. Then find a job."

"Times are getting tough these days."

"Can't say it's easy."

"Aren't you worried about how to feed your family, what with this dry spell and all?" I asked as I walked back to check on the children. Ugh. They would need three baths to get the muck out of their hair.

I looked at Lester pulling weeds as I walked back to my bench. He looked emaciated, but then he hadn't changed much since I first met him years ago. A tall, thin man, he always looked to be on death's door ready to meet Jesus in raggedy clothes.

"No, ma'am. The good Lord's taking care of us." Lester paused and I waited, sensing he had more to tell. "My biggest worry may be poverty, ma'am, but my biggest fear is riots. You see, my family slid out of Tulsa back in '21. I saw a few of them white hoods. I was just a kid, but I learned then that all white folks ain't as kind as the Trimbles and the Popes."

"Sorry you had to see the bad side of people," I said, touched that he'd share his thoughts. He wasn't usually this talkative.

"Course, sure is glad for the work your mama gives me." Lester didn't have to say any more about Tulsa. I knew about the riots. Hundreds of black folks had been killed and thousands of homes destroyed. Lester learned first-hand about hate and fear. Hopefully, Shawnee was different.

Papa had his own opinion, basically stating that people received what they deserved. His phrases resounded in my head. "If a man refuses to pull himself out of the mire, he is doomed. The destitute have failed to better themselves. Our first task must be to re-train those who insist on remaining at the bottom." My unconventional father loved to spout words no one understood.

Papa didn't care for black folks, but I'm sure he was talking about folks in poverty as much as those in the black community. Those in poverty now included my own family.

I gritted my teeth. People like Lester should never have to worry about riots or such things, no matter their color or economic status—no person should. Wasn't our country based on freedom for all people? From what I saw and heard, the greater problem in Shawnee was feeding the masses. Meaning—trust God for the next meal. Most of us in town had that in common.

Bath time lasted longer than usual that night. Margaret, my right-hand helper, and Judson, my lively boy, had never been so clean.

"How is gym class this year?" I asked Blanche when she came by my house after school on Monday. I was exhausted after spending the day at Mother's doing laundry.

"I have a prissy little teacher with a good figure and a face like a bulldog." Mean words just flowed out of Blanche's mouth, uncensored.

"What do you mean?"

"The teacher accused me of having T.B. Said she thinks I have it because I'm so skinny."

"Why would she say that?" I asked half-heartedly. Margaret sat in front of me on a kitchen chair stacked with magazines. I tied a towel around her neck to catch the curls and began to trim her hair.

"My teacher asked me what I ate at home. Did I eat beans? Yes, I told her. I eat beans every day. That's no lie. We live on brown beans and cornbread." Blanche's face fell. "She probably thinks I should be living in some institution."

I sympathized with Blanche. Tuberculosis and consumption scared all of us. One of the two sanatoriums located in Oklahoma for T.B. patients was south of Shawnee. The Indian Sanatorium. WPA people had been working on improving the building.

"My teacher upset me so much I started shaking." Blanche's voice grew louder. "I know all about T.B. I do *not* have it. How can she even ask?"

Blanche, unfortunately, did look like a totem pole with awkward limbs. But she didn't have any coughing or fatigue. Although her teacher was wrong, maybe I should get my sister outside more.

"What did Mama say when you told her?" I said as I snipped strands of Margaret's hair.

"Mama was furious. She stomped up to the school and got my class changed to Glee Club. I wanted out of gym anyway after the way the teacher acted. I don't want any more to do with her. It's good I love to sing."

"You do have a beautiful voice."

"I'll enjoy the year much more now."

I gave her a sisterly smile. "And Blanche, you do *not* have tuberculosis."

Instead of getting irritated with my obnoxious sister and turning away, I tried to understand her. Feel what she felt.

"Jump down Margaret. We're finished." I took the hair-covered towel to the back door and shook it out.

Love expanded inside me and my heart went out to others. I empathized with the needy. Understood the downtrodden. It amazed me how a person could grow so much in a few short years. Maybe trials did that. Helped me see others differently because I definitely began to see Lester and Blanche in a new light.

Chapter Thirty-Three

May 1937

Mama and I seldom sat and talked, so I cherished time with her. We sat under the low-pitched gabled roof supported by brick pedestals, swinging on the porch swing that hung from the ceiling. She listened as I expressed my concerns about recent disasters.

I crocheted and talked at the same time.

I had listened to the radio and heard about the Hindenburg airship crash. Thirty-six fatalities. Then just as I was processing that catastrophe, listening to comments until late in the night, Amelia Earhart disappeared while flying over the Pacific. How could this happen to the woman of the century? Was this whole world full of disasters? Would we ever find peace and stability again?

My concerns spent, Mama and I quietly watched Margaret and Judson play in the front yard for a few minutes. They laughed, throwing a ball at each other, until Judson got tired of playing and stomped the ball, deflating it.

Mama and I began to discuss the Eastern Stars, the organization she belonged to and where she spent so much time. Frances and Blanche occasionally went to meetings with her and would sit in the lavish lounge. They also waited while Mama attended fancy afternoon teas served in demitasse cups, or were patient during the informal luncheons.

Informal, meaning the table was set with china, linens, watercress salad and squares of pimento cheese sandwiches.

Mrs. Marland, an Eastern Star friend, was wealthy because her husband owned a chain of M&P grocery stores. A few years ago, she played the piano while Mama sang on the KGFF radio station. When she learned that Mama was clear out of food, she brought a few groceries over. Mama was delighted that someone cared so much.

Lately, the Eastern Stars paid Mama and the girls to wash dishes after the meetings and formal dinners. Sometimes they cleaned up until one o'clock in morning, and Mama would get between five and ten dollars. She also could take home leftovers, a plus.

Mama complained about the wilted stuffed tomatoes and molded grapefruit salad she took home last week. How could she complain if the food was free? She was going on about the lack of decent leftovers when we heard Blanche yell from inside the house.

"What happened to my dress?"

Mama grimaced. "Oh, dear."

Blanche stormed through the front door carrying her blue satiny dress with a gathered waist. I cringed. A burn on the skirt was shaped like an iron.

"I was trying to help," said Mama.

"Don't you ever try to iron my clothes again."

My eyes widened. I'd never heard Blanche speak like that to Mama.

"Don't worry," said Mama. "I won't."

Blanche turned and went back into the house, slamming the door behind her.

"The last time I washed her blouse in the wringer machine, all the buttons came off." Mama grimaced. "Guess I'll let her wash her own clothes from now on."

"She gets so angry," I said.

"She thinks I'm harder on her than the rest of you kids. Claims you didn't get bad treatment because you didn't have me as a mother during this depression."

Blanche. Blanche. Why did she have to stir up trouble all the time?

The children tired of playing kick ball and picked up sticks, pretending to fight with swords. They chased each other all over the yard.

"Your papa quit making child support payments over three months ago," said Mama bitterly. "I've tried to be patient, but we need food on the table."

I steadied my breath, wishing I had good news or money to hand her. Papa hoped to get a bank examiner's position when the new state banking act passed. Fourteen examiner positions would be open. I didn't hold out much hope for him getting the job, because of his connection with the previous Commissioner Barnett. He was too close to the scandal. Not to mention the ramifications of the public divorce.

I shared the latest news with Mama about Barnett. His petitions for a re-hearing on the misuse of funds had been dismissed. Barnett would most definitely stand trial.

My mind wandered as I thought of a catch in the Barnett evidence I didn't understand. Papa had been the auditor who selected the specific Ardmore banking records to be destroyed, the records that were burned. Barnett claimed those records could have helped exonerate him. Papa said the documents were inconsequential. Who was telling the truth? Did Papa intentionally destroy pertinent records? If he did, why? The thought made me queasy.

Mama interrupted my thoughts with talk about Calvis. "Weekends, Calvis still goes to Spring Lake Park and sings at that dance place. I'm sure your papa knows nothing about it."

I shook my head of disjointed thoughts and relaxed. Glad Calvis had not completely given up music as he claimed he would. "I'm sure Calvis enjoys the singing. He's always dreamed of joining a band and touring with a famous group."

"Cal said he sang with the Andrew sisters when they came to town."

"Wish he could find his place in music. He has a clear, moving voice."

"Why doesn't your papa let him alone? Calvis is working at the bank, isn't he? Your papa beats all."

Mama and I got quiet. I did remember. I remembered a lot. Trying to please Papa had consumed my life until Fremont came along. Maybe Calvis also tried to please Papa. Tried to follow his way to get approval.

"I got a call from Marjorie," said Mama. She jumped from subject to subject quicker than a flea bites.

I raised my eyebrows. Marjorie was living in Phoenix with Kelley, against everyone's recommendation that she forget him and come back home. A man who runs off with another woman should not be chased.

"How's she doing?"

"Been working as a waitress. It's pretty bad, from what she said." Mama sighed. "Kelley's knocking her around again."

I turned toward Mama. "What?"

"Yeah. He got jealous at her for flirting with some guy at a juke joint."

"A knock-out like Marjorie attracts the wrong kind of fellows."

Mama shook her head, which was covered in curlers hidden underneath a scarf. "Clearly, Marjorie wasn't doing anything wrong. But he stomped through the house and dumped mustard and ketchup all over the floor. Made a horrible mess."

"I don't know why she puts up with him." I reached into my basket of crocheting and kept my hands busy with a newly-learned pattern, keeping my anger at bay.

"That's the funny part. Larry was watching and got enraged with his father. He ran over to Kelley, punched him and kicked him on the legs." Mama laughed as she said it, obviously pleased at Larry's outburst of anger.

"But Larry could have gotten hurt. Kelley could have hit him." I found no humor in it. I felt sorry for my little nephew. A child's fury against his dad could create an ache that might never go away.

"No, Kelley just laughed. Took hours for Marjorie to clean up the dirty floor though."

"Is she going to stay out there? If he's acting that way, she should come back home." I looked at Mama to see her response, dropping a stitch. I stopped crocheting. I would have to start this line over.

"She's still out there, Kelley's bad temper and all," Mama said. "Oh, and listen to this. Some guy wanted to rescue Marjorie, saying he would take her to another country where she would be safe."

"She won't go, will she?"

"Of course not. Some safety. He'd probably make her a slave."

"Marjorie's weakness for nice-looking men and flattering words will get her into trouble." I let out a deep breath.

"It almost caused her to succumb this time," said Mama. "I'm glad she managed to say no."

Marjorie, always Mama's favorite, even when she lived miles away. But then it didn't matter anymore. God loved me. I wanted Mama and Marjorie to feel his love, too.

"I can't believe *that man* kicked Marjorie out of his house and made her go back to Kelley," said Mama.

I knew she was talking about Papa. She wouldn't let us get over the divorce. Like the old saying, all roads lead to Washington, every conversation with Mama always led back to Papa.

I sat still and prayed silently, "Lord, reveal your love to her."

How long would I have to pray this prayer?

Chapter Thirty-Four

June 1937

Mother Pope taught me more about life and homemaking than I thought possible. My mama put little effort into creating a happy atmosphere, her focus was on what society friends thought or putting down Papa. Mother Pope, on the other hand, never said a bad word about her husband, laughing at his shenanigans and enjoying his company. Their relationship delighted me and I wanted Fremont and me to have the same closeness.

I spent a lot of time with Mother Pope, going to her house for laundry once a week, helping her bake and do garden work. I loved to bask in her wisdom, for wise words seemed to spew from her mouth. She could squirt a line of wisdom out of the blue and it would be exactly what I needed.

One Friday evening, Mother, Margaret and I sat under the catalpa tree in the front yard, several bowls in hand. Eight months pregnant, I balanced the bowl on my round belly. We sat in a circle. Irene and Ruth pitched in to help snap the beans. Fremont's young teenage sisters agreed to assist in exchange for a free night on Saturday. Tension existed between Fremont's sisters and I because they thought I had tricked him into marrying me. Thought I was not good enough for him. Maybe sisters are like that.

We snapped so many green beans my fingers turned numb. I'd never seen so many. Not that I hadn't snapped beans before. I had. Everyone in the country knew about snapping green beans. But because the weather had been hot as wild fire, they had grown well. At least something flourished in this hot weather.

"This is the first good crop we've had in years," said Mother. "I think we're about finished here. Times goes by fast when you're working together. I'll be ready to can the beans in the morning."

"Could you teach me how to can?" I asked, wanting to add to my homemaking skills. "Please. I've never canned before and I want to learn."

"As long as you're up to it. I'm sure Irene won't mind getting out of the chore." Mother laughed. "Come over early. I'll start before the rooster crows."

The next morning, Fremont, the children and I arrived as the sun rose, its first rays stretching across the vast Oklahoma sky. The children followed Fremont down to the shed to help milk the cow and feed the pig. Later they would water the garden. Dad had planted tomatoes beside the house, just below the retaining wall. A trellis supporting the plump red vegetables was loaded and would be more so as the season went on.

"Green beans should be picked every two or three days," Mother told me looking out the window.

Mother must have considered me a city girl who had never walked through a garden. She wasn't completely wrong, but I didn't say so. No one told Mother she was wrong, lest of all her daughter-in-law. I merely hoped to keep up with her. My days had become tiring, taking care of the children and the house while growing as large as a full moon.

We took pails of beans outside to the water well to wash them before beginning the process. The pulley squeaked as I pulled the bucket up from the well, the bucket overflowing with cold, sparkling clear water. I took the metal cup and drank from it, water running down my chin. The fresh, clean water tasted heavenly.

Mother yelled at Dad, who was hoeing in the garden nearby. "Make sure the beans get plenty of water!"

"I know. I know," said Dad wiping his brow with a red bandanna. "No water, no beans."

"And don't forget to leave green beans on the vine. We'll be needing beans pods next year."

"You're worrying too much, woman. I've been doing this for years."

"Make sure those seeds are completely dried before you store them. We ruined seeds last year because they got damp and moldy."

"Mother, you go on about your business and I'll do mine."

Mother shook her head. "That man."

We carried the pails back into the house and set them on the kitchen counter, pouring water into the big pans.

"Sibyl, bring in another bucket of water."

When I got back, Mother was checking the rims of a dozen or so glass jars for nicks or cracks. She washed the jars before dunking them in scalding water.

"It's best to keep everything hot," she said. "Heat the water to near boiling to cover the jars and keep the lids in warm water. Mixing hot and cold can shatter the glass. Now pack the hot beans into the heated jars, leaving about an inch at the top."

I did as she directed.

"That's the way. Shake the beans down and pack them in tight." She added a spoonful of salt to each jar.

"Take this wooden spoon and put it down the side to release any air bubbles. Add more water if you need it. Remember, one inch below the top edge of the jar."

I helped Mother by taking a tea towel and wiping the jar rims, then we put on the two-piece caps and tightened the bands.

"Now if you get too tired, you go right ahead and sit down a spell. No sense in wearing yourself out."

"I'm all right so far," I said, determined to let nothing slow me down. I felt proud of our accomplishment.

"You're doing great," she said.

"What's next?" I asked, taking time to jot down notes so I could remember the steps. Mother had a monstrous pressure canner, something I didn't have. Canning seemed to be a social affair, not as easily done by yourself.

"The hard part's over. Simply process the quart jars for twenty-five minutes."

I sighed. The process was longer than I'd expected.

"Go on and sit down," said Mother kindly. "You stay there while I clean up. A watched pot never boils."

By the time my breathing slowed down, Mother had the kitchen straightened and glasses of iced tea poured for us. Pregnancy made canning an onerous task.

Sweat poured down my back as I took the jars out of the canner. Why did green beans have to grow in the heat of summer?

"Good. Good. Now set them on that clean kitchen towel over there, away from drafts, mind you. We'll leave them alone for the rest of the day until they're cool."

I counted sixteen quarts of green beans by the time we finished.

Exhausted more than I cared to admit, I sat at the table to rest. Mother pulled off her long apron, its bib catching on her braids. Then she bent over and loosened the buckles on her shoes and joined me.

"Add this to your note taking, Sibyl. After the jars cool, test the seals. If you can pop the lid up and down, they didn't seal properly."

"What if they didn't seal? Do we start over?"

"Oh, my no, child, if the jars didn't seal, eat them in the next few weeks." Mother explained that it takes a certain amount of pressure to seal a can of green beans, just like it takes pressure to seal a marriage. There were other similarities. Takes a lot of hard work. A relationship may sometimes be hotter than fire and sometimes has to cool off. Be patient—that was the advice I needed.

I had learned another skill to help my family through. I was proud of myself. I'd mastered a lot since I married Fremont. Mother's wisdom was endless.

Now if the baby would only quit kicking, I could enjoy the rest of the day.

Chapter Thirty-Five
July 1937

Perhaps due to Fremont's job and our move uptown, I refused to get depressed during this pregnancy as I had during the previous two. Even Mama and Blanche's criticism about having too many children couldn't get me down. I sewed baby clothes, crocheted booties and caps, and received gifts from family and friends. The perfect little nursery layout was prepared and waiting.

Nine months and ten days after we moved into the new house on Draper Street, a baby boy blessed our home. After a difficult birth because of his size, Keith was born on the third of July, 1937, right on his due date.

Keith, at ten and a half pounds, looked halfway grown when he was born, more like a six-month-old baby than a newborn. He was a beautiful child with brown hair and eyes. Healthy in every way. This new bouncy infant promised exciting days ahead. The discouraging days were over. He represented a new start and a promise for a brighter future.

"Biggest newborn I've ever seen," Dr. Fortson chuckled. "Probably put him to work right away."

I collected baby Keith and held him in my arms, rocking him back and forth. This child instantly captured my heart. His olive complexion and brown hair matched mine and my heart softened. I nursed him easily, without the problems I'd had with my first two children.

How I wished Marjorie was around to share this joy. I would let her know that she wasn't the only one who could nurse a baby. I didn't need her assistance this time. I was a good mother.

"Isn't he adorable?" I said to no one in particular.

Margaret, like a second mother, held his bottle and patted him on the back to put him to sleep while Judson merely made faces at him trying to make him laugh.

A citywide parade on July twenty-second celebrated the completion of the Deer Creek Dam, the place where Dad and Fremont had worked. It took longer to complete than they planned due to the cutbacks, but the whole city went all out for the celebration. I wanted to assume they were celebrating the birth of my third child. At least that's what I celebrated.

My Sunday school class called themselves the Win-some class. The ladies gathered around me enamored, oohing over Keith's cute fat cheeks. They pitched in and bought a gift for Keith. It was a tiny metal baby cup with a handle that had the name "Skippy" engraved on the side for the cartoon character people loved. The sweet ladies, always assisting someone in the area, chatted about helping the tornado victims in Maud and the work needed. I enjoyed volunteer work when I was not at home caring for my growing family.

Keith came to us as an optimistic, innocent child, unscathed by the economic hardships, family problems, and social despair of the decade. He brought hope to all of us.

I determined to be the best mother in the world. To shield the children from the world's problems and create an atmosphere of togetherness. If I couldn't be a successful leader as Papa wanted, I could still be a successful mother and housewife. I breathed deeply and shoved my shoulders back, swaggering in knowing the importance of my job.

I loved Keith so much and it felt like our family was complete. Fremont reluctantly agreed with me that three children seemed to be the right number, two boys and a girl. I almost applauded.

Chapter Thirty-Six

August 1937

Fremont's twenty-sixth birthday arrived on August seventh, and I wanted to plan something special for him. After all, he never complained about the chaos surrounding the children or my family's idiosyncrasies. He remained as solid as the big pecan tree in Dad's backyard, never wavering. He deserved a party. He worked days this month instead of nights because he was filling in for a mechanic who broke his arm.

On Sunday before his birthday, I quietly invited some church friends to our home the following Saturday. Fremont, as had become his usual way, didn't attend church often, but would occasionally go. Too busy working and supporting his family.

Monday morning, my friend Effie came over to help plan a surprise for Fremont. For a decoration, from a cardboard box we created a large sign which read, "Happy Birthday, Fremont!"

The morning of the party dawned and I fretted. Fremont left early for the daytime job. Still recovering from Keith's birth only a month ago, I worried all day about what to wear, rummaging through my bare closet. To keep my hands busy while pregnant, I had crocheted a lot. One item I'd made, after baby clothes and a doily, was a white hand-crocheted dress for myself. Tonight would be the perfect time to pull it out and wear it. I laid it across the bed and chose a nice pair of high-waisted trousers and a shirt for Fremont.

I washed my hair and rolled it up in rags. I usually used bobby pins, but I wanted loose curls today. Grandma Bennett had used rags and showed me how to twist the hair around and tie it.

Using Mama's recipe, I baked a chocolate cake early in the morning to let it cool before decorating. Chocolate cake creates about the best smell in the world. While the children napped, I spread frosting on the cake and hid it on top of the ice box.

Anxiety grew as I worked. The closer it came to five-thirty, the more nervous I became. I didn't know if I could keep the surprise or how Fremont would respond. I had not completely recovered from Keith's birth and my moodiness had increased.

I bathed the children early and had them ready. Keith, nursing every few hours, never seemed to be satisfied. I supplemented his meal with a bottle of goat milk.

Fremont walked through the back door, his work clothes covered with grease and oil. His face streaked with dirt.

"Why don't you clean up while I set the table?" I had prepared a light supper, which wouldn't take long to heat.

"What's going on?" Fremont yelled from the bedroom when he saw our nice clothes laid out. "Something's mighty fishy around here."

"Don't fret so. Your mother invited us over after supper for ice cream," I said, crossing my fingers behind my back. "Go ahead and change clothes."

I set the meal on the table, a chicken and vegetable soup made from yesterday's leftovers. Neither of us said much during the meal and I, normally a slow eater, wanted to hurry through but slowed myself down.

"Would you wash the dishes while I change clothes?" I asked, trying to hide my nervousness. I slipped into the bedroom, brushed my hair and fluffed it around my head. Fremont would understand if I took extra time, because he usually had to wait for me.

A knock sounded on the front door.

"Would you open that?" I called from the bedroom and entered the living room.

Fremont threw the front door open.

"Surprise! Surprise!" Effie and Doug, Opal and Carl, Irene and other friends barged into the room. Effie carried a balloon while Irene held up the big sign.

The children gathered around Fremont.

"Are you surprised, Daddy?" asked Margaret, hugging his leg.

Fremont picked her up. "I had no clue, young 'un."

Effie, about my height and plump with dark brown hair, was a sweet girl who liked everyone and everyone liked her. Pregnant with their second child, she was dodged by their son, Robert, who was a few months younger than Judson. Opal brought a freezer full of chocolate ice cream to go with the cake.

"Here you go, old man." Doug handed Fremont a shiny new yellow fishing lure. "I made it myself." Doug worked as a carpenter and set up a shop in his garage where he made bows and arrows. He also crafted wooden cabinets in his spare time for extra cash.

I'd pondered long and hard about what kind of gift to give Fremont. With money still scarce, I'd been saving extra pennies for months. I selected a pair of new gloves from Sears and Roebuck's. Fremont smiled when he opened the box, and I knew I'd made a good choice.

Someone had purchased a six-pack of Coca-Colas for the event, and we poured a bit into every person's glass.

The party lasted well into the night. It had been a whopper of a day and I felt weary.

We played three rounds of Dominoes and I took a break to feed baby Keith. Then we began a word game called Dictionary, my favorite.

As always, I started the dictionary game. I selected the strangest word I could find from the dictionary, said the word out loud and spelled it out slowly for the players. After our friends wrote down their made-up definitions, they handed me their slips of paper. I shuffled them, along with the real definition, which I'd written myself. I read the meanings aloud in random order. Everyone but me voted for the definition he or she believed correct. Then they guessed which definition was the true one. If no one guessed the true meaning, I won. Maybe that's why I liked the game. I usually won.

The group laughed as we played and warm feelings filled the room. When it was Fremont's turn, he took almost ten minutes to find a word.

"Odalisque," he finally said. No one had heard it before.

Each person scribbled out their imaginary definition and handed it to Fremont. Doug, the last one to finish, labored to pen a ridiculous meaning. "Two donkeys standing in front of a red Oldsmobile."

No one came close to knowing the answer. "Tell us, Fremont," someone said. "What is the real meaning?"

Fremont hesitated. "It means a female slave, a concubine in a harem."

Everyone laughed and I froze. A female slave? Why did he choose that word? Is that what I was to him? A slave, like Mama said she had been to Papa, doing his housework and every bidding?

"Fremont, how could you?" I squealed, knowing my thoughts were ridiculous. No one cared for me as much as Fremont.

"I thought it was a mighty good word. Took a long time to find it."

The minute after I dashed out of the room, I felt ashamed. My touchiness alienated my friends. Tears stung my eyes. I had certainly overreacted, but where had it come from? Perhaps the tension of the day exhausted me. I'd pushed myself too far, caring for two children and a newborn was enough work by itself.

Whatever the reason, I scolded myself for my behavior. Why couldn't I be more self-controlled like my husband? I had improved from a few years ago but still needed more self-discipline.

When I walked back into the room, the game had ended.

"I shouldn't have yelled like that. I apologize," I said to the group.

"You must be exhausted," said Opal. "What with the party and the new baby and all. Here, let me help you clean up."

I let go of my anger but remained cool toward Fremont, although he seemed unaware. He had no idea anything was wrong with me.

Still troubled early the next morning, I gazed out the bedroom window at the sunrise. Fremont had left for work and the children slept. Why had my emotions exploded? The hurt inside agitated me. Partly from my embarrassing eruption and partly because I recognized some truth in the idea that I felt enslaved to a life I didn't plan. No one understood my frustration and exhaustion, not even Fremont. Three small children were more work than I'd expected. I should never have planned a party so soon after giving birth. I bowed my head and let the tears come.

Then I heard the soft words in my heart. *I understand.* God understood? Yes, of course, God knew my heart even better than I did. He knew about my lack of sleep, the dirty diapers, and the children sleeping in the adjoining room. He knew my disappointment with myself and my fear of our perfect little life falling apart.

I turned quickly to the book of Peter and read, *"Casting all your cares upon Him; for he careth for you."*

My heart found comfort in knowing someone understood my intricate, complicated life. Someone saw my struggles and cared for me anyway. He wouldn't let my world fall apart, would he?

Chapter Thirty-Seven

Summer heat almost destroyed the farm in Sulphur where Grandpa Bennett, Mama's father, had been living. After some discussion, Uncle Louie sent him back to Mama's house. Grandpa agreed to move in with Mama and the girls only because Papa no longer lived there. He was one of the few people happy about their divorce.

Over the years, Grandpa Bennett and Papa had wrangled about the Civil War. Papa had insisted his children adopt his viewpoint. He bought a book about the Confederates and explained the economics involved, boring us with details. To erase Papa's influence, Grandpa lectured about how the North freed the slaves and saved the union. Mama hated listening to the arguments and tried to hush them both.

"You've never been around Grandpa Bennett much," I observed as Fremont and I walked over to Mama's house. "Don't be shocked. He's quite a character. Not your regular died-in-the-wool, yellow-dog democrat."

Fremont laughed. "Don't worry, our family has some mighty strange characters too. Remember Uncle Raleigh's long-winded sagas?" He pushed Keith's buggy while I held Margaret's hand. Judson bounced between us.

When Grandpa came to live with Mama, she had another mouth to feed and another bed to make in their small living area. The twenty dollars he received every month from the government helped, but with four living together, the house became crowded.

I walked into Grandpa's room and helped him straighten his belongings on the dresser. His comb, straight edge razor, and shaving mug. He'd also brought his fiddle and a few changes of clothing.

When I noticed Grandpa's faded black-and-white picture of Grandma Bennett on the dresser, tears formed in my eyes. I missed Grandma Bennett more than ever. No one understood me or supported me the way she had. She died a few weeks after Fremont and I married, and in a way, I still connected marriage with her loss. But the Lord had forgiven me for that time of disappointment in myself. The time I had to marry because I was pregnant.

Grandpa Bennett, a lumberjack and carpenter, had moved through life wherever big jobs needed men. He worked on building a bridge over the Merrimac River and built two houses for Grandma and enough furniture for a dozen families. He built the pine breakfast table and benches in the breakfast nook where we ate.

Blanche and Frances came into the house about the same time. They greeted Grandpa and left to find Mama in the kitchen.

We gathered around, found seats and ate like we hadn't eaten in a week. I certainly enjoyed every last bite of chicken and dumplings piled on my plate.

"I couldn't even offer you a decent meal tonight," Mama said.

"Nonsense. It was delicious, as usual."

"Boiled chicken wings and flour dumplings are an everyday meal. Not for visitors. It's all your papa's fault. He hasn't given us a penny in months. How am I supposed to feed his daughters?"

Ignoring the remark, I helped collect the dirty dishes off the table. Fremont and Grandpa carried chairs and rockers to the back porch, where we gathered to watch the golden orange streaks of the sunset across the huge sky. The bouquet of Clematis blooming close to the house filled the porch with a sweet smell. The outline of the children's playhouse created a surreal backdrop. Rose bushes covered the front of it, thorns sticking out along the side, darkening as the sun went down.

Judson, sitting on the steps beside Margaret, grabbed a handful of flowers, squeezing the blooms in his little fist.

"Boy, I dunked your Uncle Louie in the rain barrel for saying bad words," Grandpa Bennett said without missing a beat on the platform rocker. He bent his head full of grey hair down toward Judson, shaking his finger. "That should be a lesson on what might happen to you for plucking Grandma's flowers." He sat back up and stroked the calico cat curled up on his lap.

"Nobody needs lessons tonight," Mama protested.

"Grandpa, please tell us a story about Mama when she was young," said Frances.

"Not now, child," Mama's voice scolded. "Maybe later."

"Cheer up, Mabel," said Grandpa. "Life could be worse."

"At this point, I don't see how."

Grandpa picked up his fiddle. A natural-born musician, he would patter around the house singing, annoying Mama no end. Her grumpiness never deterred him.

"What do you want to hear?" Grandpa asked, scanning the circle. Fremont and I sat to his left with our children while Mama, Blanche and Frances completed the circle to the right. "I can play anything, long as I've heard it. Can't play it if I never heard it." He laughed at his own joke and hopped up, sending the cat screeching toward the house. He loved to dance and sing while he played the fiddle. His nearly six-foot frame swayed to the rhythm of the music that came from deep in his bones.

I watched him, his love of music apparent in his dancing toes and moving fingers. The source of my love of music dawned on me. My handsome Grandpa had passed his musical talent on to his clan. My feet tapped and I laughed, wanting to join him.

I glanced at Fremont, but he was watching with a straight face, his perfect profile motionless. As usual, he remained calm, showing little emotion. It puzzled me. How could he not feel it? How could he not sense the deep spark inside the soul that was inspired by music? The need to move, to cry? To laugh and jump for joy? It seemed so natural to me, like a dog begging to be stroked. I could hardly stay in my chair and dropped my hand down to Margaret's shoulder to encourage her to join in the dancing. She and Judson buzzed around Grandpa like a jigsaw.

Frances jumped up, dancing smoothly in ballet style, showing off her tap dancing lessons like it was a regular shindig. Her skirts ballooned around her.

Grandpa brought joy to the family in the middle of our troubles. He'd been a good-looking man when he was young, with clear sapphire-colored eyes and a head full of dark hair. He remained good-looking now, even though he stooped a little and his hair had faded. For the next song, he played a ragtime, the old-fashioned kind with a lively back and forth sound. The spry old man danced while he played, his violin and his dancing intertwined around him together.

Mama, after grumbling that Marjorie would have loved to dance with them, finally dropped her ill temper and joined in. I stared down at the floor. Then, from the corner of my eye, I noticed Fremont's foot tapping. He probably didn't even realize it. I smiled. Deep down, music touched him like it did the rest of us.

Grandpa, although fun and happy, tired out rather quickly. Twenty minutes later, he plopped down into a chair to take a breath and sip a glass of iced tea.

"Papa never danced," Blanche said in a flat voice as if she'd just realized it. She hadn't gotten up to dance, but maybe she was still in that self-conscious teenage stage.

"He learned to dance only to get me to marry him," said Mama, breathing heavily. "He never danced after we married."

Fremont and I exchanged glances. We preferred to avoid discussing the merits of dancing. It remained too touchy a subject, not mentioned since before we married. We decided not to ever go to honky-tonks or speakeasies again.

"You haven't told us a story about Mama yet," Frances begged.

"Always got a story for you, young lady," said Grandpa, breathing heavily. "When your mama was a little tyke, she had these two calves that followed her 'round like pets."

"Baby calves? For pets?" Margaret's eyes opened wide.

"Sure enough. And one day they up and followed her right into the house. Her mother was downright aggravated when they tracked mud on her clean floor. Then those calves nibbled every last piece of cornbread in the house 'til your Grandma Bennett ran them off with a broomstick. You never saw such a sight as that scrawny woman flying around with a broom in the air!"

Laughter rolled through the gates and down the street.

"I remember riding a train by myself when I was only five years old," said Mama.

"At five, Mama?" I asked. "You couldn't have. Why, that's not much older than Margaret."

"I was under the conductor's care. I rode all the way to Indiana to see Uncle Watson Clay."

"That reminds me," Grandpa said, his eyes twinkling, "Do you know what your Aunt Adah did one time . . .?"

The lights stayed on late until Grandpa Bennett lay down on his cot by the side of the house. "Got to get my forty winks in." He frequently slept outside because it was cooler.

No one wanted the night to end. My heart filled with joy. We were fine, God-wrapped in a warm cocoon, despite Papa's neglect, the depressing weather and our family problems. Fremont and I had a place to worship and we had food on the table. God was good.

We thrived even if we didn't have much. Happiness and warmth spread through me. Three beautiful children. A good family. A stable husband. A joyful grandfather. What more could any spirited girl want?

Chapter Thirty-Eight

September 1937

"Are you coming, Sibyl?" asked my friend Effie after church. She watched as I straightened Margaret's hair ribbons.

"The children need naps," I said, "but I think we can go for a little while."

"Bring blankets. We'll spread them under a tree."

Fremont and I relished rendezvous with friends. After I packed a bag for the children and made a coleslaw, Fremont drove us to the outskirts of Shawnee. Opal's parents had a hundred acres east of town. When the weather permitted on Sunday afternoons after church, several young couples would travel out and set up a picnic on their land.

The scene was memorable. We picnicked in a small clearing where we could see the North Canadian River nearby. Besides Opal and Carl, Effie and Doug, Anna Clark and her husband Joe came. Anna visited our church women's group occasionally, but her mother disapproved because she was from a different denomination. Anna shifted back and forth in her religion like a see saw. It didn't help that her husband avoided church altogether. Neither Carl nor Doug went to church either at that time.

We aligned our large brimmed straw hats, dusted off our small-print, shirt-waist dresses, and took off our shoes. I loved to go barefoot, as did the children. We spread the blankets and shared food. The picnic was a huge success.

For desert, Opal made her famous vanilla ice cream and my mouth watered. She had packed the ice cream churn full. Homemade ice cream with fresh eggs and cream. Oh, my stars. I could eat it all myself. She packed ice chips around it to keep the tin bucket cold. I was glad it was already churned.

After eating, the ladies pulled chairs under a shade tree to chat. Nothing as sweet as my friends' company. Friends, especially during hard times, were a valuable asset.

We fanned ourselves and our babies, who played on blankets in front of us as the older children ran in circles through the blackjack oak trees. They played cops and robbers pretending to chase Pretty Boy Floyd and Mad Dog Underhill.

In reality, Pretty Boy Floyd had been raised in nearby Earlsboro, which meant he didn't plunder nearby. But Underhill, of the most-wanted-bandit list, had been ambushed in Shawnee on East Main a few years ago. The little boys overheard the talk and loved to reenact the scene where Underhill was chased to the McAlester Feed Store sixteen blocks away. The exact location was known to almost everyone in town.

After we ate our fill of cold ice cream topped with plum preserves, the guys discussed what to do for the rest of the afternoon.

Doug pulled a Bull Durham package out of his pocket and took out a pinch of tobacco to chew. He offered some to Fremont. "How about going shooting at the river?" Doug said. Shooting guns at the North Canadian River bend was one of their favorite pastimes. The fellows practiced by throwing sticks or tin cans into the running water and aiming at them.

That decided, Fremont climbed into the back of Doug's old pickup with Carl and Joe. I watched as Doug drove through an open field to reach the river. In the tall grass, something jumped in the meadow.

"A rabbit!" Fremont's voice carried. I could see his straw hat in the distance.

Doug stopped the truck, stuck his head out the window and looked back. "Hey, grab your bean shooters!"

Fremont nodded. Meat was scarce and a rabbit hunt would be entertaining just when life in Shawnee seemed dullest.

Fremont cocked his dad's twenty-gauge shotgun. Doug, the best shooter by far, and Carl, who owned a newer rifle, followed suit. Joe wasn't far behind as they jumped out of the truck bed.

Fremont spotted another hare in the field. He shot and within seconds I heard another gun ring out. Fremont ran over and picked up a rabbit by its hind legs, holding it high.

Doug drove on and I heard more shots in the distance.

Pleased as peach pie, the boys came back and offered us their haul of rabbits. For their efforts they received both repugnant *ohs* and admiring *ahs*.

"Jack rabbits!" said Fremont, disappointed, his thumbs anchored in his suspenders. "All we've got are a bunch of skinny jack rabbits. No cottontails at all."

"Yeah," Carl added. "The girls could have fried up some plump cottontails and we would have had a feast."

"I say." Fremont pulled his shoulders back. "But no matter. The shooting was a mighty big success, right fellows?" Even if the rabbits weren't as good eating as cottontails, it was something the fellows could be proud of—proof they could hit a moving target. And proof they could provide for their families.

"Reminds me of those rabbit round-ups I heard about," said Doug. "Over in the panhandle."

"Thousands of long-eared critters are eating up their crops."

"Girls, let's do something with these rabbits." Effie said. "Can't waste anything these days."

"How about canning them?" I proposed. "Never canned rabbits before, but we can try."

"No sense throwing them to the dogs."

"Shake a leg, fellows! We're heading out."

The fellows piled the gunny sacks of rabbits into the back of the pickup while we gals packed up lunch and the young ones. We borrowed Mother's pressure canner and drove to our house. Fremont and the guys skinned the rabbits and handed us a tub full of bare hares. With the girls' help, I cooked them until they became tender. Then together we stuffed rabbit meat into glass jars and poured hot liquid up to the top, leaving one inch, as Mother suggested. Her lessons were fixed in my mind.

Sealed inside clear glass jars, the meat looked almost edible. We each claimed several.

"Honey, jack rabbits are as tough as old codgers," said Fremont, chewing on a hunk of tobacco. "Not fit for a hobo to eat. We may as well keep 'em for a souvenir though."

I frowned at him, at the dark juices on his lips—lips I liked to kiss. "Either the tobacco goes, or I go."

Without saying a word, Fremont opened the back door and spit. He stepped back into the kitchen. "Didn't like it much anyway."

I let him know how much work we had done on the rabbits. "I just spent hours preserving what meat I could get off the bones."

He cleared his throat and said, "I imagine jack rabbit and dumplings might be good."

During the cold winter when money got scarce as hen's teeth, I could cook up a bunch of those rabbits and try it out. Fremont's job down at Norton's driving a wrecker barely paid the bills. We skated by on leftovers.

Chewing tobacco was not welcome in our home. And jack rabbit had to be tastier than a pot of week-old brown beans.

The following week, Fremont's sister Irene had a birthday and I thought her seventeenth year would be a good time to do something nice for her.

My heart went out to Irene. The Popes lived on the poor side of town and she didn't have fashionable clothes, makeup, or fancy handbags—

items high school students needed to fit in. Her mother was very strict and Irene rebelled in her own way. Her group of friends thought church catered to old folks.

Mother Pope kept Irene at home as much as possible, but she liked to sneak out to the corner streetlight to meet buddies and share cigarettes. She still went to church because her mother made her, but many Sunday evenings I saw her slip out the side door.

Irene invited her teenage friends to her birthday party, girls she had introduced to me. I told the girls they could invite whomever they wanted.

I prepared a fresh apple cake, beating in the eggs, sugar and Mother's homemade churned butter. I added white flour with a little baking powder and stirred it before adding two cups of grated apples. I greased and floured two round cake pans and baked the cake in my unpredictable oven. After the first twenty minutes, I checked the cake every five minutes and didn't leave the kitchen until it was ready to remove.

Fremont, who didn't care for girl parties, went dove hunting with Doug that day, carrying his rifle and burdened down with whistles and bags and such.

The children helped me spread our nice table cloth and napkins and we put a bouquet of flowers on the table. I made punch from apple juice and lemon soda, called 7UP.

Seven girls arrived with Irene. Irene, with her seductive blue eyes, had developed into quite a beautiful, buxom young lady. Always talking, she led the conversation about school, movies and boys. Mostly boys. Some thought she was pushy and a bit bossy. I didn't know about that, but I did see some self-centeredness in her.

I heard a knock on the door.

"Hello, Ma'am." The boy's voice cracked like an adolescent. "I heard Irene is having a birthday party." Two boys stood behind him.

This wasn't what I'd expected, but I let them in.

I chaperoned closely, a difficult chore with that many bouncing teenagers. At a decent hour, I shooed the youth out the door, satisfied in my role of making Irene feel loved.

I felt good about the party. I hoped this generous feeling would stay with me always.

Chapter Thirty-Nine

October 1937

A few weeks later, I took Fremont's work clothes off the clothesline and walked into the house. Blanche jumped up from the sofa. She smelled like freshly cooked taffy. She must have visited the Shawnee Candy Company on her way over.

Blanche begin to pace back and forth like a caught hyena.

"What's wrong?" I asked. "Is Mama all right?"

Blanche didn't speak. She kept chomping with a frown across her forehead. Something was on her mind.

"You can at least nod your head to let me know. Is Mama okay?"

Blanche nodded her head slowly. Yes, Mama was fine.

"Then what's got into you? You look troubled."

Again, the nod.

"Well, just spit it out. What's the matter? School? Family? Papa?"

"Don't you know? You gave Irene a birthday party."

"I did do that. Does it upset you?"

"Upset me?" Blanche screamed as she turned to me. "Upset? Why would I get angry at my sister for giving her husband's sister and my schoolmate a birthday party and not inviting me?"

"I thought you didn't like Irene."

"I can't stand her. But you're my sister and I expect to be included in high school parties you give. Even if I despise the person."

I had no idea she'd want to come. Truthfully, I never thought of inviting her. Blanche was not always pleasant to be around.

"You've never given me a party."

"I didn't know you wanted one."

"You didn't ask."

I'd tried to do a good deed and it backfired. However, if Blanche had been present, it might have backfired even more.

I could never please Blanche, the sourest person I knew, tart as a green apple. Her anger at Papa rotted her viewpoint. When I tried not to speak badly of Papa, she thought that meant I took his side against Mama's. Now, by giving Irene a party, I'd made her spitefulness worse. I couldn't win no matter how hard I tried.

"All right. If you ever want a birthday party let me know and we can put one together." I wasn't sure what friends would come since she had so few. Even though she was one of the smartest students in her class, she wasn't well liked.

I was disheartened. Blanche felt like an outcast and I didn't know how to help her.

"You don't have to do *anything* for me." She stomped off.

Mother Pope was prim and proper. She carried herself with poise. Once a year, she hired a downtown seamstress to make her a new Sunday dress. She'd keep the dress in the closet for a year and then she'd wear it.

People would say, "Oh, you have a new dress," and she'd say, "This old thing? Dear, I've had it for a year." She didn't want to think herself better than anyone else. Successful dressing, in her opinion, was the avoidance of pride and over-decoration.

While Fremont slacked off going to church with me, I got more involved. I sang in the choir and attended the Women's Missionary Union, or WMU. Each week Mother taught us about men and women in other countries who took the message of Christ to the nations. The meetings gave me a chance to meet other women who were poor, who were from the wrong side of the tracks, as it was sometimes expressed. Women who, like me, wanted to help others but didn't know how.

However, my greatest inspiration came from Frances.

"I don't feel like I ever had a father," she told me one evening that week while we sat on our front porch steps. "I seldom saw Papa before he left home and now I hardly see him at all."

"Oh, sweetheart, that's so sad." It made my heart putter—to think she had never been close to Papa, never felt his love. Never known him well.

Frances shrugged. "My own father doesn't want me and doesn't care about me." To her, Papa was simply a nice man, a man who occasionally brought exciting gifts. I put my arm around her shoulder and pulled her close.

She was still a child. Why did emptiness invade the life of a child?

"I wish I could change it all, but I can't." The helplessness surrounding me felt like a slipknot tied around my hands. I wanted the best for my struggling sister. I didn't want her to experience the heartache I had known. "I'm sorry. I didn't know you felt this way. But you still have Mama and Blanche. And me. I love you."

"Oh, you don't have to worry anymore," said Frances looking up at me with a twinkle in her eye. "I feel much better now."

"Better? Why?"

She stood and faced me. "I went into the backyard last night and lay down on a pallet, out by the playhouse. I was crying real hard."

"Oh, dearie." I wanted to hug her again, but she wasn't finished with her story.

"Then I looked up at the stars and prayed to God. I told him I was sad about not having a dad like other kids." She paused. "And I told him he could be my father. I think he's happy to take care of me. Made me feel tickly all over."

Frances and I smiled at each other, sharing a joy bigger than chocolate candy. Tears stung my eyes. She sat down beside me and I stroked her hair.

I'll always remember the last words she said that night.

"Now I have a real father!"

Chapter Forty

December 1937

Mama's patience wore down to nothing. Papa had refused to pay the monthly child support since July. Six months. Grumbling all the way, Mama filed a court order against Papa. It required that Papa appear and show cause why he should not be committed to the County Jail for contempt of court.

The court scheduled a hearing for five days before Christmas.

Papa responded with his own petition to modify the divorce decree. He stated he had been unemployed since July. The state bank auditing department had been revamped and he'd been left without a job. He wasn't selected for any of the bank examiner positions. He claimed it was impossible to make the child support payments, therefore he filed to modify and reduce the amount.

Mama burned with anger. "Papa still has his fancy rock house, all his lease holdings, new cars and no telling what else. He's always kept secrets from me. And he wants me to believe he's broke? Rubbish."

I walked with Mama into the same Shawnee Courthouse and the same courtroom where Mama and Papa's divorce had been broadcast two years ago. Granite panels still hung above each doorway, impressive as much now as back then.

Papa's fury raged at Mama for suing him. They saw each other in the hallway outside the court room, and I thought another world war would explode. His face was red and his beady eyes scrunched in hate. What caused his anger? Was he being truthful about his job situation?

He practically whined, "How could I possibly have been married to you twenty years and survived? A mistake if I ever made one."

Mama spit at him.

Papa held his fedora in his hands as he stood before the judge a few minutes later. He had always been fastidious. He shaved under his arms and used Odorono deodorant, walking around with his arms up to let it dry before he dressed. But today, I could see sweat running down the back of his collar.

"Your Honor, these two children don't even want me around. Why should I give her money for them? I'm not obligated. I never wanted them to begin with."

The severe-looking judge leaned forward. Papa's involvement with Barnett may have colored the judge's demeanor. After all, former Bank Commissioner Barnett was from our hometown of Shawnee. He still owned a local lumber company.

"Mr. Trimble," the judge said, "it doesn't matter what you think is right or wrong. You are ordered to pay the back amount. You're three hundred dollars in arrears. And you must continue paying the fifty dollars a month, or you'll end up back in this courtroom."

"I refuse!" Papa's face scrunched in anger, his eyes flashing. "You have no right to make me do something so ignorant."

"I can find you in contempt of court if you refuse."

"I don't care," Papa retorted. "That's a ridiculous order. This establishment is like all the rest, out to hurt the underdog . . . ." His continued his diatribe for nearly five minutes, his words running into and over one another.

Mama and I looked at each other, speechless. We shook our heads. I didn't know if Papa liked being cantankerous, if he was out of his mind, or if he simply hated Mama so much he refused to give her a nickel. His arrogance reminded me of Hitler, the German dictator who'd just marched into Austria, a man who thought he could take over the world without fear of consequences.

It hurt to see Papa digging himself deeper into what appeared to be quicksand. He was getting farther away from the truth. As I sat there, I prayed for God to intervene and soften his heart.

"You leave me no choice," the judge interrupted. He pounded the gavel, which resounded like God's wrath. "Take him away!"

Sheriff Evans and two guards grabbed Papa by the arms and marched him out of the courtroom. They took him to the Shawnee jail.

Mama won the child support payments and reveled in the thought of Papa incarcerated.

My papa, the one I'd adored as a child. Papa, my former hero. Thrown in jail. Maybe he was more like his folks than he'd ever believed. Papa had occasionally rambled on with stories about his family, their shenanigans and misdemeanors, but he claimed he wasn't like them.

Papa's father, William Slaughter Trimble, originally from Camp Hill, Alabama, was a small, dark and aggressive man. He left his hometown and ended up in Bowie, Texas, where the Slaughters lived, another part of his family. He married Lavalet Blanche Andruss and my papa was born in Bowie in 1888, right in the midst of the wild west cowboy days. Those Slaughters had a bad reputation, some of them a mean bunch of criminals. Maybe Papa was more like his family than he liked to think.

Looking at Papa now, stubbornness may have also been one of his family traits.

Chapter Forty-One

Christmas holiday brought another gift, a snuster, which was a mixture of dirt and snow. This snuster reached blizzard proportions. Couldn't even make snow ice cream from the dirty snowfall. Every snow bank held a mixture of unclean dust and ice crystals. The storms had created damage and suffering that our dejected Shawnee did not need. However, our little corner of Shawnee ignored the weather and celebrated as if the world weren't falling apart outside.

Fremont and I spent Christmas Eve with the Pope family. Homemade pumpkin pies, candied popcorn, and sweet spicy applesauce cake highlighted the evening. We ate like royalty. Dad read the story of Jesus' birth aloud from his big, worn Bible. After decorating the Christmas tree, the children and Mother made fudge. We enjoyed it, along with hot cocoa diluted with Carnation milk for Margaret and Judson. The Pope family didn't expect much of a Christmas, finances so tight.

Christmas morning, a Saturday, Margaret and Judson woke up with delight on their faces. They ran to the living room and dumped out their stockings. An orange, a few pecans, and store-bought candy. I'd beaded a bracelet for Margaret and Fremont had whittled a whistle from a sweet gum tree for Judson.

Since Fremont had a job now, I had stashed away jars and cans of vegetables in case of another catastrophe. Like a squirrel stashes pecans in his hide out, a good mother provides for herself and her offspring. I pulled out cans of peas, corn and potatoes. Christmas was a time to celebrate.

Keith laughed at everything and everyone. He could hardly keep from grabbing anything in his path and babbling over the colorful wrapping paper I'd saved last year and reused. His bright eyes were full of mischief. I finally held him so he wouldn't destroy the decorations on the tree.

My sweet Fremont bought me a used book, *Gone with the Wind*, a highly acclaimed paperback. I loved him for it. He knew how to make me smile.

On Christmas Day, we visited Mama's. With little money, we'd agreed to not give each other gifts. However, we did have plenty to eat, a feast of honey ham and sweet potatoes topped with Mama's mouth-watering peach cobbler and decorated sugar cookies for the children.

Our Christmas meal had already ended when Calvis showed up. He drove down alone from Oklahoma City in his 1934 Chevrolet.

Calvis yelled as he entered the room where we were cleaning up the tall stack of dishes. "Mama, you ruined my Christmas by locking Papa in jail. How could you?"

Papa still languished in jail?

"I didn't lock him up. His own big mouth did," said Mama. "Contempt of court."

"But you're the one who took him back to court."

"I had no choice. His money keeps us alive."

I'm not sure who paid Papa's bail, but he was released within the week. It would be a long time before I could forgive Papa's hateful words against my sisters, claiming he didn't feel obligated to take care of them, that he never wanted them.

And he still refused to pay Mama child support.

Even in trying times, Shawnee's Main Street was extravagantly decorated for Christmas. Light poles held up wreaths. Red ribbons and greenery adorned storefronts, while angels and reindeer lit up glass windows.

Sunday morning, the day after Christmas, Calvary Church sparkled with decorations and the nativity set up for a program. The play would include most all the children.

"Hold still, Margaret." I draped my five-year old with an angel costume and pinned wings to her back. The holiday season was the busiest time of the year, and even Margaret had trouble sitting still. "Now, you're ready."

"Wait," said Mother. She placed a halo gently on Margaret's beautiful, dark curly hair, which I'd managed to tie up in rags the night before. The girl was a darling.

Our family sat on a wooden pew near the front, chatting before the program began. Mother and Dad with Ruth and Irene sat near Fremont, who held a squirming Judson through the whole program. Next to them sat Mama, Blanche, and Frances. Baby Keith slept in my arms.

Margaret scooted on stage and sat on one side of the platform while another angel sat on the opposite side. My child, shy but adorable, stared ahead the whole time. Later, I recalled an incident during my grade school days.

When Marjorie and I were young students, we walked home from school together. As the eldest, I was responsible for Marjorie but I could never keep her in check. A talkative child, she said hello to everyone we met while walking the six blocks home. Her golden curls bounced as people admired her spunk and sassiness.

"Sibyl's hard on shoes," I overheard Mama tell Aunt Adah. "She wears them out faster than a buzz saw, breaking the heals or scuffing the front." I owned few shoes, so after hearing those words, I slowed down to preserve my shoes. Instead of chasing my sister, who ran in circles, I would stop and wait for her before continuing home.

My clothes wore out quickly, too. Or were soiled, stained or torn. That's why I shouldn't have been surprised at what happened when Mama came home from shopping in Oklahoma City—back when we had money. Boxes, sacks, and tissue paper littered the living room when we returned home from school that day. Excitement rose with the messy pile.

"Marjorie, I'm glad you're home. Come look. I want you to try on this dress I found." Mama held up a darling outfit.

Marjorie, anxious to impress others in grade school with her expensive clothes, scurried over. She was thrilled at the dusty rose percale dress with a white pinafore over it. She grabbed the dress and dove for the bedroom to try it on.

"Did you buy me a dress, too?" I asked in a timid voice.

"Oh, you know, dear," said Mama offhandedly. "You know how you loan clothes to friends and they come back torn or dirty. Why, last month someone destroyed that darling blue skirt with the sash, and as I told you, there's no use buying you new clothes until you learn how to take care of them. I'm sure you agree, don't you?"

I remembered the skirt. My friend Elizabeth had begged to wear it and I couldn't refuse. How could I say no to a friend? Was it my fault if my friend got tea stains down the front?

"You must never let other people borrow your clothes," Mama scolded.

The severe pain of that day remained, along with the guilt. It was my fault. I had failed to take care of my clothes, so Mama didn't want to buy anything else for me. Looking back now, I saw it a little differently. Was I so wrong to loan my clothes to friends? I certainly paid a heavy price all those years, years when Mama favored Marjorie over me.

The sweet voice I'd learned to love sounded in my heart. *Your generous heart was the better way.*

I recalled a verse in Luke I'd memorized in WMU class. *Give and it shall be given to you: good measure, pressed down, shaken together, and running over* . . .

A burden lifted. A burden I hadn't been aware of all these years.

Chapter Forty-Two

January 1938

On Monday, I needed to get out of the house and shopping was a good excuse, even if I couldn't purchase anything. While Fremont went back to work, I bundled the children and pushed the baby carriage three blocks down Draper Street toward downtown.

Try as I might, I couldn't keep my feet from stopping in front of J. C. Penney's to admire the window display. The invigorating cold air brought back fond memories of past Christmases when Papa had dashed home with surprises, clothes and toys galore. He'd been an exciting father, bringing laughter to a dull household.

Window shopping only reminded me how little we had. I gazed at mannequins outfitted in up-swept coiffures, dresses with full skirts and veiled millinery. The frilly evening attire and Drindle dresses looked beautiful and I longed for one.

While I ogled the mannequins in the store window, Judson slid in circles in the snow.

His scream startled me.

I turned, expecting to nurse a skinned knee or wounded finger.

"Look, Mommy. See what I found!" Judson held up his tightly squeezed fist as if grasping a precious diamond.

"Let me look at it, dear."

Judson opened his hands wide, proud of his discovery. "Can I keep it?" he exclaimed, revealing a shiny object, a man's expensive watch.

"Where did you find it? Now show me exactly."

"Here, in the snow on the sidewalk." Judson bounced near the big display window, begging, "Can I keep it? Can I keep it? Please."

"No, someone must have lost it. He'll be looking for it." After many inquiries with store owners, I posted a sign on the Penney's front door. Snow began to fall, a dirty, sandy color and we hurried home before the weather worsened.

A few days later, Mama heard that Mr. Johnson, one of the wealthier men in town, had offered a reward for the return of his Stauer dashtronic watch. Mama told me, but by then, everyone on the block knew about the watch, what with Judson boasting about his find.

Judson and I walked down Bell Street to the Johnsons' house and knocked on the massive front door.

Mr. Johnson, a kind looking man with untidy hair, opened the door and looked down on us. Judson simply opened his fist and handed him the watch, obviously reluctant to let the shiny article leave his tiny hands. Proud of my little son, I patted the top of his head.

Thrilled to get his watch back, Mr. Johnson held out ten dollars.

"Ten dollars? Are you sure?" My eyes widened at the large amount.

Mr. Johnson smiled and nodded.

Mother would declare it a miracle when she heard the story. She'd say, "God surprises us sometimes."

I wanted to go back through town past Penny's, but having money for food and rent was much more vital than a new dress.

God had provided, albeit in an unusual way. A lost watch? But however God supplied, the ten dollars in my pocket would help us through the next month. I couldn't wait to share the news with Fremont.

I took Judson's hand and made my way home to my little family. My steps a bit lighter. My mind a bit clearer.

As my large baby grew, his charm and cheerful personality attracted everyone who saw him. Bubbly and sociable, Keith responded to people and laughed a lot. He soon became a favorite of the whole family as well as neighbors and church workers. Fremont began to go to church with us more often.

"Hello, baby Keith," said the pastor when he stopped by our pew on Sunday morning. "It's good to see such a healthy, robust child." His routine attention to Keith tickled me. I wasn't the only one enamored with my third baby.

The pastor continued, "So many of our women have lost babies during the drought that we're cautious to get attached to new ones." He tussled Keith's hair. "But this child is a winner."

Fremont bounced Keith on his knees to keep him quiet, because the child jabbered louder than the preacher. Everyone loved him.

Keith brought a fun and happy disposition to life, but he wasn't a tranquil child. I introduced him to bottled milk and he gulped it down like a starving street urchin. He swallowed anything put near his mouth.

During church service, Keith threw his glass bottle down. It shattered on the wood floor. The pastor paused his sermon, the church service interrupted. I rose and carried Keith out of the auditorium, deposited him in the nursery and snuck back in to sweep up the broken glass. After church, people laughed and pinched his cheek as if broken glass bottles were the special music they expected every Sunday morning.

I marveled over Keith's ability to babble so early. As Margaret and Judson got older, I had taught them to read, to add and subtract, and to draw pictures. I smiled when they learned long words like *Mississippi* and *Constantinople*. I clearly had three bright children.

With Keith, besides wanting to teach him, I felt freer and less reserved. Better able to show affection without inhibition. His openness actually helped me hug the other children more. Affection had been absent in my family growing up. Papa believed learning was more important than endearment.

Unsure how to hold and kiss Margaret and Judson at first, I was now experiencing the importance of touch. And I liked it.

"When the children are old enough," I insisted, "I'll teach them to swim and play tennis . . . and dance."

Chapter Forty-Three

February 1938

F remont decided to purchase our first automobile. With his love for motor cars, deciding which one to buy was the hardest part. He didn't have enough money for the snazzy new car he wanted. Although I loved to drive, I couldn't tell the difference between a Ford and a Lincoln, so, needless to say, any type of transportation would make me happy.

We walked to Norton Motor Sales on North Union Street where Fremont worked. They offered the best cars in town. Fremont looked over the 1937 Chevrolet Six. "Low as $475," he read. "Improved clutch, down draft carburetor, counter balanced crankshaft, and improved six-cylinder engine. It runs up to sixty-five miles an hour."

He'd obviously been eyeing the car for a long time.

"I can't believe its speed," he said. "Accelerates from one to thirty-five miles in six point seven seconds. Mighty fast." Fremont touched the slick body constructed of wood and steel. "I wish I could afford this car. Someday, honey, someday."

We couldn't afford a brand new car. We both knew that, but we enjoyed looking.

Doug, Fremont's friend, had a used 1926 Chevrolet for sale at his house. We went to look at it. Other than a few dents on the front fender and some work needed on the timing valves, which Fremont said he could fix, the car appeared in good condition.

I stood nearby as he walked around the vehicle several times, touched the curves, got in, honked the horn and revved the engine.

He opened the hood and stared. "I've never seen one so clean." The car suited him. "He's asking only ten dollars down and six dollars a month for a year—with interest. It's a great deal."

"It's not too fancy, but it beats walking."

We climbed into our new purchase and Fremont released the break, let the clutch fly out, and promptly stalled the engine. Chagrined, he tried again and succeeded.

Fremont spent the afternoon waxing the rough paint until the original dark shiny black appeared again. He tinkered with every part of the car, tuning it until it purred like a kitten. Finally, he installed a heater.

"A heater?" That part tickled me no end.

The next afternoon, we left the children with the Popes and took our new Chevrolet for a drive.

"Go faster!" I shouted over the engine's roar. I loved the car, if not for its engine, at least for the power it brought to our lives. Power to leave Shawnee and take a drive in the countryside. I hoped to drive our new car soon. I learned to operate a vehicle back in '32 when Mama got her new Chrysler.

"I think we could tour the world in this!" yelled Fremont as we drove.

"Go faster, Fremont!" I hollered back. We both loved road trips.

Fremont shouted again, ignoring my pleas to drive faster. "I need to fix Mr. Wheaton's vehicle next Saturday. It'll bring in a little extra."

I nodded and smiled at him.

We flew like eagles on our first ride. On a good, straight stretch of two-lane road with no other cars in sight, the speedometer hit forty-five and the wind blew my scarf like a waving flag. I caught it and threw my arm out the window, letting my scarf blow in the wind.

Fremont sped up.

"You're going too fast," I screamed over the roar of the engine, holding onto the dashboard.

"Make up your mind!" Fremont glanced at me and his eyes twinkled.

I tossed my hair out of my face and raised my chin. My heart skipped a few beats at this dapper man driving me around. "Watch the road!" I yelled back.

We laughed all the way back to Shawnee.

A flood of rain came that week and although thankful for the rain, I wished it would hold off until summer when the vegetation was scorched. Unfortunately, not enough water soaked into the parched land.

By Saturday night, the sky cleared and the air smelled like fresh dew.

We cruised down Main Street for entertainment. The stores kept their lights on unusually late. Businesses bustled and people ventured out from their cozy homes. Fremont waved to neighbors as we tootled, stopping to visit with other couples in coupes and sedans and speedsters. Baby Keith sat on my lap, sleeping soundly nestled against me, while Margaret and Judson sat in the backseat bundled in blankets.

We passed another automobile and recognized Doug and Effie and their children in the backseat. Fremont slowed the Chevy and we pulled over to talk. We learned the news of a foreclosure and who had a new baby to show off. The visiting beneath the downtown lights lasted until around nine o'clock when stores closed until Monday and the crowds headed home.

We finally had a life worth living. A family life. A good life. I hoped this dream would last forever. A promise of good things to come. Now that Fremont was working and our family had made it through the worst hard times intact, I could breathe easier.

At least I was successful at being a mother and wife, even if I had a lot to learn. I felt like a warm blanket had wrapped around me, and I snuggled in its comfort.

Chapter Forty-Four

As a young woman, Mother Pope spent several years in Waco with her sister, Susan Frances Castleman who married Feggan Whitten. Mother's parents had passed away when she was young and as the last of seventeen children, she had plenty of older siblings to take care of her. Called Fannie, the eldest sister was like a mother.

Aunt Fannie died February the fifth. She was seventy–nine. Uncle Feggan had died less than a year before.

Fremont and I and the children climbed into the back seat of the Pope's sedan to travel out to Waco for the funeral. We drove up behind Uncle Raligh and Aunt Woodlie's vehicle. Clyde and Inez got out of the back seat, Clyde carrying Marvin.

The clapboard Baptist church sat on the corner of Okay and Waco Roads. Comforting, worn and rickety, it was still used on Sunday mornings and for weddings and funerals. Model-Ts, beat-up trucks, horses and buggies, and wagons were parked to the east of the building.

Aunt Fannie had eleven children, four of whom died before her. She also had a slew of grandchildren and great grandchildren. I couldn't count how many came. I did recognize Mother's sister, Mary Florence, who drove in with her husband from Cushing and one of Dad's sisters, Josie Pope, who had married a Fannie Whitten boy.

The pastor preached for nearly an hour, the adults growing as weary as the children.

After the church service, the large congregation of family and friends gathered on the south front lawn of the church. The Waco folk were the kind that gave bear hugs, everyone hugging everyone from the dog to the new neighbors. I felt awkward but cared for at the same time. My family had not been affectionate. Judson, the little rascal, ran from the scene to his grandpa, who picked him up. Margaret stayed by my side, holding my hand.

We loaded up and followed the horse and wagon carrying Fannie's body down the dirt road, going half a mile south to Black Cemetery. The small cemetery was shaded with post oak trees and spotted with stones from families who had lived in the area. Besides the many babies and Whitten family members who had passed away, there were stones for the Mitchell family and many of the Stapps.

Some of Mother's family took Margaret and Judson with them in their vehicles as we made our way back to the Whitten home for a meal. Food seemed to appear out of nowhere. The spread from dried beef gravy to canned tomatoes and okra was meant to comfort and console the family.

I had met a few of the clan, but not very many. However, Mother, Dad and Fremont knew everyone and their cousin's cousin. Feeling left out, I wandered toward the back room where several of Aunt Fannie's family sat together.

"Come on in and have a seat," said Effie May when she saw me. She was a Whitten who married Fremont's cousin, Joe Pope. The Castleman, Pope and Whitten families had certainly connected over the years.

"We're just talking about mom."

I sat on a stool in the corner of the spacious area and listened in.

"That woman had more energy than a tornado."

"What an inspiration she was."

"She never had an enemy."

"Loved the Lord all right."

"Couldn't have had a better mother."

I thought about how much Aunt Fannie's children loved her and loved each other. That's what I wanted, a home like hers. Like the Whitten's. Like the Pope's. Loving, godly, welcoming to strangers.

So different from my family full of squabbles, pettiness and spats.

Chapter Forty-Five

April 1938

Mama sang at the Eastern Stars' bridge parties and cooked for their formal luncheons. Her extra job washing party dishes afterward began to dry up. As money got tighter, the social functions stopped altogether and Mama's work ended.

"I'm happy to never eat Shrimp a la Newburg again," she exclaimed.

I laughed. "And you'll never have to pretend to like oyster bisque."

"Yes, but those occasional dollar bills and leftover sweet rolls kept us going. I didn't like washing hundreds of goblets and mountains of silverware, but it helped a lot."

Mama became desperate and sold her fur coat to pay the food bill.

Mulling over how to earn money to survive, Mama decided to rent out a bedroom in her home on Beard Street. Before long, a couple rented the room for five dollars a month.

Lucy spoke with a thick Cajun accent and talked of nothing but her home in Baton Rouge, chatting incessantly until the family knew all her stories by heart. Unfortunately, it turned out the pair wasn't married.

"I can't have that, not with two young girls in the house," Mama told me. "I asked them to leave." When the couple moved out, Lucy left a yellow kitten crying in the closet and Mama claimed it as her own.

I heard all about Mama's renter problems. How the tenants invaded her privacy by sitting at the kitchen table while Mama cooked a meal.

How one woman stole Mama's salt and pepper shakers, and how another left food out on the table all night, collecting insects.

"Can you believe it? Ants were all over the dish when I went to make the morning coffee." Mama fumed.

"Pensioners might need a place to stay. You could talk to some of them."

"Most only get a few dollars a month, which won't buy paupers' peas. It would help if I had more rooms to let."

"There's a solution, Mama. Remodel the house to create separate living quarters."

"I can't afford that."

"Come. I'll show you a way." I led Mama through the house and showed her how it could be rearranged and divided into separate compartments. For over an hour, we discussed the different possibilities and how to minimize the cost and how to find a place for Grandpa who might become disoriented for a few days.

"You can use the side door for your entry way." A French door opened to the south, and sweet honeysuckle covered the lattice over the side porch, which held a three-seater rocker. The rocker was nice, as was everything Papa purchased. Concrete steps led down to the front sidewalk where Mama kept a little red wagon she used to haul groceries from the store.

Mama took her last month's rent income and sent Fremont to Bell's Lumber. He was instructed to find cheap material to change the layout of the house. Mama enlisted Lester, the handyman, to help Fremont with carpentry work. Lester worked full time as a janitor at Nortons, but he still came around and helped Mama when she needed it.

Fremont came home from work early that evening to work with Lester on Mama's house. Sawdust flew, hammers pounded and within an hour, a hole in the wall appeared. The men worked all evening, framing a new doorway, sheet rocking and repairing broken plaster. They completed the major work by late evening.

This new doorway opened through the bedroom. After the construction, the house contained three separate living areas. By using only the back master bedroom and porch room for the family, Mama would be able to rent out two suites in the rest of the house.

Lester returned the next week to finish plastering and hang the doors. He seemed grateful for the extra work. Mama paid him two dollars and a bag of potatoes.

The next time I visited, Mama and the girls had painted their two rooms a faint mauve color and the other rooms white.

"Come help me with this!" hollered Mama. "We need to move the furniture."

Mama and I pulled the Persian rug from the living room into her bedroom and rearranged what furniture we could squeeze in. Mama carried packed boxes to the abandoned playhouse in the back yard.

Mama stored the boxes in a corner of the playhouse and said she would go through them later when she had more time. She couldn't cram all her furniture into her condensed space, so she gave us the wooden oval dining table.

Blanche, as usual, complained about everything. She was stuck with Grandpa, twin beds on either side of the room, and she complained that they only had a bathtub. We had a shower and a concrete floor in our bathroom where water ran out into a sewer. We had three bedrooms while they had only two rooms. Jealousy didn't look good on her.

I stayed all day and helped Mama create a small kitchen in one corner of the bedroom. We set up a cook stove and a tin basin to carry water from the bathroom to their makeshift sink. Since they only had one bathroom in the house, the family would share it with the boarders. This new arrangement would give Mama and the family some privacy while also supplying much-needed rent money.

We rested at the dinette table, exhausted from the day's work. Mama yawned and propped up her feet.

Frances, who'd been in the backyard rummaging through the playhouse, came running through the back door, surprising us. She held up a large piece of white material.

"Look what I found!" She lifted up a cotton cloth, which seemed innocent enough.

I held my breath. It was a KKK hood. Definitely a hood. It was pointed on top and had slits for eyes. Frances had no idea she carried a dreaded symbol of bigotry. My heart pounded as I stared at the offensive object.

"Where did you find that?" I asked, shocked at seeing such a thing with the family's belongings. I looked at Frances questioningly.

"It was in one of the boxes in the playhouse. There's a white sheet with it."

Mama looked at me and shrugged. "It's your papa's. He was a sheet wearer. Here, Frances, let me have it. Now stay out of those boxes."

"We should put it in the burn pile," I said.

"We can use the fabric for something." Mama took the hood from Frances. "No use wasting it."

Papa's hood. I would never have guessed he was involved in anything so sinister. Here was one more piece of the Papa puzzle.

I remembered Governor Walton's political rally Papa took me to when I was a little girl. I recalled Walton had been ousted from office. He campaigned against the Klan yet unofficially colluded with them, so I heard. Did Papa know that? A stone as heavy as the Shawnee dam lay in my stomach. The more I learned about Papa, the more I questioned his beliefs. Part of me hoped I'd never find any more of his puzzle pieces.

Still, in a corner of my mind, I remembered the job Papa had offered me. If I went to work in the city and sent money back, we could afford better living quarters and things like health care. I should keep the possibility open.

"We should be thankful. We have electric lights, a fan and the Victrola," said Mama, continuing as if nothing had happened. Like everyone found white hoods in their storage.

I pushed back from the table and wandered into the living room where the piano still rested. I ran my hand over the wood, touching where small holes branded the finish. Some of Marjorie's guy friends had laid their cigarettes on top.

"The piano stays in the living room with the boarders," called Mama from the other room. "We don't have room for it. Blame your papa."

I would miss playing the piano, almost as much as I missed my sister, Marjorie, singing along with me. I used to play for hours while she belted out Gene Autry's "Goodbye Little Darlin,'" her clear voice raising the rafters. I wished she hadn't moved to Arizona.

The boarding rooms were empty, and I sat on the velvet covered piano bench and gazed at the black and white keyboard. I played "The Blue Danube," my fingers running smoothly over the keys for Strauss's familiar waltz. My mind wandered as I played. How many thousands of notes had I played on these keys?

How many thousands of thoughts had I had in life? How many struggles? Was it possible to stay married and still follow my vision of helping the poor? To do something important in life? I felt restless and pounded loudly as I considered my best chance of success. Be a good wife. Be a good mother. Create a perfect family.

The past few years had brought many losses and losing the piano represented another. Would I, like Calvis, give up on my dreams? I stopped playing and took a deep breath, feeling stifled. Yes, I could try to solve life's many problems, but would my heart survive?

I didn't want to be like Mama, crowded out of my own house.

I would focus on my family. Focus on creating the best, most caring, godly family in the whole state of Oklahoma. Save my pennies and buy my mama the best Victorian house on Broadway. Some day she wouldn't need boarders.

Determination was my second name.

Chapter Forty-Six

May 1938

Mama and my sisters rearranged the furniture, crowding into the two rooms. They brought in a few more boarders and I was relieved they now had enough income for staples.

Word floated around that the owners of the Greater Seminole Field still practiced unbridled oil production. I read their excesses had much to do with the push for state oil and gas reforms.

Then oil field workers heard about Mama renting out rooms. Wildcatters, field hands, and roughnecks knocked on her door. The 1920's boom was gone, but by the late thirties, the fields around Seminole became the largest supplier of oil in the world, or so they claimed. With the ongoing work, fellows needed a place to stay. An oil field couple moved into two connected bedrooms and another moved into Mama's living room and kitchen.

Many field hands were not married to their women, at least not the ones who inquired at Mama's house. But under the circumstances, she couldn't afford to decline a paying renter, so she learned to accept their choices. Even tolerating that, being a landlord was not all that rosy.

I prepared to walk to Mama's, and loaded Keith's ornate baby carriage with my pocketbook, a can of pickles, my crocheting and Judson's wooden toy trains. Judson loved his trains, and I needed something to keep him out of mischief. Margaret would sit quietly in the corner and read a book, but not my boys. Keith, especially, had the curiosity of a stray cat.

I rolled the carriage to the side of Mama's house, the new entryway. She came out to help unload, kissing me on the cheek as usual. I took the pickle jar and walked into her little kitchen to set it on the makeshift table. The glass jar slipped from my hands and crashed to the waxed floor, shattering into pieces.

"Oh, no!" I cried. I'd worked hard canning those bread and butter pickles, measuring the right amount of vinegar, mustard and celery seed, turmeric and sugar, as Mother Pope had guided me. I wanted to show Mama my latest canning attempts.

"Stay in the backyard, kids," Mama said. "I'll help your mom clean up."

Mama picked up the glass while I wiped the floor. Afterward, when I walked into the shared bathroom to wash my hands, I saw another disaster.

Obviously, one of the roughnecks had arrived filthy from work. Black grease and muck coated the sink. Dark, filthy clothes lay in a heap, and blackened boots and once-upon-a-time white socks smelled like the whole rig had moved in.

I wasn't sure how the oil workers got the dark smudge and mud out of their clothes, much less out from under their fingernails. Oil and gas field work was definitely grim manual labor. They worked long, hard hours.

The locals didn't care much for oil field workers, or so I'd heard in my typical eavesdropping manner. Their loose lifestyles, drinking, and carousing didn't match our city's morals. Fresh money coming into the area was appreciated though.

I turned to walk out of the bathroom and bumped into the boarder. His wet hair hung around his ears, his face still smeared in places, and his whiskers stuck out like porcupine needles. Two fingers on his right hand were missing, a common hazard of working on a rig.

"Sorry, miss." His eyes looked kind and gentle, unexpected traits for a roustabout. "Sorry about the filth. I'll clean that up soon enough." He turned and grabbed a cloth and began scrubbing the black grease away. "My wife usually picks up after me."

Maybe these fellows had feelings too. Maybe they needed kindness and understanding just like the rest of us.

Scrubbing or no scrubbing, I wasn't sure Mama's bathroom would ever be sparkly clean again.

"Mama, who washes the boarders' dirty laundry?" I asked when I returned to the kitchen.

"I do. Of course they pay me, and I change their bedding. You can't imagine how much laundry I have."

No. I couldn't imagine Mama doing laundry for all of them. Until now, I had not thought about that pile of greasy clothes Mama would stuff into the wringer. It made my family's laundry seem insignificant. Nor had I thought the oilfield workers deserved to be treated with dignity like the rest of our work force. They had been invisible to me.

How did God keep opening my world larger and larger to include people so different from me? How had he managed to pry my eyes open to other peoples' needs?

Maybe godly love looked like Dad Pope when he carried a bucket of tomatoes to the widow down the street.

Chapter Forty-Seven

June 1938

The Morning News stated that President Roosevelt would travel through our town on Saturday afternoon at exactly 3:10. The Rock Island train would stop at our passenger station and, for the first time in history, a United States President would speak to the residents of Shawnee.

I was overjoyed at a chance to see President Franklin Roosevelt. Everyone talked about it. I waited until the evening to mention it to Fremont. We sat on the front porch to catch a breeze, Fremont propping his boots up on the low wall.

"Fremont, we have to go. We can't miss this opportunity."

"He'll only speak for ten minutes."

"We missed Mrs. Roosevelt when she stopped in March and I'm not about to miss this."

I scrambled to open the morning newspaper and summarized what I read. "They're expecting a huge crowd. All businesses are suspended for an hour. Paul Boone's going to lead the high school band in a concert before he arrives."

"We probably won't be able to see anything, and it'll be blazing hot this time of year."

"The station will supply ice water," I said hopefully.

"Ice water's good."

"Two loud speakers will be provided, one for the President and one for the chief of police. Can you go with me? Please. Do you think your mother can watch the children while we go?"

"Hold on, honey. One question at a time."

"Mama's going. We can meet her there."

Saturday morning after breakfast, I dressed the children and they ran out to the front yard while I cleaned up and put on my favorite summer dress. Fremont, always ready earlier than me, waited outside.

As I walked out the front door, I saw a mentally disabled neighbor boy wander into our yard. Keith ran toward him, his arms outstretched. Keith was a large child and Willard, this neighbor boy, was nearly my height. This sweet-natured child was unable to attend school, but he loved to play with Keith, a magnet for anyone who loved playfulness. Willard and Keith became daily playmates.

I rounded up my three children.

"I go too," said Willard.

"Not this time." He lowered his head as I stowed the children in the backseat of the auto. Keith frantically waved goodbye to his buddy.

Mother Pope was prepared for the children. I could smell cookies baking. She hugged Margaret and Judson and picked up Keith, kissing his dirty face. I think she favored him a bit.

The northeast side of Main Street toward the train station was packed with people. I held onto Fremont's arm so we wouldn't get separated. With his handsome profile, square jaw and straight nose, I felt proud to be with him.

The intense heat of the afternoon made rivulets of sweat run down my back, and based on the smell, others were in no better condition. A sea of umbrellas lay in front of me. Body odor and noise permeated the air. Paul Boone's music ended.

I heard the train engine getting louder and my heart felt like lead. We would never be able to get near the Rock Island tracks. And it would be impossible to find my mother among the thousands of people crunched together. Everyone who lived in surrounding counties must have come. The crowd pushed forward as the train ground to a stop.

"Where did you say the train will stop?" Fremont raised his voice over the crowd. Confusion caused us to hesitate. Then I heard the whistle sound and the massive train cars screech as they slowed down.

"Can you see anything?" I couldn't see much because men taller than I wore hats that made them even taller.

"I see the last train car rolling in. The rear platform must be Roosevelt's special car."

"What else?" I yelled over the noise.

"Special guards are coming out first. They're looking around. Probably scoping the place. There. Now I see Roosevelt's gray head on the platform. He has on his wire spectacles."

I pulled on Fremont's jacket sleeve urging him to continue.

"I recognize Will Rogers from when he gave me a ride to the city years ago. Yep, and Governor Marland. I don't know the other fellows. They're waving to the crowd like they're meeting old buddies."

He couldn't tell me who else traveled with the President but Pottawatomie County was an important stop for the many politicians shaking hands and passing out fliers. I remember candidates stressing that "as Pottawatomie goes, so goes the state."

"Ladies and gentleman: The President of the United States."

The President's voice came crackling over the loud speaker. "My friends," he said, trying to speak over the noise. "I am glad to be here. Glad to see the progress this great state of Oklahoma has made. I remember when I was a boy, this state was known as Indian Territory."

The police chief's loud speaker competed with the officials' speaker. "Please step back. You must get twenty feet from the President."

The crowd stepped back in unison.

After Roosevelt introduced the dignitaries accompanying him, he introduced his son Elliott, even taller than his father. The proud father stated, "My son and I have inferiority complexes because we are the runts of the family." The crowd erupted in laughter.

When Roosevelt's ten-minute talk ended, he peered around the corner of the train to see the vast throng packed into the streets for blocks. That was when I caught a fleeting glimpse of him. He wore a light-colored suit, as did most men that day, but he was without a hat, which was unusual. He looked tan and was leaning on his cane.

After the presidential train left, Fremont and I pushed toward the sidewalk to escape the horde. We saw Blanche standing beside a store window. Fremont grabbed my hand and shoved through the crowd toward her, knowing Mama would be nearby.

Mama was looking up and down the street, frantic. She turned and saw us. "I'm looking for Frances. Have you seen her? I can't find her anywhere."

"You brought her to this raucous turnout?" I asked Mama. "She's too short to see over anyone's heads."

"Well, she wanted to come. Maybe she headed back home."

"We can't find her in this crowd."

How could Mama lose a child? I would never do that.

"Here she is!" yelled Fremont from several feet away. He led the eleven-year old by the hand. "She was going the wrong way."

Mama grabbed Frances's hand.

"Did you see the President, Mama? Did you hear the speech?" My mind rushed in circles around the consequences of this, even if no one else seemed impressed. Most of the crowd appeared agitated, annoyed at having traveled so far to see so little.

"A waste of time if you ask me," said Mama. "All of this hullabaloo for nothing."

I didn't think so. Even a glimpse of the President made the chaotic day worth it. I felt like a part of history. However, I realized after seeing the slew of men on the train with the good old boy mentality that I did not want to be in the political arena. Others might like the chaos of passing out fliers and shaking hands to swarms of strangers, but I didn't want to add that to my crazy life. No matter how much my papa had pushed me toward politics, I didn't need it.

Chapter Forty-Eight

July 1938

On his way to work, Clyde dropped off Cousin Inez for the afternoon. Although they still lived in Bethel, west of town, I occasionally saw Inez at church or family gatherings where we enjoyed visiting.

I encouraged her to walk with me to Boy Scout Park, the neighborhood playground.

We loaded up crackers and cold sausage, blankets to sit on and an empty glass jar full of water. I pushed Keith in my baby buggy while Inez pushed Marvin in a new, fancier contraption. Inez's son Marvin was almost two years old now. She pushed the buggy while my two children, Margaret and Judson, skipped along beside us.

It only took a few minutes to walk the four blocks. The wind blew circles around us.

WPA gangs had built a tennis court at the park, in addition to the play area and children's wading pool. The children thoroughly enjoyed the pool in this atrocious heat. It was good to hear them laugh. My heart soared like the world was noble, parenting was rewarding, and my children would grow up to be admirable citizens.

"How do you manage with three children?" asked Inez. "Don't you get tired?"

"I'm worn to a frazzle most of the time. Really takes the starch out of you. What with diapers to wash, dinner to prepare and beds to make. I'm overloaded. Sure could use a good night's rest. Keith still doesn't sleep through the night. I've given up on that."

Inez, her sweet self, nodded like she understood. Then I looked at her son Marvin and felt two-feet tall.

"Has Marvin improved?" I asked. "You told me about his seizures and stiff neck." I reached out and admired Marvin's new leather booties with the adorable ivory buttons on the side. Aunt Woodlie purchased her only grandchild every newfangled treasure she could find.

"Not much better," said Inez. "When he was small, he was a fussy baby and had trouble sleeping. He doesn't cry as much as he did."

Marvin hadn't developed as he should have. The poor child could barely hold his head up.

"His eyes don't focus well and he has a problem eating," continued Inez, anguish sneaking through her soft voice. "I don't know what to do."

"Maybe he'll improve." I read about drugs given to mothers to deaden the childbirth pain. Drugs that caused a high death rate. Could drugs have caused Marvin's disorder? But Inez claimed she took no drugs.

I hesistated and then I remembered her appointment. "Have you taken him to that specialist in Oklahoma City like you planned?"

She nodded. "Last week. I forgot to tell you. The doctor said Marvin may always be like this. It was probably caused by the measles. Remember that high fever right after he was born?" Inez paused and her words fell to a whisper. "Sibyl, how could I know high fever would damage my baby for life?"

"I'm so sorry. I don't know what to say," I shook my head slowly.

"It's my fault." Tears came to Inez' big blue eyes. "He can't sit up and he's two years old. He can't talk or feed himself."

"Aren't you afraid?"

"The good Lord's given me a measure of grace. It isn't easy, but fear is not my enemy since God helped me years ago."

I put my arms around Inez and hugged her tight. What else could I do? "At least you have some answers." That seemed a lame response, but at times like this, encouraging words evaded me.

Keith, my chubby, happy toddler, ran toward us, his charisma drawing other children to follow him.

Inez squatted as he came close and he practically jumped in her arms, babbling nonsense. She covered him with kisses like he was a balm to her sorrow. My sweet cousin certainly loved children.

My complaints about my three rollicking offspring dissolved as I watched Inez set Keith down and wipe the slobber from Marvin's chin. Conflicted, I felt glad to have healthy, rambunctious children, but at the same time I felt horrible for Inez and Marvin.

Her tragedy made my heart beat fast. I stood helpless looking in from the outside, almost like last month with what happened to Bob Renegar.

It had not rained all spring and the ground was dry as a sow's bone. Bob and his son were out plowing a field a few blocks from the Pope's house, at the dead end of Farrell Street. Suddenly, a little shower popped up in that small field. No other rain in town, mind you. Bob and his son ran for cover, but while running, forty-nine year old Bob was struck by lightening. His hat torn to shreds. He didn't survive.

Why does tragedy happen? Were we helpless to change the course of life?

Chapter Forty-Nine

October 1938

Mother Pope loved children. Since her daughters were already teenagers, the three grandchildren became a beacon of light to her. I think she felt a bond with them, almost like another chance at influencing young hearts.

Irene, the talkative, silly teen of the family, hated to study, nearly flunking out of school. I worried she might not graduate from high school at all. Ruth, Mother's junior-high daughter, was beautiful and graceful and mature enough that older boys flocked around her. Keeping her under wraps was no small task.

My children spent the afternoon with Mother Pope. They loved to help gather eggs and make mincemeat pies. Mother seemed to take the children under her wing like a mother hen.

I walked away from the children Saturday morning as Mother headed toward the chicken coop, her apron full of grain to feed the chickens. The little ones tagged along behind her as she scattered the corn. I heard Mother saying, "Here chick, chick, chick." The chickens gathered around her.

Then I heard a scream.

I turned and bolted to the back yard.

A chicken attacked Margaret, flapping its wings and squawking. I grabbed her up and calmed her down. I gave her a glass of milk and set her on the porch where she could watch Mother and the boys from a distance. When I knew she would survive, I sighed and hurried to meet Effie for a quick soda.

After a long day of shopping and buying groceries, I arrived back at the Popes' in the afternoon to pick up the children.

I could hear Keith howling from inside the house.

I panicked. My baby was hurt. Another child in distress. What in the world?

I rushed through the screen door and stopped. Keith was snuggled up in Mother Pope's big bosom, sniffling. Her arms were around him and tears ran down his chubby cheeks.

"What happened?"

Margaret knelt on the hooked rug near Keith, patting him on the back like a big sister who worries too much. She was such a responsible girl, I could have left an infant with her. She looked up at me for approval and I nodded.

Keith seemed inconsolable. I held out my arms to take him but he refused to come, content to stay in Mother's arms. A warm, comfortable spot. His crying stopped and his eyes drooped in sleep.

"He burned his arm on the cook stove," said Mother quietly. "I put salve on it."

"My poor baby."

Keith drew trouble like flies. Thanks to his curiosity, something always seemed to happen to him. He embraced each new day and each new experience.

I looked around for Judson, but he was nowhere in sight. Probably in the barn helping with Dad as usual. Dad and Judson were like two monkeys in a barrel, couldn't keep them quiet if the day depended on it.

I found them sitting on a bale of hay. Dad could entertain little ones in a sticker patch. He was paring an apple, and I watched as he cut the apple from the top to the bottom in one long pare. I was as amazed as Judson.

My, what a day. Two scares were enough to make me want to hibernate for the next week. Good mothers always kept their children safe from harm. If anything serious happened to one of them, I'd be devastated, but so far, my kids were safe and healthy.

As I rounded up the children and directed them out the front door to go home, I hugged Mother. "I'm so thankful for all you do."

She said, "Oh honey, it's a gift to have grandchildren, don't you know?"

Gratitude welled up in me, gratitude for a happy home and people who loved my children as much as I did.

Chapter Fifty

November 1938

Mama's boarders left the house on Thanksgiving to visit relatives, which meant Mama could open the living room door to accommodate the family.

We arrived early and I set down a hot squash casserole, a new recipe I'd found in the newspaper. Some of my new dishes were delicious, others a complete failure. I hoped this dish tasted as good as it sounded. Did Fremont like my cooking? So far, he had never complained, even claiming he liked burnt toast.

Mama and I chatted as we set boards on cinder blocks for tables and brought in chairs, including Grandpa's carved bench.

Relatives started arriving. Aunts and uncles and cousins who had never met my children. Aunt Adah's and her family drove in from St. James, Missouri, and Mama's brother, Uncle Louie Bennett and his family came from Anadarko. It was like a reunion, gathering Grandpa, the three siblings and many cousins together. The overflowing house made it feel like a holiday. Excitement kept us scurrying.

Everyone dressed to the hilt. Women with feathers in their hats, lace collars and chiffon gowns. Men wore pique waistcoats with linen handkerchiefs in their coat pockets. It was a sight. The chatter and tall tales would be memorable.

Marjorie and Larry still lived in Arizona and couldn't attend. But Calvis and his young wife, Evie, drove down from their apartment in the city. They wore the latest fashion. His narrow neck tie and silk hat must have been newly purchased.

"Calvis, so glad to see you." Mama kissed him on the cheek. She turned and tried to kiss Evie, but she turned away. It seemed she and Calvis had been squabbling.

The house felt warm and humid after all the cooking. Mama took the turkey out of the oven, lifted the lid to let it cool while she made gravy. The smell drifted through the house and out the propped-open windows. I smelled yeast rolls baking and my mouth watered, looking forward to a hot roll spread lavishly with butter.

A commotion came from the porch. Grandpa Bennett rushed through the door pulling a bedraggled man behind him. A tramp had wandered around to the side of the house.

Everyone took a step backward. Calvis nudged Evie behind him and a scowl covered his face.

"Who is he?" someone asked.

"Does he belong here?"

"He looks like a tramp to me," said Calvis. "Mama, do you always let people like that into your house?"

"Sorry, sir." The grungy man backed up. Family members' well-coiffured hair and stylish dresses added to the man's discomfort. "I'll be leaving."

Mama shushed the grumbling. "We'll turn no one away. This is Thanksgiving Day, after all."

"But we can't allow just anyone to walk in. This is family."

"Yes, and a generous family," I added. "God told us to welcome strangers and that's what we're doing." I took the man's arm and guided him toward the back room.

"You think you're the Mother Carey of Shawnee, don't you?" I heard Blanche spit out.

Grandpa followed me and ushered the ragged man into the bathroom to clean up. Dirt and a nasty smell followed him. I left them and went to help Mama.

As ice clinked into glasses and tea was poured, folks begin to gather around the tables waiting for the blessing. I tried to list in my mind all the things for which I was thankful.

Surviving the terrible snusters of last winter, dirt and snow swirling together.

Baby Keith's first steps.

Fremont's job at Norton Motor Sales.

Mama's boarders bringing money to support her.

My missionary class, where I could share my heart.

Yes, I was mighty thankful, as Fremont would say. Would this perfect life last?

Calvis found his way around to Mama and I heard him whisper, "Sorry, we have to go. We have another engagement." He nodded toward Evie and lowered his voice even more. "She wants to leave."

I'd overheard Calvis muttering about keeping up appearances and not for a second did I believe Evie was the reason they wanted to leave. The hobo had probably infringed on Calvis' desire for a fancy-dancy world. Calvis had not always been that snobbish. He had changed over the last year, perhaps trying to please Papa. What would I have been like if I had not married Fremont? If I had not learned about God's love?

What did Fremont think about Calvis' response to a vagrant? He had been one himself a few years ago.

Grandpa's tramp cleaned up well. His hair was slicked back and he must have used Grandpa's razor, because his whiskers were gone. His odor had significantly improved.

The *Shawnee News* social reporter called about our Thanksgiving festivities. It was reported in the newspaper the next day.

"Mable Trimble, North Beard, had guests for Thanksgiving. Calvis and his wife Evelyn Frances from Oklahoma City, Sibyl and Fremont and children Margaret, Judson, and Keith of Shawnee, and relatives from St. James, Missouri, and Anadarko."

No mention of the tramp. And no mention of Calvis and his bride skipping dinner. Or my only brother following Papa's ways.

Chapter Fifty-One

December 1938

The temperature fell below freezing and the town blew their no-school whistle. Shovels scraping piles of snow sounded from the streets. I bundled up Margaret and Judson with extra socks and hand-knitted mittens. They went outside and built forts, fought snowball battles and got soaked from head to toe.

Steam clouded every window in the house. The cozy embrace of a welcoming kitchen and chicken soup on the stove brought squeals.

After being cooped up in the house for several days and bumping into one another as we moved around, Fremont and I braved the weather and stomped over to Mama's. Unfortunately our car wouldn't start in this weather. I carried Keith, and Fremont scurried on ahead with the two older children following him, shrieking as they slid on the frozen earth.

When we arrived, Mama took one look at the children's pink cheeks and rushed to get hot pads.

"What are you doing out in this weather?" scolded Mama. "You're going to give these children pneumonia." I wrapped the blankets tightly around Margaret and Judson.

"We're going to the church and check on the water pipes. Fremont volunteered to help this month. Can you watch the children?"

"Got your own family to worry about, I say. You shouldn't be so concerned about the church building."

Mama took Keith into her arms but he scrambled down and climbed on a chair to get a biscuit off the table. With his voracious appetite, he larger than Judson now. He loved people and people adored him. On Sundays before church started, he would run through the aisles pausing to talk to men and women sitting on the pews. He gave everyone a hug, no one a stranger.

"We'll be gone only a short while. We'll hurry."

"He's a good baby, even if I do say so myself," Mama exclaimed as she retrieved Keith. She covered him with a quilt and bounced him on her lap. He laughed out loud as she crossed her eyes and made faces at him. His delightful passion and love for life had brought our family closer together. In many ways, Keith opened our hearts.

Lifting my chin proudly, I said, "I received a Cradle Roll Certificate for him last week. Signed by Pastor Sewell. God favored me when he gave me a baby like Keith."

"You could bring him to our church once in a while." Mama had joined the First Baptist Church choir again. The new song minister, Warren Angel, Dean of the College of Fine Arts and Professor at Oklahoma Baptist University seemed to appreciate Mama's operatic voice, one of the most powerful in the congregation. I was glad she had gone back.

Mama agreed to watch the children if Blanche would help. "Fremont, before you go, there's a tree limb blocking the back door. Could you move it out of the way?"

"Sure, I'll be right back."

"I'll put Keith down for a nap while you watch Margaret and Judson," Mama said to Blanche. She disappeared into the bedroom with the baby.

Judson had never warmed to Blanche. The skinny, wiry boy ran behind the couch where Blanche couldn't reach him. He slid out from the other side and ran around the coffee table, taunting her in his deep, scratchy voice. She grabbed for him.

Twisting out of her arms, he knocked over a glass of tea sitting on the coffee table. It spilled over the sofa and rug.

I ran to get a washrag. That's what I typically did with Judson—clean up his disasters. Why couldn't he be a perfect child? I had done everything I knew to teach him to behave, but he didn't listen. What kind of mother was I?

"I'll never, ever babysit that rascal again," said Blanche.

Judson, apologetic, ran up to Blanche and said with his low voice, "I love you, Auntie." He sounded like a little old man.

"Your behavior is atrocious." Blanche swatted his arms away. "No child should behave so badly. Shame on you for being such a bad boy."

"He is not a bad boy," cried Margaret. The sensitive girl almost started to cry, her lips quivering.

I gave Blanche a stern motherly look and patted Margaret on the shoulder. "Don't worry sweetie, I'll take care of this." I caught Judson, scolded him and set him on a chair. I turned to Margaret and calmed her down in a gentler voice than I would have used before Keith was born.

"Don't fret, dear," I said to Margaret. "Be a loving big sister and watch your little brothers while we're gone."

The door flew open and Fremont stomped back into the house. "We'd better get going. It's getting mighty nasty out there."

At the church, we wrapped the outside water pipes in cloth and left the water dripping so the pipes wouldn't freeze. Fremont might not often go to church on Sundays with me or discuss spiritual lessons, but he willingly helped with church maintenance.

Icy snow stayed through Sunday and made it impossible to walk or drive across town to attend Calvary Baptist, especially by myself with three children in tow.

I hadn't missed a service since we'd married so I decided to visit a church nearby. Many Baptist churches in town had a missionary ladies group. I hoped to discover the date and times these church women met so I could attend meetings without having to traipse across town on foot.

I dressed the children in several sweaters and wrapped scarves around their necks. Margaret and Judson trudged behind me as I pushed Keith's carriage the five blocks to Emanuel. Poor children had to be tough in this kind of weather, but it was better than being stuck inside.

Emanuel Baptist Church had the most awe-inspiring architecture in town. An impressive rock building with towers, it looked like an English castle dropped down right on Main Street. We passed it every time we went downtown or walked to Mama's house. To me it looked like a great rock cathedral with its beautiful spires on top. It was welcoming with a gorgeous stained glass window.

Actually, Shawnee had a multitude of magnificent church buildings, like the Emmanuel Episcopal Church, with its glowing painted window depicting the nativity, and First Presbyterian with its huge columns. The First Methodist had an adorable, quaint auditorium, and First Baptist Church, too, was massive and impressive.

Worshipers in our town built incredible tributes to God. Had he abandoned us through the decade to wind, disasters and hardships? Were we being disciplined? Whatever it was, I hoped it was over. Only eleven more months before a brand-new decade would begin. The forties had to be better than the thirties.

A lady greeted me as I took off the children's heavy outer garments. Near my age, she led me to their classes. As I followed her back to the auditorium, I asked about their missionary program.

"Oh, honey, we'd be glad to have you any time. You don't have to bring a thing, just walk on over with those precious children."

"My Grandma Bennett always inspired me to help others," I said. "And WMU is one way to do that. I'll drop by when I can."

I missed my grandma bustling around at twenty miles an hour preparing mashed potatoes and corn on the cob. It had been six years since she'd died. She was intelligent and from a good Michigan family. She inspired me when she explained how, when younger, she took care of street kids living on Mayor Street. She would have approved of my WMU work. Would have also encouraged me to teach the children to help others.

Chapter Fifty-Two
January 1939

S omeone banged on my front door.
I yanked it open and my heart nearly burst out of my chest.
"Marjorie!" I screamed as I hugged her. "What are you doing here?"

When she didn't answer, I stepped back and studied her. Marjorie didn't look overjoyed to be back in Oklahoma. Her hair fell unkempt around her face and her usual flamboyant attitude had disappeared.

"What happened?" I asked. "You look like you've been run over by the Santa Fe."

Desperate, Marjorie had left Phoenix to come home with no way to carry her trunk full of personal belongings. Life with her husband had evidently taken a turn for the worse. Afraid to reveal her intentions to Kelley, one morning she left for work as usual and took five-year-old Larry to the babysitter, promising the overdue payment as soon as possible.

"I just wanted out, sis," said Marjorie, slinging herself on my sofa. "When I went back to get Larry, the babysitter wouldn't let me have him. 'Not until you pay me,' she says. So I hitchhiked back to Oklahoma by myself."

"You did what?" I was shocked. "You left Larry in Arizona?" I was trying so hard to keep my family together and here was my sister, abandoning her little boy thousands of miles away.

"What was I supposed to do? I don't have a penny to my name. Now I'm trying to get money to go back and get him."

"No one around here has anything to spare, except maybe Papa."

"Can you go with me to ask him, lovey?" Marjorie confessed she didn't want to approach Papa alone. "Dearie, can you help? Please. I'm in a terrible bind."

"Don't you know anyone in Phoenix who can help you?"

"There is my old boyfriend, sis. Remember Speedy with the motorcycle? He's out there and helped me out of a few jams."

I heaved a sigh. Old boyfriends were not a remedy to life's problems. "You'll have to get cleaned up. A hot bath and a clean set of clothes will do wonders."

"You said it, sister."

That afternoon, I rang up Calvis from a neighbor's wall-mounted telephone and explained Marjorie's situation. He drove to Shawnee the next morning and Marjorie and I climbed into his Chevrolet for the drive to Oklahoma City. Our vehicle had broken down and Fremont had worked on it relentlessly.

Staring out the window on the trip, I read Burma Shave warning signs along the way. "Don't stick your head out the window too far. It may go home in another car." And "Don't lose your head to gain a minute. You need your head. Your brains are in it." Warnings.

Marjorie and I ventured inside Papa's house while Calvis waited in the car. Calvis and Gladys were not on speaking terms.

"You'll have to do the talking, now," I said to Marjorie. "I'm just here for support."

Papa's eyes widened when we entered the house. "Well, well. The prodigal child comes home." He kissed Marjorie and I on the cheek. "And what occasion brings my daughters traipsing into my house today? Marjorie, I didn't realize you'd returned from your venture to Arizona."

Marjorie stood with her hands behind her back, staring at the floor.

"Out with it, girl. I know you want something."

Marjorie didn't speak.

"Sit before you fall," Papa ordered.

Marjorie and I both slid into chairs.

"Papa, dear," Marjorie plunged in. "I need money to go get Larry and bring him back. He's in Phoenix."

"Tell me what happened." Papa listened as she described her living conditions, Kelley's abuse and her inability to save enough money, even though she worked like a slave as a waitress.

Papa's piercing eyes narrowed as he listened. Then he simply shook his head. "I won't loan you anything. Now pull yourself together, get a job and start saving. I can get you and your sister a job at the new bank here in Oklahoma City where I work."

Marjorie sobbed. "I may have gotten myself into this, but please don't blame Larry. It isn't his fault."

I slipped over and put my arm around Marjorie. "Papa, can't you do something? We can't just leave the boy out there by himself."

"Sorry. Marjorie's a big girl now. She needs to solve her own problems. She'll never learn responsibility until she can survive without help from me. I'm tired of giving handouts."

"I'll pay you back, Papa. I promise," begged Marjorie, moving to the edge of her cushioned seat. "I'll pay you back."

I wasn't sure where my forthrightness came from, but Papa and I had always talked openly. "You preach about charity. Here's a chance to practice it. Your grandson needs you to step in and help."

Papa's eyes bore into me. "Christianity has belied this generation. You want handouts? Go to your local church. People should be forced to respond in a charitable manner for their own good. Socialism, if administered correctly, will see to that."

"You can't force people to behave like Christians." I leaned forward as I faced Papa, gathering strength. "Charity should be a free choice, and . . . and socialism can't change the heart. Sure, churches aren't perfect, but I've seen more love in Fremont's church than anywhere else. They would help if they could."

"So, you're preaching to me now?"

"Not preaching. I think you're mistaken."

"I believe many churches are evil." Papa pulled at his shirt collar. "At the least, most so-called churches have failed to function properly. They deny responsibility for the evils which shape our country."

I took a deep breath before I answered. "How do you propose to eliminate evil, Papa? Tie up the bad guys? Kill everyone who disagrees? Isn't there a bit of evil in all of us?" I could never understand Papa on this point. "And if you're so good, then why won't you help your own daughter?"

Papa stormed out of the room.

I picked up Papa's glass ashtray and threw it to the floor. It broke. Marjorie and I walked out arm in arm.

When we slid back into Calvis' car, tears streaked our faces. She lowered her head into her hands and bawled. Great heaves swept over her. My heart ached for Marjorie and Larry and I seethed with resentment.

"How did it go?" Calvis asked slowly, knowing the answer before he asked.

"I never want to see him again in my life." Marjorie's words spit out. "He's no father to me."

I hated Marjorie's predicament. And although she may have gotten herself into the situation, Papa's refusal further revealed his character. What kind of man turned away his own daughter and grandson? How could a person honor such a cruel parent?

Torn in shreds, I felt so angry I would have jumped a train myself and gone to rescue poor Larry if I'd had two nickels to spare. All I could do was offer a few dollars. If, or when, I had a job, I would have enough money to go after Larry.

Mama asked an attorney for advice and learned that no one could legally keep Marjorie's child away from her. Not even if she owed that person money.

"I won't come back without him," Marjorie promised the next morning before leaving Mama's house to go back to Arizona.

She probably hitchhiked.

When the children returned from the Popes, I fed them bowls of vegetable soup, wiped their faces and put them down for a nap.

My bedroom had become the place where I examined my thoughts and discussed them with God. But today I felt so overwhelmed with my feelings, I couldn't focus. Every time I thought of Papa and what he'd done to the Marjorie and the family, I cringed in dismay. He was a scoundrel. A downright unreliable, horrid man.

I pressed my hands to my temple.

Even his religious ideas burned me. As Mother Pope would quote, "Many have quarreled about religion that never practiced it."

I couldn't go through life with this anger inside. How do you get rid of it? The papa I'd loved so much turned out to be a man I couldn't admire.

Grappling with my feelings, I sunk to my knees. Tears spilled from my eyes, and I sobbed. It felt like I'd lost a loved one. I had resisted, hoping for years that I was wrong. Or mistaken. Or he would change. But I had to face the truth. All my faith in God had not helped him.

The hurt became unbearable. A sword pierced my soul.

"Lord, how do I live with this pain?"

Deep inside, I heard the whisper, *forgive*.

I remembered in the Bible when Peter asked Jesus, "Lord, when someone won't stop doing wrong, how many times must I forgive them? Seven times?"

And Jesus answered Peter something I was only beginning to understand. "You must forgive them seventy times seven."

I bowed low to the ground and asked the Lord to help me forgive. Peace filled my heart and I felt different. The irritating disappointment in my papa disappeared and left sadness. I released the animosity that had grown in me and clung to God, my rock of tranquility.

Chapter Fifty-Three

The morning bolted alive with the smell of smoke blowing in from the south.

I rushed Fremont out the door to find out the details and see if help was needed. Thankfully, he had fixed our car. Working the night shift at Norton Motor Sales, he could get news about disasters before the newspapers.

Impending doom clouded over me. I checked to make sure the children were still sleeping. They were. But I felt a foreboding, something was amiss.

He came back quickly.

"Honey, it's the Poor Farm. It burned down early this morning. There was a big explosion too."

I gasped. "Was anyone hurt?"

"One poor chap didn't make it out. Old man Dudley was living out there and the Bayliss fellow. They're both safe."

The Pottawatomie County Poor Farm was located three miles south of Shawnee on Beard Street. The rambling two story structure held at least a dozen aged or crippled residents. Folks from our county.

"What happened?" I asked.

"Don't know the whole story yet, but it looks like the fire came from coal in the basement. The police are trying to find the residents a place to stay. They got out with only the clothes on their back."

"Mama has a room open. I'm sure she'll help."

At first, Mama didn't like the idea of housing a destitute elderly man. She already had Grandpa Bennett roaming through the house. But by noon, she agreed. Why wouldn't she? She had an empty living space and the city would pay the rent.

Toward noon the next day, I made Mama a casserole and a batch of butter cookies to help out. The children and I walked across town to her house. I opened the front door and heard rattling and banging in the kitchen area. My sisters would be in school, so it must have been Mama moving around like a runaway locomotive. I sniffed and smelled chicken soup cooking.

"Is something wrong?" I asked after the children and I unloaded our haul. "Where's the fellow from the poor house?"

Mama mumbled. "Police brought him in last night. What will the neighbors think?" She slammed down a bowl. "I found bed bugs. And he can't even feed himself."

"It won't be for long. They said only a few days."

"Well he can't stay long, that's for sure. What with Grandpa wandering around at night like he is lately. He's likely to scare this fellow right out of his britches."

A small, feeble man stumbled into the room. He grunted. The bald man wore a set of Grandpa's pajamas and looked nervous, frail, ready to blow over in the Oklahoma wind. He slowly passed me without speaking and sat down at the table.

"Don't just stand there, Sibyl," said Mama as she poured hot chicken soup into a bowl. "Pour us some tea while I take care of this moocher. And don't start thinking I'm some kind of nurse maid. I'm not."

Mama tied a bib around the fellow and pulled up a chair beside him. She tested the soup to make sure it wasn't too hot. Then she smiled at the man and held up a spoonful of soup to his mouth. He opened his mouth like a child and she fed him. Bits of soup dribbled down his chin and Mama wiped it off. Patiently. Gently.

"Don't stare," said Mama. "He needs clothes since he lost everything in the fire. What he wore, I had to put in the wringer to get rid of the bed bugs. I can buy socks and things, but I can't afford much." Mama fed the fellow another bite. "Does Fremont have any old shirt or trousers to spare?"

I held back a smile. Mama cared. She might have been bitter at Papa, but she fed beggars at her back porch and helped old people eat. My heart went out to her and admiration surfaced. Kindness. I saw kindness.

"Sure. I can pack up one of Fremont's warm shirts and a pair of trousers. I'll bring them over tonight."

Grandpa came into the room and helped himself to one of our cookies.

All three children stared at him as if he had stolen peanuts from the drug store. I nodded and the children giggled and grabbed a cookie.

My mama might have her problems, but deep down, she really was a good person.

Chapter Fifty-Four

April 1939

In the early spring, I rushed around helping Irene and Blanche prepare for high school graduation. Time sped by making prom dresses, discussing prom dates and deciding on graduation rings and yearbooks.

At the same time, Effie and Opal and I made plans to attend a meeting in Muskogee regarding missions work. None of my women's group had ever gone to the annual, state-wide WMU missionary conference before. Energized, we spent hours deciding what to wear, where to eat and where to stay the night. As a leader among the young married women, I was thrilled to take a trip with my friends.

Keith came down with a slight temperature. "Don't worry, Sibyl," Fremont said. "I can take care of the boy. You need your time away." My little family functioned quite well, I must say. Fremont considered my mission work important. And yes, I needed to do this. I had been planning this trip for months and the other ladies wouldn't go without me.

I drove to Opal's house to pick her up and then to Effie's. We reviewed my list to make sure we brought all the essentials. Bibles, notebooks, hairnets.

Fremont and the other dads would stay home with the children. Opal had one little rambunctious girl at home, and we laughed at how our husbands would find out what it was like to take care of children and a house for two days.

"Keith's a little sick," I told Effie as we drove away. "It seems to be minor, though. Fremont's such a dear to keep him for me." Effie had two small boys about the same age as Margaret and Judson and she was pregnant. I wasn't sure she should be traveling, but she refused to stay confined.

I shared with my friends about our broken window. Hopefully, Fremont would have it fixed before I returned home. Keith, playing in the living room, had seen his best friend Willard, the handicapped neighborhood child, looking in the window from the outside. Keith squealed and ran to jump in Willard's arms. I laughed as I told how Keith didn't see the clear glass between them. Needless to say, the glass shattered and terrified both children. No one was hurt.

Then the conference took my mind away from family life.

Several hundred women from across the state attended the Muskogee weekend conference to learn about leadership in mission work. Effie, Opal, and I spent the night together in a hotel room, chatting into the early morning hours. We talked about marriage, children, and the true meaning of life. The next day was worth our efforts to be there. Effie's special interest lay in teaching young girls through Sunbeams, the mission program for children. She attended a separate session and later would share what she learned.

Elated, I glowed with excitement as Opal and I listened to Edna McMillan, the Oklahoma WMU president for the past ten years. "A rich man is one who has enough for himself and enough left over to help others" she said. According to that, I was a rich woman. I felt valuable, worthwhile. I had accomplished my goals of creating a smooth-running household, and raising beautiful, well-mannered children—excluding Judson's shenanigans. I supported a noble husband, and was inspired to encourage him to go to church with me more often.

The women involved in state mission work voted to name the Season of Prayer for State Missions after Edna McMillan. After listening to

Miss McMillan speak, I strongly concurred. Her heart was dedicated to others, more than anyone I had ever met, and I wanted to be just like her.

As I listened, I realized how much church work needed to be done. I found another purpose in life—sharing Christ's goodness with those around the world. I also would keep teaching my children and praying for Fremont. I scribbled my usual list of notes. My elation lasted throughout the trip home.

I arrived home from the conference on Sunday afternoon and hugged Fremont. Margaret and Judson jumped around me and I gave each of them long hugs, too. I went over to check on Keith and knelt by his crib. His skin felt extremely hot and he seemed worse than he had when I left. I felt terrible for leaving him. How could a mother leave a sick child?

"He's doing mighty poorly," said Fremont.

All that night, I sat beside Keith, bringing him water or carrying him to the bathroom, where he sat on the stool for long stretches of time. He was constipated and lay in his crib and screamed, crying out with abdominal pain. I asked Fremont to run over to Mother Pope's for the bottle of castor oil and I administered a small dose to Keith. It made him vomit.

Nothing helped. We tried all Mother's remedies, even bathing the baby in cold water to reduce his fever. Five-year-old Margaret sat beside his bed, which sat in our living room, and washed his face with a cool washcloth. She wouldn't leave his side. Such a caring child. She hated to see her baby brother suffer, and her face showed worry like a child's should not.

I remembered the rare skin disease my sister Blanche had as a baby. I was ten years old and cringed at her body covered with blisters. She went into convulsions, which scared me more than the blisters. I thought she would die. Mama took her to Dr. John Coley, Papa's cousin in Oklahoma City. He gave Mama some blue tablets, Bichloride of Mercury I learned later, to bathe Blanche in. Mama immersed her in the blue water and claimed it saved her life. Dr. Coley has since passed away and the blue stuff might not help, but I thought about the remedy. Mothers will do anything to help their children.

Dr. Fortson arrived early Monday morning and ordered Keith to be taken directly to the hospital.

Shawnee City Hospital sat on the corner of Center and Walnut. We approached the three-story red brick building that sat on a hill about six blocks from our home. Fremont carried Keith up the tall set of stairs. Inside, the long narrow hallways seemed to echo like St. Gregory's Abbey north of town.

Fear gripped me. I thought about Inez's baby, Marvin. He would never develop past the intellectual stage of a two-year-old. His brain had been permanently damaged.

What would happen to Keith if his fever didn't go down? Would he end up like Marvin?

A headache threatened to blind me.

Fremont and I took turns sitting with Keith in the hospital. Intermittently, we held his hand or wiped his brow as he tossed and turned. We tried to console him as best we could. I sang every lullaby I could remember. My friend Anna knitted Keith a baby cap and brought it to the hospital. I felt sad as she tucked it on his head. She hadn't been able to have a child and she adored Keith.

The day seemed endlessly long. The tension never lessening.

The doctor arrived but seemed puzzled. He examined the pale child and his protruding stomach. "Possibly an intestinal blockage," Dr. Fortson said. "Possibly peritonitis. Just wait. We've taken all the tests we can."

"Maybe we should pray," I whispered to Fremont after the doctor left. I slumped in a chair on the opposite side of Keith's bed.

"My dad always said, 'Faith should be as easy a walking across the room,'" Fremont looked down at Keith's face. "Why is it so hard to pray?"

"Sometimes it's easier than other times. Or maybe we just get so busy we forget."

Fremont and I gazed at each other across the baby's bed. We had never prayed together, not really, not on a regular basis. Especially not since Fremont's faith had cooled and he'd drifted off track.

He stretched his big hand out across the white sheet and I entwined my small fingers in his. Tears streamed down our faces and I saw my own fear reflected in his eyes. Our words sounded incoherent and disjointed.

I poured my heart out to God, pleading for him to hear us and take care of our precious baby. Fremont's voice broke as he expressed his sorrow, his heart.

Nighttime shadows appeared, the hall light breaking into the room and shining on our baby's pale face and dark curly hair. The smell of antiseptic surrounded us.

Many visitors came to see Keith during the next few days. Mama dropped in late one morning to see her little grandbaby. I could tell who it was without looking up because I smelled Ivory soap. Mother Pope smelled of homemade lye soap. Mama embraced me tightly and then turned toward Keith lying in the hospital crib. Pale and unresponsive, sweat glistened on his brow. A visitor had given him a pink rosebud, an unusual gift for a child, but he clutched it tightly in his baby fist. He appeared as if nothing was wrong, just a sweet, innocent, sleeping child.

"What can I do to help?" Mama asked.

"Nothing much to do. Just wait," I said. "The Popes are taking care of Margaret and Judson."

"Keith's such a good baby. Everyone loves him. He'll be all right." She patted my hand and slipped back out into the hall.

Night descended with little improvement. At least his thrashing stopped. Fremont and I kept our exhausting vigil until I finally relented and went home for a few hours of sleep.

Chapter Fifty-Five

I heard bits and pieces of the story over the next few days. Bits and pieces I didn't want to hear, but needed to hear. Fremont filled me in because he was there.

Toward morning just before sunrise around 6:30, Fremont rose from his chair to check on Keith. He saw our baby's eyes flutter slightly and watched him stir uncomfortably and become limp. Fremont reached out and touched his soft face. Keith's breathing stopped.

"Nurse! Nurse!" Fremont called out.

People came running. Two nurses on staff tried to resuscitate Keith. Fremont stood to the side and watched as the nurses frantically tried to restore his life.

But Keith was gone.

"There's nothing more we can do," a nurse said.

"My head fell and I sobbed," Fremont told me. "Sibyl, nothing ever hurt me as much as this. My heart tore in half, gouged from the inside out. Our baby was dead."

I reached out and touched Fremont's face. I should have been there. I should never have left. "Go on," I said.

"I could hardly manage to get up from the chair I collapsed into. I hated to leave Keith, but I had to tell you. I ran down the hall to the lobby and picked up the telephone on the wall and turned the hand crank. You know the rest from there."

"You called Mrs. Martin and begged her to come get me even though it was nighttime."

Fremont finished the story for me. "I told her, 'It's Keith. Run to my house. Tell Sibyl to come quickly.'"

I had run the six blocks to the hospital and up the stairs and through the front door. I almost collided with the nurse.

My throat constricted. My heart froze as I entered the room.

I should have been there.

In those hours immediately after our loss, April 23, 1939, I fell apart. The child I loved, the one so much like myself, was gone. Had God not heard my prayers? Or if he had, why had he chosen to do nothing? How could I live? I could never go back to our house. I could not bear to see Keith's empty crib or the corner where he loved to play.

In recent years, I'd tried to be faithful to my loving Lord, and now—now he'd taken my child. A chill traveled down my whole body and I shook uncontrollably.

Mama came to the hospital. She took my hand and led me to her house.

"There must be a reason God would do this. There must be," I muttered as I curled up across Mama's bed. "I just don't understand." I grieved for three days. I couldn't eat. I couldn't return home. Fremont and Mother Pope planned the funeral. When asked what I wanted, I simply didn't know.

How could I go back to Fremont and the children with my world torn apart? I had never known such loss. I felt useless.

I failed baby Keith. I hadn't even there when he'd left this earth. This child of hope, this child of promise. The baby I loved beyond time lived for twenty-one months and nineteen days. I relived each of them in my mind. Depressed, I yearned to hold my baby like a starving child grabs at a crumb of bread.

My dream as a young girl was to leave home and do something important, help mankind as I promised Papa. I'd tried to fulfill that promise by being the best parent I could and have a perfect home. Now I failed. I lost my baby. I couldn't succeed at anything, not even being a mother. I squeezed my eyes shut and despair crept over me.

Perhaps what I really sought all these years was a loving home. I had wanted folks who loved each other no matter what. A good family like the Popes. All this, I had found, I'd had it all. Now it was gone. Unsuccessful at being a mother, I couldn't face Fremont.

The pit of my stomach churned and fear made me tremble.

Chapter Fifty-Six

I glanced at the obituary in the Shawnee Morning News. Fredrick Keith Pope's funeral would be held on April 26th at Gaskill's. I stopped reading. Gaskill's Undertaking was a pretentious building located on Union and sat near Norton Motor Sales where Fremont worked. So close together—life, work, death.

The funeral home couldn't accommodate the crowd. So many attended the funeral that people stood around the edges of the room and flowed out into the hallway. The windows were opened for those in the yard to hear.

Fremont held me up at the back of the funeral home as I leaned into him. The crowd hushed when they saw us.

The town hadn't seen such a crowd since the 1920s.

People arrived from our home church, Calvary Baptist, and also from Emanuel. Mourners came from the Trimble's church, First Baptist and other churches in town.

Many former classmates from Shawnee High School, where Fremont and I had graduated, came. They must have read the notice in the Shawnee paper or heard the news in town.

High society people sat beside dirt farmers who lived in Waco.

Bankers who knew Papa came in their dandy suits and ties and sat in the back beside poor women in flour-sack dresses. Mama's friends from the Murrow Chapter of the Eastern Stars came.

White people came. Black people came. The owners of Norton Motor Sales came, and so did Lester Morris, Mama's handyman. I saw him sitting in the hall with his wife, Mattie, and their children.

My baby had brought hope. Hope after the worst economic depression anyone could remember, and now that hope was dashed, wiped out like the green pastures that had once graced our land. Death carried a heavy weight and we mourned together.

People cried into their handkerchiefs. Men wiped their sleeves. Children clung to their mothers. The whole town seemed to hurt—family and friends who loved us and our precious son. A child who promised a glimpse of an optimistic future. Our community grieved as one.

I clung to Fremont's arm as he led me to the front pew. Our family filed in behind us. Mama and my sisters. Family from Sulphur and around the state. Grandpa Bennett, Aunt Adah, Uncle Louie, their families and other relatives I hadn't seen in ages. Clyde and Inez sat behind me, and Inez placed her hand on my shoulder. The Popes sat a few rows back, Margaret and Judson safely tucked in beside them. I didn't see Papa, but I was told he sat in the back, far from the family.

Flowers surrounded the casket and graced the whole front of the room. Flowers most people couldn't afford but sent anyway.

I noticed the pink rose clutched in Keith's fist and I wheezed, panic clutching my throat. I began to weep. My friends Opal and Effie must have sent the small pink roses, like the one he clutched in his little fist before he died.

I let out a loud wail and couldn't stop. Fremont put his arm around me and began to cry with me. I could only recognize my own pain. It was so deep and personal I felt like I was the only one in the whole world who'd felt the agony of losing a child.

"Something's wrong with Mommy," said Margaret from behind us, loud enough for me to hear. Margaret and Judson spent the funeral morning at Mother Pope's house, where she'd bathed and dressed them in good clothes.

I clung to the edge of the pew when I heard Margaret whisper again, "I need to see Mommy."

Fremont had told Margaret that baby Keith went to heaven. Margaret knew we missed Keith terribly, so perhaps she thought I needed comforting.

Mother whispered in a deep, lowered voice. "She can't be bothered right now, dear."

Fremont glanced back to make sure Mother knew to take care of Margaret. I prayed she could console my daughter.

"I need to tell Mommy something." Margaret jumped from the pew, rushed to the front and stood right in front of us. She folded her hands across her chest, her teary eyes grave.

"What do you need to say, child?" Fremont asked.

"I need to tell Mommy not to be so upset," Margaret began to wring her hands. "We're still here. She still has Judson and me."

Fremont couldn't handle any more. He hung his head and sobbed.

"Go on back to your seat," Mama whispered to Margaret. "Judson needs you."

"No. Mommy needs me!" Margaret yelled.

The whole town gasped. People in the church cried out and loud sobs echoed through the room. Sobs not only for Keith and our family but for themselves as well, it seemed. They grieved for the never-ending battle to get past the sorrow created during the past decade. The depression, the hunger, the drought, the thirties. When would it be over?

I grabbed and hugged Margaret so tight she whimpered again. Tears washed her face.

Mother came and pulled Margaret away from me and took her back to sit beside her. Pastor Baily Sewell from Calvary Baptist Church presided. The congregation sang "Be Thou my Vision" but I didn't remember the words of the service.

After the program, the family was whisked out and driven to the Fairview Cemetery, northeast of town. The scent of dry dirt settled around me as we stood by the grave site. Dry and brittle, like my heart. So far, this year had brought little spring rain.

Fremont picked up Keith's miniature casket and carried it toward a back road beside a WPA-built rock wall. After a few words, he lowered Keith into the hard earth, into the cold ground that took away our livestock, our vegetation and our babies. Fremont led me away, back to the car.

I had no strength to talk and no words to say. There was no way to share my deep loss. I couldn't even share my grief with Fremont— especially with Fremont. I had trouble carrying my own pain and felt helpless to console him. Sharing Fremont's pain would have broken me. His pain made me ache for a strength I didn't have.

Family and friends arrived at Mama's house to offer condolences. Neighbors and friends brought food for the family—chicken casseroles, custard pies, and home-canned vegetables. Food they couldn't spare but brought anyway. Flowers and potted plants filled the home.

Would life ever be normal?

Chapter Fifty-Seven

Mama made a jar of homemade bath oil—corn oil mixed with a dab of shampoo. She made me soak in it for relaxation. I slept through the next day. Then I stirred and couldn't sleep, crying when I overheard Keith's name or thought about him. My mind couldn't grasp the thought of my baby being gone. Fear, pain, and nonsense rattled around in my brain.

A week later, I woke feeling a bit better. Mama brought me a clean set of clothes and said, "You're stronger than you think. Now, get up out of that bed and do what you have to do."

The time came to return home and put things in order. To begin anew. I would try, even though I still ached inside. Still felt like my heart dripped with pain.

Fremont and I took the children to the Popes' home. When I walked in, Mother was sitting at the table, reading her Bible, tears dropping onto the pages. She rose immediately and embraced Margaret and Judson, kissing them on the cheek and squeezing them in a bear hug. She was always more affectionate than anyone in my family, and I hoped she could comfort them.

"The children can stay here as long as necessary. We aren't going anywhere."

"That means a lot, Mother."

"Dearie, how are you doing? Been praying for you to find peace through all this. Been hard on everyone."

"I still don't understand why it happened."

She patted me on the shoulder and said, "This side of heaven, we may never get a clear mind about it. But God knows our sorrows. He's a crying with you."

Our house was stale. No one had lived in it since Keith's death. I went in alone while Fremont left to get a few needed items. I walked timidly through the silent rooms, afraid I might see remembrances of Keith. Someone, perhaps church women, had removed Keith's clothes, his blankets, and his toys, thinking I wouldn't want to see them. Somehow I wished they hadn't.

I entered the kitchen and opened the refrigerator door. Refrigerator yeast dough had taken over and the rising dough flowed in mountains inside the enclosed space. The overwhelming odor of yeast hit me and pushed me backward.

Gulping, I ran to the bathroom and vomited.

I'd have to scour the house immediately. I opened all the windows and spent the next hour cleaning the refrigerator and wiping the counter tops with vinegar to get rid of the odor.

Yeast. The horrible smell stuck in my mind. I would never be able to make yeast bread again.

Fremont arrived, but by then the disaster was over. I pulled myself together to finish cleaning. Rambling around the house, I gathered clothes to be washed and piled them in front of the washing machine. I opened the lid and reached inside.

I pulled out some clothes from the washer. Keith's baby clothes. Staring at them at first, my voice broke into a low moan, which kept growing. Fremont came running.

"What's wrong? What's wrong?" He stopped when he saw the baby clothes. "Oh no, I thought they'd taken everything."

"I can't do it. I just can't." I collapsed as Fremont pulled me into the living room and onto the couch, his strong hands guiding me.

"I know it's mighty hard, but we can make it."

I buried my face in Fremont's shoulder and soaked his shirt with my tears.

I finally stopped crying and sat up and saw tears running down Fremont's face. My deep pain was mirrored in his eyes. Deep, lasting grief.

Fremont took my face in his hands and said, "I know it isn't going to be easy, honey, but we *will* make it."

"I'll do the best I can, but I'm not promising anything."

That night while getting ready for bed, Fremont fell apart.

"He climbed the ladder a few weeks ago," he said. "And he loved to eat, remember? I can see him trying any kind of food. Why, he even tried Dad's buttermilk and liked it."

Fremont had been strong when I hurt, but now his composure crumbled. His self-control and calm demeanor disintegrated.

"Why?" he asked. "Why did this have to happen? Nothing is more important than a child."

He paced the floor, crying out to God. Begging for understanding. "The innocent ones. Why the innocent ones, Lord?"

I had never seen Fremont so distraught. I saw outside my own grief and realized the jolt of losing Keith had shaken Fremont as much as it had me. Life hurt, but I didn't want Fremont to hurt like I did. It doubled my pain.

"My own son. Why my son? Why?"

"God's ways are not our ways." I remembered some of Mother's words. "Some things we'll never understand until we get to glory land and ask him."

"After all our hard times and now this!" Fremont's voice broke as he walked back and forth. "God, are you trying to talk to me—tell me something? I admit I haven't been doing what I ought."

I could do little but watch him as he fumed.

"I've been ignoring God," Fremont confessed. "I haven't put him first. Haven't gone to church. Haven't been praying. Yeah, I tried to live a good life and not do anything wrong and work hard to support my wife and kids."

"There's nothing wrong with that." I took his hand to slow him down.

"Maybe there is."

"God can give comfort. Even in the middle of death." I kept my voice low, tried to be comforting, as he'd so often comforted me. "I don't know how, but maybe he can bring some sense out of all this."

"I haven't paid much attention to God lately, honey. Too busy taking care of the family. Sure, work *is* important, but God is more important. Everything is temporary. What matters is our relationship to God. Nothing matters but Jesus. Do you understand, Sibyl?" His voice got louder. "Do you understand?"

I understood like I had never understood before.

Fremont lay down on the bed beside me, holding me in his arms.

His cries jolted me awake. He sat straight up in bed, trembling. "No! That's my baby!"

Words I didn't want to hear. Words that pierced my heart.

I shook him. "Fremont, wake up. He's gone. You can't do anything about it." My heart lurched, a flood of torment overwhelmed me.

We sat up on the side of the bed and I put my arms around him. Rubbed his shoulders. Fremont hadn't woken with a nightmare in a long time.

"Honey, we need God's help with this. Will you pray with me?"

We hadn't prayed together since Keith first entered the hospital. "I can't. I can't even pray."

"You don't have to. I'll pray for us."

Fremont held my hand tight and his deep base voice began hesitantly. "Lord, we're in a mighty bad way here. We're needing your help. Sibyl and I are hurting and don't know what to do. Can you give us a little understanding?"

He opened his eyes. We stayed still for several minutes.

"I've been thinking about my nightmares," said Fremont. "About that bitty girl on the trail. Maybe I can't do anything about the children, the starving ones. And maybe I can't do anything about Keith."

His voice lurched and I squeezed his hand.

"Keith is in God's hands now," he said. "It's time to let Jesus take care of him and all the other tots. He loves them more than we do. I'm ready to talk to him now about my life. About the future."

Fremont and I slid to the floor, kneeling together. We prayed and prayed. We prayed until my knees ached and we kept praying. Fremont dedicated the rest of his life to telling people about Jesus. To telling folks that Jesus is present when you need him. It was a dedication I never thought I'd hear Fremont express. But it felt right. He'd come back to his faith. Faith would get us through. Our faith had grown strong enough to weather any storm.

His words soothed me. I would never understand. Why had it taken Keith's death for Fremont to return to God?

The next day I opened the front door searching for Mother Pope, who was to bring the children back home.

On the steps sat a child. Willard. The big, lanky tender-hearted boy who loved Keith.

I sat down beside him. "What are you doing here?"

"Waiting Keith. We play." He rubbed the sleeve of his jacket.

"I'm sorry, but Keith is gone."

"Can he come play?"

"Keith won't be able to play anymore." I caught my breath, struggling how to explain Keith's absence, not sure how much Willard could understand. "He got sick and went to live with Jesus. He's gone far away."

"I go too."

"You can't go, Willard. Someday, but not now."

"I want Keith. We play." His voice rose and I thought he might lose control. Tears wet his face. He looked at me with his big, innocent eyes, trying hard to explain his need. "I want Keith!"

"I want Keith too, but he had to leave us." I wished with all my heart that Keith were here to play with Willard. The boy's face was full of confusion and pain. "We'll remember him forever, won't we?"

He nodded and I put my arms around this sensitive child and pulled him to me. We wept together.

Finally, I took his hand and led him back to his mother. The pain in his shuffle burned into my heart.

Chapter Fifty-Eight

May 1939

A knock sounded on the front door.
Papa pushed it open and walked in before I could answer.

Tuesday afternoon and I had plopped down after washing dishes. I jumped up.

He pulled off his suit jacket and hung it over the back of a chair. Then he sat and stretched out his legs, admiring the toe caps on his new white wingtip shoes. He would never have worn white shoes before marrying Gladys.

He'd driven down to express his sorrow. I hadn't seen him since Keith's funeral. He muttered something about Gladys being unable to come but sending her condolences.

I didn't care to chat. My mind swam with hurt. My baby had died. Didn't Papa understand I couldn't function as normal? I could barely brush my hair in the mornings.

"It happened so quickly," I said sitting back down. "I don't understand."

"If I'd been notified," said Papa, almost accusingly. "I would have done something to save the boy. Why didn't you call me? We could have gone to the best doctors in the state."

Was Papa suggesting we hadn't tried hard enough to save him? "Dr. Fortson did all he could. No one could have done any better. God has a plan, even if I don't know what it is."

"I'm a believing man." Fake patience made his voice scratchy. "I know what's best and you're flat wrong about God. If you had left Fremont and taken a job with me, this would never have happened. You would have had enough money to help the boy."

"What are you saying, Papa?" I squirmed in my chair and looked over at him, his cruel words searing my heart.

"You heard me. Poverty killed your boy and Fremont's a poor man. He'll always be a poor man. Survival requires money and dedication. Poverty killed your baby."

My jaw clenched and words came slowly from my mouth. "No, Papa."

"Never thought your marriage to a poor man would work anyway." Papa rose and stood over me like a sergeant and spoke in his thunderous voice. "You've made enough mistakes. It's time to move on. You should come to the city and get a decent job. Your family needs it."

I closed my eyes, steam rolling from my head. My body shook. Had Papa's soul not softened through all these troubles?

Papa stood and brushed imaginary dust off his trousers. "I expect you to leave soon." He eyed the few possessions in our house with contempt. "You're stubborn, but it should be clear after what's happened that you'll never get out of this situation if you don't make a change."

My blood pressure must have risen a hundred points. "You have no idea what you're talking about."

"Give your family a chance. You need to do this or your children will grow up as worthless dirty bums. If you can earn money, you and Fremont can pull yourselves together and do something useful with your lives."

Words came from somewhere deep within. "Useful? Like you're useful? A person who won't even take care of his own children?"

Papa looked at me in disgust. "Children, like the downtrodden, are expendable, Sibyl. What's more important? Salvaging this world or mamby-pambying to a couple of kids? Use your head, girl."

He kicked Margaret's doll away and shook his head. "Your children need more than you and your husband can provide. Your neglect is obvious."

I stood so fast the chair toppled and crashed to the floor. I flew up and faced him. "You're unfaithful at home and at work. You've been an atrocious father, a worse grandfather and an all-around terrible person. I want no part of you and your distorted beliefs."

My angry words didn't faze him.

"You'll change," he said. "Someday you'll come begging for help." He slammed the door as he left.

The gap between Papa and I widened more that day. God had used life's difficulties to teach me. He had used my marriage, the children, the storms, the poverty, and now, my baby's death to teach me how much I needed him.

But Papa . . . Papa seemed to believe he could solve all the world's problems by himself with his intellect and money.

My earlier frustration melted away and a feeling I'd never connected to my larger-than-life Papa replaced it. Pity.

Papa had never known contentment, never been able to trust in a superior power. He'd depended upon himself and his grand ideas. Papa had espoused his beliefs while hoarding his wealth and judging those he deemed beneath him, including his own family members. What kind of belief condones such narrow-minded blindness to the suffering of others?

But then, his nasty words seeped into my heart like a cancer, and fear took hold of me.

My fear, far greater than my disappointment in Papa, crippled me. Was Papa right? Had I failed my children? If I'd gone to work for him years ago, if I'd had more money, would Keith have lived?

I cringed at the thought. I *had* failed. Failed at being a mother. Failed at saving my sweet little boy from death. Would I fail the other children as well?

I loved my family more than anything and couldn't let them down.

Margaret and Judson needed their daddy. Fremont was a good father and would always have Mother's help. He could care for the children while I focused on earning money. Papa's way offered possibilities. It offered hope.

I could take the job in the city.

It was a choice. Not the choice I wanted to make, but probably my best choice.

Chapter Fifty-Nine

At first, the children wandered through the house listlessly. Even Judson was subdued. I hugged them often, hoping to alleviate some of their pain. I didn't realize how much I needed to see their faces and hold them in my arms, every minute of every day. However, soon the children were back to their normal energetic selves.

Wednesday morning Margaret and Judson finally collapsed in a state of exhaustion after scrambling through the house, over the furniture and out the back door, running for almost an hour. Nap time was hit or miss with them. I limped into our bedroom and shut the door.

I stumbled around the small bedroom, growing more and more tense. On a pass by the window, I slammed it shut and returned to the dresser.

I paced back and forth, crying repeatedly, "Lord, please help me. I can't go on. I can't do this!"

Depression had been a battle since Keith's death. Sadness sat like a boulder on my chest and I could barely look up. Hopelessness weighed as heavy as a mountain. Prayer should have been my first choice, but I stubbornly followed my own thoughts. I would not fail my two remaining children.

Our small suitcase was perched on the top shelf of the closet and I pulled it down. I slid several blouses and dresses off the hangers and stuffed them in the suitcase. Then I opened the drawer to pull out personal items. I grabbed the small black pocketbook, my small stash of bills that had grown in the last few years, thanks to Fremont's job.

The process of packing was slow. My energy spent. I would leave a note for Fremont. He'd understand. Then I'd drop off the children at Mother's house on my way out of town. Take the train to the City and talk to Papa about a job. I wouldn't be gone forever. Just long enough to save some money. Then I'd come back.

I walked out of our bedroom with the suitcase in my hand.

Margaret burst into the room. I dropped the suitcase and it echoed off the floor like a bomb. I would have to explain to the children.

Margaret saw the suitcase sitting in the middle of the living room floor and slid to a stop. She looked up at me, her face quizzical.

Judson, awakened from his nap, stumbled in behind her. He began to bawl.

"Shh . . ." Margaret grabbed Judson's hand. "We have to be good so Mommy won't leave."

I knelt before the children. "Tell me, Margaret, why do you think Mommy's going to leave you?" My heart pounded as loudly as theirs. I knew they were confused about seeing the suitcase.

Margaret looked at me, distress revealed in her large blue eyes. "Baby Keith left. He went to heaven and now you don't want to be here anymore." She pointed to my suitcase. "You're leaving, too?"

My heart stung with her words. "Just for a little while."

"We'll be good, Mommy," Margaret whimpered. "I promise. If you stay, we'll both be good."

I looked at my children as if seeing them for the first time, really seeing them. Tears left streaks down their gloomy little faces. Margaret's curly hair was unruly and her short dress hung wrinkled from the day. She rubbed a scratch on her leg where she'd fallen down. Judson appeared thin, his clothes crumpled, like he'd worn them for days. He had gone barefoot outside earlier, as he liked to do, and dirt colored his toes. He yawned.

I remembered myself as an unhappy little girl and tears welled in my eyes. I'd been a lonely, unwanted child. A girl whose busy Mama didn't favor her and whose Papa was gone most of the time. Neither of my parents truly cared about my needs. How isolated I'd felt. Only when I met Fremont did I learn that God knew me and cared about the emptiness in my heart. God's love changed my whole life. He had never left me. He was still here. A warmth enveloped my body—the warmth of knowing God had not abandoned me.

I pulled my children closer to me.

"Mommy, are you leaving us?" Margaret understood what was happening. She looked up at me like her world had been crushed. Tears pooled in her eyes. "You don't want us?"

Margaret, hurt and scared, would never know a mother's love if I left her. She would feel unwanted. How would the children learn to trust God's love if they doubted their mother's love? God, the great wise father, would show me the way. I drew the children near, my heart full of love—overflowing love.

I could never leave them.

My children needed me, needed my love, needed me to be their mother. I didn't want to lose them as I'd lost Keith. They should have a chance to grow up unafraid. Not as I had been, unsure of my place in our family. No, I still had work to do, responsibilities, a home to tend. I had scratches to kiss and lessons to teach and games to play with these little ones. I had a purpose—and a good one at that. It didn't matter if we were poor as field mice. My children and I belonged with Fremont. Other mothers may have made a different choice, and that would be all right for them. But for me and my situation, I would never let anyone, not even Papa, convince me to abandon my family.

Papa hadn't been there for me through the trials. But God had never left. A familiar peace flowed through me. I didn't understand the purpose in our suffering, but I trusted God to be with us.

I couldn't stop the tears. I would have to forgive my Papa again. How many times was that? Seventy times seven.

"Don't worry, sweetie. I love you." I pulled Margaret to me. "And I will never, ever leave you. Now, let's go unpack my suitcase."

Papa may have thought my children didn't need me, but Fremont and the good Lord thought otherwise. They desperately needed me.

Chapter Sixty

At six-thirty on Sunday night, a short while after Keith's death, Fremont and I placed Margaret and Judson in the back seat of our Chevy and drove down Beard Street to Calvary Church.

We slid onto the oak pews near the back. The congregation sang, "The Little Brown Church in the Dale," while many old friends came and sat around us. Few spoke, but their presence felt like a reassuring home coming. I basked in it.

Music about my precious Lord had always touched my soul. Did love always bring pain? I grabbed Fremont's hand and squeezed it.

When I was six years old, I had to leave Mama to start first grade. I refused to go. I screamed and cried, resisting as much as any little girl could resist. Unsure of my parents' love, I'd clung to them with all my might. Leaving home felt like the worst form of punishment. Grandma Bennett was visiting that day and took it upon herself to see that I made it to the school. She pushed me across the field until we reached the schoolhouse. I yelled and whimpered to no avail. When we arrived at the school yard, Grandma got down on her knees, put her arms around me and hugged me. I buried my head in her bosom.

"Sweetheart, I love you," said Grandma, stroking my hair. "I'm sorry for hurting you but it's for your own good." She took my face in her wrinkled worn hands and said quietly, "You have to face the tough things in life and go on, even if it hurts."

Grandma Bennett had been right all those years ago. My mind centered on Keith. The pain subsided as I recalled his enthusiasm for life, his unrestrained love and outgoing personality. Oh, how much Keith had helped me see the good in life. He'd helped me accept people. Perhaps his short days had served a divine purpose after all.

The preacher spoke, his voice rising as he told us how much Jesus cared about our predicament and listened to our pleas. The dirge wouldn't last forever. We must trust in God because he alone knows the plans for the future.

The last song of the evening was by Fanny Crosby, "All the Way my Savior leads me." It melted my heart. Sinking down into the wooden pew, I bowed my head and prayed. I desperately wanted to know that whatever happened in life, the Savior would be beside me. Guiding me. Helping me. *"Please, Lord. Please lead me through life."*

God offered peace. Even in the midst of trials. The truth of his compassion and love sank deep into my heart and a river of harmony engulfed me. The steady flow of God's presence melted the pain around my heart.

Two days later, we were waiting inside the front door when Fremont arrived home from work. Margaret and Judson wore their good Sunday clothes, hair combed and laughter sparkling in their eyes. I had bathed, dabbed on perfume and slipped on a clean print dress. I tied a ribbon around my hair.

"What's this?" Fremont had a lightness in his voice. "Is this really my wife and kids? I feel honored."

"Times have changed. And we have another surprise for you." I led Fremont by the hand into the kitchen. The two children suppressed a giggle as they followed.

I'd cooked a meatloaf dinner and set the table with cloth napkins. A jar of daffodils sat in the middle of the table.

"We picked them for you, Daddy!" Margaret said. "Mommy took us to gather flowers in the field behind us. She said today is a special day."

I handed Fremont a package wrapped in brown paper. "What's this? It's mighty heavy."

"It's for you...or for us. I'd saved money for the hard times."

He looked at me curiously. "What money?"

"In an old, black pocketbook. I never told you about it."

Fremont tore open the wrapping and held up a big book. A family Bible. A place to record all God had done for us. Our marriage. Our children's births—and deaths. A record for future generations, so they could see God's work in our family. A place to remember.

"The pain will always be with us," I said, "but we still have family. The children need us. Like you said, we're going to make it."

God's promises had not failed us and they never would. We would hold on to Keith forever in our hearts, and someday the grief would lessen.

"I've been thinking about going to heaven," I told Fremont later that evening. Darkness had enveloped our small home, music played from the Crosley radio in the kitchen and the children lay tucked in bed. "I miss him so much."

"No. Don't even think about heaven yet." Fremont almost jumped to the edge of the sofa. "I need you down here. You're important to me. Besides, I can't take care of work, the house and two children by myself."

"No, no." I almost laughed. "What I mean is—Keith will be waiting for us, and someday we'll be able to hold him again. If God wants the sweet boy with him, then we have to accept it, even if it leaves an empty spot inside."

Fremont smiled sweetly, one of his adoring, understanding smiles, his broad, handsome face peaceful and his eyes sparkling like diamonds. He kissed me on the cheek and held me close.

"Fremont," I said a few minutes later, kicking off my shoes and pulling my long legs onto the couch. "Do you believe we were meant to be together?"

"What a silly question. How could I not fall in love with you?" Fremont leaned back beside me. "A beautiful brunette with golden skin and big brown eyes? God worked mighty hard to make you special."

"But what about the future?"

"Well, I've been thinking about that. I'd like to become a Sunday School teacher in the church, maybe teach young men. That is, if you agree. It would mean a mighty lot more time and responsibilities. Do you think I should look into it?"

"Of course you should." My heart warmed at the thought of my husband following his parent's teaching whole-heartedly. What a kind heart. He would make a great teacher. "But I'm talking about us. How many children do you want to have? I mean, is it too early to have another one?"

Fremont cocked his head. "And what exactly do you mean by that?"

I smiled. Here, in front of me, was a good man. God must have known all along we were meant for each other. "I do believe I'm ready for another child, sir. Not too far from now either."

Fremont's blue eyes lit up like connected to electricity. "You mean you're . . ."

"No, silly, I'm not pregnant. But I think it's time to start thinking about it again. And this time I'm delighted about the idea. Scared, too. Life goes on, but I think a new baby would be a blessing."

The song "It Had to be You" played softly on the Crosley radio.

"Remember this, Fremont?"

Fremont stood up in front of me. For the first time in our marriage, he put out his strong, working man hand for a private dance. I placed my long, pale fingers in his and rose.

"I love you, honey," he whispered in my ear. "I'm happy to be going through this life with you."

Nothing could defeat us. Not as long as we danced through life together.

The end.

Author's Notes

Thank you for reading this book about my grandparents. My closet holds enough boxes of research for a dozen more books, or at least a few. It was difficult to choose what antedotes to include and what to leave out. I've tried to stay true to all dates, including births, weddings, deaths, etc., which are usually easy to verify.

I began research for this book in 2001, interviewing many of Sibyl and Fremont's friends and family members, copying documents, and organizing data and newspaper articles. Many of the interviewees have passed away since I began.

Sibyl Trimble, the ever up-and-down, emotional but brilliant lady, did her best to make a great family. Seeking God, she studied, taught, and shared about Christ. She put her heart into working with the Women's Missionary Union, the WMU. Most of the stories included are true, like the watch story, the birthday party, and the bread lady.

Fremont Pope did indeed slip away from his faith for a few years. I remember him re-telling how Keith's death affected him and how that event convinced him to return to his roots. Until his death, he would greet people with "Do you know Jesus?" And although I don't have a copy of a letter received from the people Fremont knew in California, he always wanted to return there.

Malcolm Calvis Trimble Sr.'s involvement in State Bank Commissioner Barnett's embezzlement case is documented by many legal papers, newspapers articles, and internet research data. I found much more than I expected, even a case of Trimble being bribed to support Barnett. The stack of papers on my desk regarding the charges begins in 1932 going up through the 1940s. As of the end of this second book, May 1939, the case was still ongoing.

As indicated in Mr. Trimble's long-winded book, *Our Awakening Social Conscience-The Emerging Kingdom of God,* he truly believed in a possible universal utopia. A KKK hood was actually found by Frances in the family's playhouse after the divorce.

Mable Bennett Trimble with her daughter Blanche Trimble wrote *Nothing but the Truth, Autobiography of Mable Trimble,* and self-published it in 1982. I could write a book about Blanche because I have pages and pages of notes taken as I interviewed her. She claimed she never told a lie, and since she had an excellent memory, I believed every word she said.

I was fortunate to be able to review the Calvary Church minute book. It was recorded that Mrs. W. O. Pope (Mother Pope) was placed in charge of the Oklahoma Baptist University Ministry for Women's Missionary Union. In 1936 she was elected to the committee for the sick. Irene was elected Secretary to the Baptist Young People Union, 1935-1937. Her mother probably nominated her.

In December 1935, Mrs. F. F. Pope (Sibyl) was elected Recording Secretary of WMU. It feels more official seeing this all written down in a book.

On November 26, 1906, the Pope's 160-acre homesteaded farm at Waco, Territory of Oklahoma, Pottawatomie County, was recorded in Volume 175, Page 135. Today, the rock foundation of the Waco church donated by the Popes still exists on the northeast corner of Okay, now Highway 331 and Waco Roads in Pottawatomie County. Through John and Amanda Pope, our family traces its heritage to the First Families of the Twin Territories, meaning this family was present before statehood.

Dad Pope and Fremont both worked for the PWA on the Deer Creek Dam (at Shawnee Lake). And Fremont worked for Norton Motor Sales for years.

Marjorie, Calvis, and Irene's stories are solid. Not much has been added. It was probably Calvis who bailed his father out of jail. Calvis' wife's name was Frances but was changed to Evie in order to avoid confusion with his sister's name. The family tragedy regarding Marvin is true.

The Poor Farm fire was accurate, however we don't know if Mrs. Trimble boarded an elderly resident, but she had a boarding house at that time, so it is likely. Emanuel Baptist Church later changed their name to Immanuel Baptist, probably to avoid confusion with Emmanuel Episcopal in town. And Bob Reneger's story is factual, confirmed by a newspaper article.

During the 1930s, many banks were closed, reopened, merged and/or sold. The State National Bank was closed during the Bank Holiday and a conservatorship was set up under the name of American National Bank. I used the name of State National Bank in this series.

I pulled the information about President Roosevelt's train stop in Shawnee from newspaper articles because of Sibyl's interest in politics. Amazingly, when I questioned Frances Trimble, she confirmed that yes, she remembered being there on that day. She couldn't see much because she was only eleven-years-old.

I was surprised at how Sibyl and Fremont's families are connected or related to so many people still residing in the Shawnee area. I probably have second and third cousins there I've never met. Ties include the Whittens, the Stapps, the Stephens, and Sibyl and Fremont's best friends, the Douglasses.

Baby Keith's death greatly affected the family and townspeople. I tried to write those chapters as detailed as the events were portrayed to me. My mother still has his little Skippy cup sitting on a book shelf.

This book is as close to truthful as I could get. It would take less work to write about what is not true than what is true. The gypsy story I used was actually Blanche's, but the majority, including antidotes like the corset job and the pawned radio, are taken from family history and interviews about that time period.

Many people helped fill in the details and promote this book. Fellow writers of the American Christian Fiction Writers group where I am a member have helped a lot. Many, many other writing friends have encouraged me along the way.

My editor, Robin Patchen, found flaws that only an expert could find. She made the story plausible. Mary Ruth Hatley Sadler, very knowledgeable of the Shawnee area, and Jeri Williams helped a great deal as did Ken Landry from the Pottawatomie County Historical Museum & Historical Society.

To my huge extended family, the many who claim Sibyl and Fremont as ancestors, I would like to remind you that this is also your story. Their faith can be yours. No matter what difficulties Fremont and Sibyl faced, they committed their lives to sharing the love of Jesus, so don't let their dedication be wasted. Thank you for the joy you bring to my life.

My immediate family has been patient with my long hours of writing and publishing. My husband, Bill, deserves thanks for his support, along with our awesome children and grandchildren. Thank you for your love.

Mostly I'd like to thank my mother, Margaret Kathryn Pope Akin. Without her, there would not be a story. She spent hours and hours discussing, analyzing and reminiscing about her childhood. I love her dearly.

Kathryn Akin Spurgeon

Sources of Information

Public Documents from:

Calvary Baptist Church Minutes, Shawnee, Oklahoma
Oklahoma History Center, Oklahoma City, Oklahoma
Pottawatomie County Historical Society, Shawnee, Oklahoma
Shawnee City Directory, 1937, R. L. Polk & Co. Publishers,
  Kansas City, MO
Shawnee City Directory, 1938, R. L. Polk & Co. Publishers,
  Kansas City, MO
Shawnee News Star, Microfiche Newspapers from 1935-1939
Shawnee Public Library archives

Books and Articles

- Burke, Bob, and Dabney, Eric, *Historic Shawnee: The History of Shawnee & Pottawatomie County, HPN books, A division of Lammert Incorporated, 2014*
- *Calvary Baptist Church, 60th Anniversary Celebration, 1920-1980,* Published by Calvary Baptist Church, Shawnee, Oklahoma, 1980
- Gaskin, J.M., *Baptist Women in Oklahoma*, Messenger Press 1985
- *The American Writer and the Great Depression*, edited by Harvey Swados, The Bobbs-Merrill Company, Inc, 1966
- Gravley, Ernestine, *Chronicles of Oklahoma*. "Fifty Years Ago in Shawnee and Pottawatomie County" page 381
- Hightower, Michael J., *Banking in Oklahoma*, 1907-2000, University of Oklahoma Press, 2014
- Holt, Brad A., *Images of America, Shawnee and Pottawatomie County*, Arcadia Publishing 2017
- McDonald, Ann Lanier, *History of Disasters in Shawnee Oklahoma, Epidemics, Plane Crashes, Fires, Floods, Tornadoes. Shawnee Oklahoma History Books, 2016*
- *Shawnee, 1895-1930, Forgotten Hub of Central Oklahoma*, reprinted by permission for the Historical Society of Pottawatomie County.

- *Shawnee Today*, Official Publication, Chamber of Commerce, Shawnee, Oklahoma, Summer 1936
- Soden, Dale E, "The New Deal Comes to Shawnee", Chapter 10 in *"An Oklahoma I had Never Seen Before": Alternative Views of Oklahoma History,* edited by Davis D. Joyce, University of Oklahoma Press, 1994
- *The Art of Entertaining*, The Women's Auxiliary of Emanuel Episcopal Church of Shawnee, Oklahoma Copyright 1935 M. F. Shelby
- Trimble, Mabel and Blanche, *Nothing But the Truth, Autobiography of Mabel Bennett Trimble,* Self-published 1982
- Trimble, Malcome C. Sr., *Our Awakening Social Conscience-The Emerging Kingdom of God,* Vantage Press, 1958
- Trimble, Sibyl, *History of Sibyl Agatha Trimble Pope*, handwritten about 1960
- Yarbrough, Slayden, *The Lengthening Shadow: A centennial history, heritage and hope of the First Baptist Church, Shawnee, Oklahoma 1892 – 1992,* published by First Baptist Church, Shawnee, Oklahoma, 1992

About the Author

Award winning author, Kathryn Spurgeon has published over a hundred stories and articles, plus poetry books and devotionals. She is on the Writing Team of Henderson Hills Baptist Church, which has published eight compilations books. She holds a bachelor's degree from the University of Oklahoma and has pursued Creative Writing at the University of Central Oklahoma. She is a retired CPA from Oklahoma and loves to research Oklahoma history for her novels.

Kathryn and her husband, Bill, are blessed to have six children and twelve grandchildren. They live in Edmond, Oklahoma.

Kathryn blogs at www.kathrynspurgeon.com and can be found on Facebook and Twitter.

A review of her books on Amazon or Goodreads would be greatly appreciated.

A Promise to Break
Faith, Loss and Hope
in the 1930s

Book 1 in the Promise Series

Kathryn Spurgeon

Sibyl Trimble promises her father when she is a young girl to be part of a socialist political movement to change the world. From a wealthy banking family in Shawnee, Oklahoma, she is comfortable with fashionable clothes, cruising in a new Chrysler, and dancing at the local speakeasy. Even the Depression cannot put a damper on her comfortable lifestyle. By 1932, the timing to fulfill the promise to her father seems right.

Then she meets a handsome, blue-eyed, down-on-his-luck hobo and her life is turned upside down. The more she gets to know him, the more she learns about her world, her purpose, and God. Her love for him opens her eyes to a different way of life than she has ever known.

Based on a true story, this novel follows Sibyl through difficult choices. She must dig deep within herself to find the strength to face her upbringing and determine which, if any, of her past beliefs can be salvaged. She must decide which is most important, love or duty.

Midwest Book Review "Exceptionally well written, making it a consistently compelling read from beginning to end, "A Promise To Break" is one of those rare stories that will linger in the mind and memory of the reader long after the book itself has been finished."
James A. Cox, Editor-in-Chief

Find on Amazon at
http://amzn.to/2cHLrRe

A Promised Hope
Faith, Prospects, and Dreams
in the early 1940s

Book 3 in the Promise Series

Kathryn Spurgeon

Sibyl Trimble, a wealthy banker's daughter, gives up her status and wealth to marry a penniless hobo. Fremont Pope, her handsome, blue-eyed, husband stands by her side through the Depression, the dust storms and other difficulties in life. Just when life starts to get better, they experience one more disaster.

Why does God allow bad things to happen to her and her family? Can she continue to trust God through adversity?

Based on a true story, this novel follows Sibyl and Fremont through some difficult trials. She must find the strength to grow through the hard times and learn to trust on the Lord's overall goodness.

www.memoryhouepubishing.net

51937452R00178

Made in the USA
San Bernardino, CA
06 August 2017